The Fairlight Book of Short Stories

VOLUME I

FAIRLIGHT BOOKS

First published by Fairlight Books 2020
Fairlight Books

Summertown Pavilion, 18–24 Middle Way, Oxford, OX2 7LG

Selection and Introduction @ Fairlight Books

Individual contributions @ the contributors

The right of Fairlight Books to be identified as the editor of this work
has been asserted by them in accordance with the Copyright, Designs
and Patents Act 1988.

A CIP catalogue record for this book is available from the British
Library

1 2 3 4 5 6 7 8 9 10

ISBN 978-1-912054-68-8

www.fairlightbooks.com

Printed and bound in Great Britain

Designed by Fairlight Books

CONTENTS

Introduction

The short story is a form that has the power to instantly transport the reader to another state, another world, another emotion. It has the power to enrapture and delight. The short story is the perfect entertainment medium for our busy modern lives – a whole adventure packed into a few pages.

Over the last few years we have received a vast number of stories through our open submissions programme from new and emerging writers based all around the world, which has enabled us to build a network of authors whose talent we have proudly supported.

This anthology includes twenty-four stories by twenty-four different writers, including award-winning authors Judith Wilson (winner of the London Short Story Prize), Adam Trodd (winner of the Benedict Kiely Short Story Competition) and Sophie van Llewyn (longlisted for the Women's Prize for Fiction), all selected from our online portal. From flash fiction to mini-novelettes, there is something for every taste.

Introduction

If you feel like travelling the world, let yourself be transported to Nepal by Abi Hynes's *The Ghosts from Kathmandu*, to New Zealand by Sam Reese's *An Experience* or to rural Canada by William Prendiville's *Marble Mountain* – or travel back in time to eighteenth-century France with Sophie van Llewyn's *Mariette*. If you're a fan of flash fiction, you'll find stellar examples of the form ranging from the quirky humour of Niki Baker's *Cold Turkey* to the bittersweet poignancy of Adam Trodd's *Locale*. If you like your fiction on the darker side, you'll find Nial Giacomelli's *My Friend Hristo* and Katherine Pringle's *Misper* irresistible. David Lewis's *Dry County* and Max Dunbar's *The Search for Atlantis* both contain a powerful combination of realism and supernatural elements, while Jasmin Kirkbride's *The Cloud Loom*, Margaret Crompton's *The Midwinter Marriage* and Sarah Dale's *Greenwood Tree* all feature a touch of magic. And if you're in the market for an incisive and original perspective on contemporary life and relationships, you'll be spoilt for choice between Anna Appleby's *Funreality*, Chloë Ashby's *Parma Violets for Breakfast*, Clare Reddaway's *Touching the Sun* and Maggie Ling's *Bird Brains*, to name just a few.

We are excited to share this excellent work with you and to introduce you to these wonderful writers.

Enjoy!

The Fairlight Books team

My Friend Hristo

Nial Giacomelli

And then there stood Hristo, eclipsing the doorway of our small classroom late one semester. He stood pale and thin, his hair combed into a greasy centre parting, a leather jacket hanging from his slender frame in a way that made him look sickly, victim to some wasting disease. He was a military brat on a temporary deployment and our classmates treated him as such. They saw little point in friendship and so he was resigned to walk the halls like some spectral figure. Not a part of our world, but apart from it.

He wore hiking boots and always seemed on the cusp of a grand expedition, preparing for some great adventure. Each afternoon he left the school bus by a remote stretch of woodland, the road devoid of any houses, and I would watch as his pale body disappeared beyond the treeline. At night I tried to imagine what he did out there, all alone. I wondered where he lived, what his home life was like. Until finally the questions became too much and I followed him one afternoon in late spring.

But I was ill-prepared for the trek and quickly lost track of him along a moss-grown path where the forest grew disorienting and began to close in around me. When I stopped to get my

3

bearings he appeared from behind the trunk of a redwood, brandishing a pocket knife. He looked beyond me, to the path, and tried to determine whether I had come alone. When he was satisfied, he retracted the blade and continued on his way without so much as a word.

I followed tentatively behind him. We walked in single file as the treeline parted to reveal a rock formation overlooking a small creek. Stashed beneath an overhang was a dirty rucksack. Beside it, resting against the rock wall, was a collection of tattered fishing rods and a badly beaten toolbox.

Set back from the creek, a few hundred feet from the shoreline, I could make out a small encampment. There was a piece of tarpaulin stretched between two stout tree limbs and beneath it a squalid-looking sleeping bag. At the centre of the camp was a pot resting above a blackened firepit. Hristo crouched before it and began to stoke fresh flames.

'You sleep out here?' I asked.

'Sometimes,' he said. 'When I can.'

He sat down and took out his pocketknife, working it into the log at his feet.

'Your parents don't mind?'

'My old man would shit himself if he saw all this,' he said.

My old man. I liked that. My father was simply: Father. Sometimes: sir. More often: Dad. Once: Daddy. Was Hristo's old man ever Daddy, I wondered?

He sucked his teeth.

I turned and looked back towards the creek, the battered fishing rods.

'You fish?' I asked.

'Sometimes.'

'My old man said he'd teach me, but he never got round to it,' I said.

'You don't need a rod to catch a fish,' he said, getting to his feet.

We walked along the shoreline, following the current downhill until we came across a tiered staircase of stone that created a small waterfall. From the bank he began to collect handfuls of crushed sandstone. We worked for over an hour, stacking the stones in a semicircle until they sat several inches above the water's surface, creating a small pool which the water trickled into from above.

The idea, Hristo said, was that fish would swim downriver and become trapped within the confines of the pool. We could leave the trap and return later, and the work would be done for us, he said confidently.

A gentle breeze made its way through the trees and the forest swayed around us. A silence descended. We were losing the light. Our project had caught us both unawares, made us oblivious to the lateness of the hour. I regarded the falling darkness with a certain sadness.

He turned to me. 'We'll come back tomorrow, yes? To check on it?'

I nodded obediently.

A glimmer of hope, I thought. The barest of flames.

The next day, as we cut through the undergrowth and made our way towards the creek, Hristo spoke of geological precedents. How fish swam into the Mediterranean through Gibraltar and then struggled to find their way back to the Atlantic. The whole Mediterranean Sea, he said, was one giant fish trap.

When we arrived at the rockpool, I was delighted to find it teeming with life. There were hundreds of small fish dancing in the shallow water. Hristo knelt beside the pool and cupped his hands, grabbing a fistful of minnows. He dropped several into my palm. Then, to my horror, he raised the fish to his mouth and began to chew them noisily, his teeth grinding their sleek bodies down to a fine paste. I forced myself to follow suit and held the tangled mass in my mouth, trying not to vomit.

'You'd need a lot more for a decent meal, but they'd do in a pinch,' he said.

'In a pinch?'

'If you had to survive out here,' he said matter-of-factly.

'Why would you have to survive out here?'

He shrugged.

'Maybe an emergency. Some toxic event. There are thousands of acres out here. A person could disappear.'

He placed his fist into the shallow pool and watched as the fish swam around it, creating a small vortex. He seemed, for a moment, to revel in his own ingenuity.

'Look how quickly the world can be taken away. Yesterday they had this entire creek. Now this is all they have. This is all they know. We did that,' he said darkly.

He stood and knocked over a portion of the sandstone wall. I watched from the opposite side of the bank as loose sediment dislodged from the bed and turned the water around him an inky black. The fish spilled out of the pool and fled downstream.

'You're taking it down?' I asked.

'Yes,' he said. 'It's important that we leave no trace.'

This, as I came to discover, was one of Hristo's primary

compulsions. He held an almost sacred belief in the semi-permanence of nature. It was paramount to him that we left no trace. He repeated the words often, like a mantra. While we worked, he regaled me with the storied history of human trap making. He spoke with reverence about humanity's affinity for subjugation, his voice taking on a lyrical quality, his body relaxing into an almost transcendental state.

'What on earth have you been doing?' my mother would ask as she tended to my soiled clothing each evening. But privately I could tell that she was relieved.

He has a friend, I imagined her telling my father in the dark of their bedroom.

A friend, at long last.

But Hristo offered little in the way of personal information. I had no idea where he lived. If he had siblings. Whether his parents were separated or otherwise. I caught only the briefest glimpses of his home life: the constellation of bruises that decorated his upper body, the long stretches of unexplained school absences, the way his voice would falter when he mentioned his father. But it didn't matter. Hristo had given me something greater than friendship. For the first time, I had a place in the world. The forest was ours. Outside lay the world, remote and murky in its confusion, but here we had claimed a part of it for ourselves. And when school closed its doors for the summer months, we conspired to live a primitive life there, sheltered from the world. I told my mother that I was staying with Hristo and he did the same, and just like that we were free.

On our first evening together we lit a large fire and lay beside it and Hristo spoke about the importance of the work that lay ahead of us. He said that people had wilfully forgotten the old ways, the necessities of their own survival. One day, by his reckoning, the power would fail without warning, the phones would stop ringing, the food deliveries would cease. And it would be caused by the pollution of the light and air, the invasion of the auditory and ocular pathways, the invisible spectrums of human conquest. Nature, he said, would eventually reclaim the spoils of man. And good riddance. To Hristo, ignorance was a trap as effective as any he could imagine building.

'My first night out here I couldn't sleep. I wasn't used to it.'

'The silence?' I asked.

'It's not silence. If you stay perfectly still, if you strain your ears, you'll hear it.'

I closed my eyes and lay still. I imagined the area around my own body. I felt the heat of the fire radiating into the darkness, but all I could hear was the beating of my own heart.

'What am I listening for?'

'The hum of the universe,' Hristo said earnestly.

'The hum of the universe?'

'The ways things are. The way things have always been. The way they will be again.'

I rolled myself over and snorted into the cool fabric of my sleeping bag.

'The world doesn't owe us anything,' Hristo said irritably, turning his back to me. 'You'll see.'

In the morning Hristo was gone. I searched the camp but there was no sign of him. When he finally appeared out of a patch of tall grass and beckoned for me to follow, I'd all but given up hope. We walked for half an hour, until Hristo stopped and took out a red journal. Inside was a sketch of a deadfall trap.

'I've built these before, but not like this,' he said excitedly as we worked to lift several large slabs of stone. 'Never this big.'

We rested each of the slabs above two carefully balanced sticks and coated a third in bait before wedging it between them. When we were finished, we climbed a nearby tree and waited. I made myself comfortable and allowed the heat of the afternoon to slowly take me. I dreamt that Hristo and I were in the forest, running topless through the trees. I caught brief flashes of his pale skin as he ran ahead of me. When he shook me awake several hours later the light had changed around us. The traps had caught a total of three squirrels. Hristo led me to each one, his breathing ragged, his eyes wild.

'They had no idea it was coming,' he said, dancing like a jester.

The animals lay sandwiched by rock, the stone kissing through them.

'This one tried to get away,' he said. 'But not quick enough.'

Its arms were sprawled out in front of it, its head bloodied, its eyes ejected from their sockets by the impact. He clapped his hands together, imitating the force of the blow. I stared at the bodies. I'd seen death before but only in passing: a raccoon curled at the roadside, a coroner transporting an elderly neighbour. In the outer world, death had a transient quality. But here, in the stillness of the forest, the concept took on a sense of permanence. We were alone not only with the body, but with the sense of the thing before the body: the life.

That night, Hristo taught me to clean and prepare the animals and we ate the meat hunched over the firepit like cave dwellers. Afterwards I told him about all of the things that had surprised me: how easily the bones had broken, how simple the body looked beneath its coat, how oddly mechanical and primitive its construction. And when he nodded his head enthusiastically, hanging off my every word, I ruminated on the act of reduction I had witnessed.

'They seemed foolish.'

'Foolish?' he asked.

'To allow themselves to be trapped.'

He leant forward, his eyes shining in the darkness, his breathing hard, expectant.

'You felt they deserved it?'

When I nodded my head, he let out an audible gasp.

It slithered out of him.

A moment of pure relief.

In the weeks that followed, Hristo abandoned any attempt at hiding the darker elements of his nature. It was as if he had suddenly realised the benefit of our partnership, and with my help he began to accelerate some internal timeline. To fully realise his cruel intentions.

We created tension traps which loosed fire-hardened stakes down upon rabbits and raccoons with a brutal efficiency. Those lucky enough died quickly; the rest fled hopelessly. We beat bushes and followed their trails, hollering like some primitive and barbarous people. And when we found their mottled bodies alive with blowflies we danced and sang.

Hristo made no attempt to salvage the meat. Instead he insisted that we endeavour to catch live game, and so we set about rigging spring snares using thin metal wire which tightened around the animals' throats and lifted them high into the air when the traps were sprung.

When we stumbled upon deer tracks late one afternoon, Hristo became consumed with the thought of catching one alive. We built a collection of Apache foothold traps, which we covered with layers of leaves and loose foliage, and for a week we waited with held breath. But when the fated deer failed to materialise, Hristo grew incensed.

The next morning we marched further than ever before into the woodland, passing a red clay gulley, and deeper still until we came upon a clearing circled by oaks and hickories where a column of sunlight cut through the trees.

We worked in shifts to dig a large pit. By late afternoon the heat was suffocating. We stripped to our underwear and crawled in and out of the earth like primordial creatures. We tossed the displaced soil over the lip of the pit, and when the pit became too deep we ran ropes through a tin pail and lifted it like a dumbwaiter.

I was working alone when my shovel hit bedrock. I called out to Hristo, but there was only silence. Above me I could see the dusk closing in. I touched the freezing dirt walls around me and felt a sudden jolt of panic. The pit was at least ten feet deep. There were no footholds to speak of. I tried to climb but without traction it was hopeless. I cried out for help, but no help came. I sat and considered my options. Eventually I dug my shovel into the pit wall and used it for leverage, hoisting myself up by grabbing fistfuls of loose branches.

I found Hristo sitting just a few feet from the pit. He'd been listening. As I caught my breath, he peered over the edge and stared at the shovel.

'You cheated,' he said disappointedly.

As we worked to cover the mouth of the pit a heavy rain began to fall. Within minutes the wind picked up and we found ourselves chased back to camp by an encroaching storm. It rained for three miserable days. When the wind brought tree branches down around us, we decamped to the rock formation beside the creek. We ate provisions that Hristo had saved or brought from home, and when the rain finally subsided we found ourselves so exhausted that we slept for an entire day.

With the weather more agreeable, Hristo was eager to check on the pit. We filled water bottles from the creek, packed tools and began on a sullen pilgrimage. We passed the clay gulley and walked carefully over moss-covered limestone and the trunks of felled trees. By the time we reached the clearing, the sun had risen to sit in the middle of an otherwise colourless sky.

We could tell immediately that something was wrong.

The netting over the pit had collapsed and beside the open mouth lay a whittled stick. Hristo froze. At the bottom of the pit lay the body of a man in a bright puffer jacket and tattered hiking boots. His left arm was bent awkwardly. The top of his head crowned by a halo of blood. At the sight of him I felt the air leave my body.

'How did he get here?' I asked, pacing the perimeter of the pit and then stopping when I felt a wave of nausea rise up in my throat. 'We haven't seen anyone in weeks. No one comes out here.'

'You're here,' Hristo said, his eyes fixed on the body.

'I don't want to be.'

'Well,' Hristo said, 'you're here.'

I sat down and began to weep. Hristo regarded me with a mixture of confusion and condescension.

'We didn't push him,' he said dispassionately.

I stared down at the body. There was something in the stillness of it.

'My God,' I whispered. 'My God, Hristo. Look what we did.'

Hristo turned and lifted me up by the lapels, walking me backwards until the balls of my feet hung over the lip of the pit.

'There's no God here,' Hristo said.

'Isn't there?' I shouted suddenly. 'You and your pathetic fucking crusade.'

He pushed me further until my body hung at an angle over the pit. For a moment I thought he was preparing to drop me. I imagined myself alone with the body.

'Please don't,' I said, clawing at his arms for balance.

He was deathly silent. I watched my fate swimming in the dark of his eyes.

'Go back to camp,' he said at last. 'Wait for me there. Speak to no one. Do you understand?'

When I nodded, he let me go.

'Help me down,' he said, picking up one of the shovels.

I lowered him awkwardly and watched as he bent over the body and began to inspect it.

'What are you going to do with him?' I asked eventually.

He looked almost startled by my presence.

'Go now,' he said. 'Leave us.'

The forest had never seemed so small as on that lonely walk back to camp. Without Hristo to guide me, the landscape felt entirely unfamiliar. The sound of phantom sirens played through the trees and I imagined beams of torchlight in the distance, search parties combing the woodland to take us away.

I thought not of the life I had taken, but of all that remained of my own.

Second by second. Minute by minute.

When I reached the encampment, I found that I was shaking. I stoked a small fire and when the flames burnt bright and good, I sat beside it and thought back to our first week in the forest. How Hristo had dipped his fist into the sandstone pool and marvelled at his own ingenuity.

'Look how quickly the world can be taken away,' he had said.

I thought again of the man. I imagined him alone in the pit. I prayed that the fall had taken him quickly. I prayed for his family. For all those who might have known him. But in response I heard only Hristo's voice: *There's no God here.*

I found Hristo's red journal and began to flip through it. There were sketches of traps, custom-built containers and cages, all manner of measurements. But as the book went on the illustrations grew steadily more disturbing, until they ceased to document traps at all, but instruments of torture.

I cast it disgustedly into the fire and watched as the pages curled and the embers floated into the early evening, and then I took a collection of spears and crude instruments he had crafted and threw them onto the flames as well. The fire rose and roared with a hunger that I sated with sleeping bags and spare clothing until the flames became a towering effigy.

Hristo appeared out of the forest in the late evening like some wretched time-haunted phantom. His entire body caked in mud, his eyes floating in the darkness. We sat in silence for a time, completely exhausted.

'It's done,' he said finally.

'We have to tell someone.'

'There's nothing to tell. The pit is gone. Tomorrow this will all be gone too.'

'People could be looking for him,' I said.

'No one's looking. His wallet was empty. He had a driving license but it expired a couple of years back. His clothes were threadbare. I think he might have been a transient. We got lucky.'

'We got lucky?'

Hristo nodded.

'We have to tell someone. If you won't do it, I will.'

'You'll tell them what, exactly?'

I thought about this. I tried to imagine the conversation. Without Hristo, I had little hope of ever finding the pit. I saw him hunch over, shielding his body slightly. In his hand he held a leather wallet.

'Did you take that from him?' I asked.

He drew the wallet close, cradling it like a child.

'He doesn't need it,' he said.

'It doesn't belong to you. You can't take a person's things.'

'A person?' He scoffed. 'You don't even know his name.'

'Tell me,' I said, rising to my feet. 'Tell me his name.'

He held the wallet out as if he were preparing to hand it to me, but as I stepped forward he cast it into the bonfire. I watched as a thin smile spread across his face. In the firelight I felt as if I were seeing him for the first time.

'A part of you wanted this,' I said, aghast.

I backed away slowly from the fire. Hristo sat motionless, watching me.

'Did you enjoy being down in that hole?' he asked. 'Because if you talk that's what they'll do. They'll lock you away. They'll throw away the key.'

I stumbled over loose branches and stone until I'd put several hundred feet between us, and then I turned on my heels and ran through the forest.

'There are thousands of acres out here,' he shouted after me. 'People disappear all the time.'

The end of summer brought with it days of isolation and grief. My mother regarded me with a certain sense of longing. She knew that something unspeakable had been lost between us, an innocence that would never be recovered. Have you been eating? she asked. And I assured her yes, yes. But even I was shocked by the sight that greeted me in the mirror each morning. It was as if Hristo was staring back at me. I'd lost weight. My skin was pale, my hair greasy, my eyes sunken.

For weeks, I waited for the news to break. For the television to show scenes of search parties scouring the woodlands, televised appeals from concerned family members. But nothing came. It was inconceivable. We had dug a hole in the earth. It had swallowed a man. How could such a thing go unnoticed? How could it not matter?

At home I took long baths and tried to scrub myself clean of Hristo's touch. I revelled in the luxury of betraying everything he stood for. But at night I lay awake and listened to the steady throb of the power lines behind the house, to the unending artificial iridescence of the outer world, and I knew that I had been forever tainted.

School began but there was no Hristo. The administration said his father had been redeployed. They left no forwarding address. No additional information. Upon hearing the news, I trekked to the creek but found little evidence of our encampment.

The fishing rods and toolboxes were gone. The tarpaulin sheets and stove pots had vanished. Even the firepit had been dug over and covered with loose leaves. I hiked to the clay gulley and searched for the forest clearing, for any sign of the pit, but I found the path unrecognisable.

Hristo had been true to his word. He had left no trace.

For months I dreamt of the pit. I imagined the man. I saw the shape of his body. I heard him crying out in the darkness. I no longer knew how to live with myself, but still I lived. Years passed in brief glimpses: the furrowing out of a meek existence. School. College. A steady stream of jobs and short-term apartment leases. Always moving on at the slightest hint of promotion or accolade. The semi-permanence of the guilty man.

I remember days of despondency, days of delinquency. Days spent waiting for a judgement that refused to come. There were relationships. Men and women. But their faces are amorphous now in my memory. Their fates sealed by a hesitation deep in the fabric of my own body. I passed through the lives of others like some half-remembered dream – but still there were moments of consciousness.

When my father collapsed on a golf course, I drove home to find excavators carving into the woodland. Men in bright vests busy digging up large swathes of ground for new developments. I prayed for the discovery of our makeshift grave, but still nothing came.

My mother died a year later. She'd gone to be with my father, the chaplain said, and it was shortly after the service, alone in the world, that I decided to confess. I sat with a police sergeant, a reticent man who correlated the dates I'd given with missing person reports, but ultimately came up empty-handed.

'Can you give us a name, anything to go on?' he asked, but I shook my head: no, no.

He requisitioned two officers and had me lead them into the forest, but after an afternoon of aimless wandering they called off the search. By their reckoning I was a victim of grief, some misremembered childhood fantasy, and they cut me loose, citing a lack of even circumstantial evidence.

'Come back to us with a name,' they said.

I packed up my parents' house and fled like a thief in the night. I searched for Hristo. There was no mention of him on search engines or social networks, so I hired a private investigator. He tracked him to Colorado through deeds and divorce records, but there the trail ran cold. It was only after an insurance company suffered a data breach that his details finally came to light. We got lucky, he said. Hristo had left virtually no footprint.

I sat on the balcony of my apartment until the early hours of the morning. When I made the call, Hristo answered almost immediately; at the sound of his voice my legs went weak. I knelt as if in prayer.

'Hristo?' I whispered.

'Who is this?'

In the background I could hear muffled conversation.

'Hristo,' I said. 'It's me.'

There was silence on the line. I pressed my ear to the receiver and listened to the sounds of a mother soothing her child. Was it possible that Hristo had a family? I looked back at the barren walls of my apartment. My pathetic kitchenette.

'Hristo, please.'

I heard footsteps and the closing of a door.

'How did you get this number?' he said irritably, his voice hushed.

'I told them what we did, Hristo. But they don't believe me. They need his name. They say if I give them his name they can look into it. They can verify the authenticity of my claim.'

Hristo exhaled slowly.

'I just need his name.'

He held the receiver so close that the sound of his breath distorted the line. He took pleasure in withholding the information. It was like we were children again: the learned teacher and the helpless student.

'I can't live like this,' I said.

He began to draw quick, excited breaths. I thought of the body in the pit. The crown of blood. The face made blurry by memory. Hristo had laid not only the body to rest, but all proof of the man. He had left no trace of our indiscretion. There could be no expiation, no hope of atonement without his blessing. He alone carried the stranger's identity and, by extension, my own. I came to him now a hollow man, a transient and unsubstantial soul. And I realised then the scope and scale of the trap that Hristo had laid. The years he had spent waiting. I saw the man in the pit, I saw myself beside him. We were one in the same.

'Hristo, please,' I wept. 'I have nothing.'

His breathing rose to a crescendo that ended with an elongated gasp. It slithered out of him. A moment of pure relief. There was silence on the line. I didn't dare speak.

'The world doesn't owe you anything,' he said softly.

I sat with the receiver in my lap and watched the sun rise in the east. It emerged from the earth as if escaping some sunken place where the dead reside, their souls inky and nameless and otherwise lost to time. Soon, I knew, people would begin to rise, and with them too the clamour of life. I sat quietly and revelled in the silence, and it was then that I heard it. The faintest utterance. A vibration deep in the earth that rose through the tenements and radiated into my bones.

The hum of the universe.

The Ghosts from Kathmandu

Abi Hynes

Leena has to starve herself for three months, but eventually her figure is boyish as his. She exercises in secret, locking her fingers over the beam above the kitchen doorframe and hauling herself up until her arms burn and her stomach muscles shake. As Anuj wastes slowly into bone and mattress, she grows lean and wiry and capable.

In the evenings, when they eat together, she observes her husband closely, and marks the rhythm of his right hand as it balls his rice to bring it to his lips. She practises mimicking his voice: the longer vowels, the softness of his tongue rolling in his mouth. His laugh she has to summon from memory, and she rehearses it in front of the mirror while he sleeps, standing naked except for one of his long shirts, her hair tucked down inside the collar. She drops her breath into her stomach and lets it deepen there. She winks, and the young man in the mirror winks back. She presses her lips to his and breathes her life against the glass. It is hot and youthful and impatient.

The Tourists have been in town for eight days. Leena watches from the window as they emerge from the Kathmandu Guesthouse a little later each morning, outrageously tipping the rickshaw drivers who disperse them amongst the backpackers and the gap year students. They have a sightseeing itinerary, although they take no pictures. Their fingers twitch in the remembered habits of phones and laptops. They compose tweets that nobody will ever read; they overlay the Buddhist stupas with imagined Instagram filters. Nashville. Gotham. Vintage. It's all so new for them, this withdrawal from the world. To Leena, they look like big, bright schoolchildren.

Their tour guide, pink and shining in his polyester shirt, is an easy man to watch. They do not know his name; they know nothing except that he will go last. He moves steadily between internet cafés, his phone buzzing in his pocket. He is Norwegian, perhaps, or Dutch, but he answers in an American accent: 'Namaste. How are you?'

Back at the house, they never answer phone calls. Each day, a note arrives for Anuj and he and Leena reply to it together. At first, he writes himself and has her copy it; she is careful to match the spikiness of his English lettering.

I'm glad you are enjoying your visit. Will you go to the zoo tomorrow? I think you would like to see the mad bear!

I hope the food at the hotel is to your liking. If not, you must come for dinner with my family. I have told them all about you.

She signs her husband's name, over and over, until she dreams about it.

Each day, the rickshaws return one fewer passenger to the guesthouse, and another room becomes available. Their clean sheets are hung to dry over the balconies like flags, and taken in again before the rain comes.

In the mornings, Anuj plots the Tourists' journeys. Leena brings his maps to him in bed and he shows her all his favourites: the bold red lines that mark the routes most difficult to track.

'India,' he tells her. 'You can fly direct to New Zealand now. Get a job as a surfing instructor, see? No one bothers you. That's one year, maybe two.' She nods.

The map in front of Leena has a jagged strip torn out of it. The whole route from Greece across to Pakistan has gaping holes in it. Syria is gone completely.

'We used to use that one a lot,' says Anuj. 'Much harder than when we lost Japan. You'll learn to change your habits quickly. Now you try.'

She takes the next name on the list. 'Singapore,' she says, stroking its shape. 'To visit friends?'

He takes the ledger from her and scrutinises the name. 'Not for this guy,' he says, his brow furrowed. The weight of the world on him. 'We could start with a trek here in Nepal, maybe, to buy some time. Could try Tibet, although it's risky. But he needs a destination fast.'

He gasps, his slight chest heaving. His skin is pale and waxy. Leena lies beside him, not an ounce of flesh between them, and they talk their grand plan through again from start to finish. She reels off the names of the men in his photographs, the names of their wives, their children, and the facts comfort them both. She measures her handspan against his and takes stock of the distance she will have to travel.

She is learning fast. Some days she feels that calm anticipation replace her fear, ready to shake off the waiting. She shape-shifts between her old identity and her new one, some days more comfortable as a boy than as a wife. She notices the small differences: her laugh is louder, and she makes more eye contact with strangers. Only her mother-in-law's forceful intrusions keep her strung tight as a hare.

'Look at you,' she mutters to Anuj on her twice-daily visits to their bedroom. Nice and loud for Leena's benefit. He lies there weakly and lets Amar chatter away to him like an infant.

'You're not very comfortable like that, are you, babu?' she asks, not waiting for an answer. 'Shall we ask Leena to help you sit up properly?'

Leena does as she is bidden, quiet and quick, and bites her tongue until there's blood in her mouth.

In the afternoons, Anuj plans the final disappearances. They are for the Tourists who will not come back; the ones for whom a few years to be forgotten will not be enough. Leena knows never to ask why these people need to disappear. Their business is in the vanishing; they are not detectives.

'Don't be afraid to get creative,' Anuj says. She likes this part. The pen keeps slipping from his hand, so she writes for him.

'Ready?'

He groans and puts his hands over his swollen eyes. 'Moped accident. Broken neck. Find a body if we need to.'

She scribbles. 'Next?'

'Secret illness. Wanted to see Russia one last time. Overdose… Wait, no. We did that one in Sweden. Better die of natural causes. We need another local one.'

'I know. The zoo – the mad bear escapes and eats him.'

He grins at her. 'Perfect.'

It's a blessing that he feels a little better when the Ghost arrives. She is shown inside before she can attract attention, before an old man passing by, who might be anyone, can see her and report it.

Anuj struggles to his feet, and washes deathbed sickness from his face and hands before he goes to greet her. His mother fusses, but the urgency is obvious, even to her. Ghosts bring trouble, and they must be dealt with.

The Ghost is a woman, no older than Leena, with a tight, hungry mouth. Her presence in the house feels contaminating. The way she looks at them is too pleading, her helplessness too obvious. She reaches out a hand in greeting and Leena shrinks away, pressing her palms to her heart instead.

'Namaste.'

She has forgotten to put her nose ring in, but the Ghost is a westerner, and will not notice.

Anuj offers her a seat. He keeps his expression severe and unreadable and rests his hands on his knees to hide the shaking. Leena serves their tea and listens from the kitchen.

'I've changed my mind,' the Ghost is saying. Her fair hair is dirty and her eyes are wild.

'You can't. You're off the map now.'

'Put me back on it, then!'

'We don't do that.'

'Please,' she says. 'You have to help me. My parents are getting old. I want to see them. I want to go home.'

The room is quiet for a moment. Leena puts her eye to the gap in the curtain; the Ghost is pulling out a mobile phone. An old-style Nokia. Pay-as-you-go. No internet, no apps, but still.

'Are you mad?' says Anuj. He snatches it from her, and in one quick motion he has cracked it open, gutted it and crushed the SIM card with his teeth. 'No. Never.'

'I thought I could just contact them. I could see... how things are. If there is any chance—'

'No chance. You think they will not find you if you use these things? No chance at all.'

The Ghost stares at the remains of the Nokia. 'But how am I supposed to live?' Her voice trembles. 'What do they do – all these people you make disappear? No phone, no name, no passport – where do they go?'

Anuj sighs. The sound rattles. 'We do not ask that. We do not even think it. We vanish them – they don't come back.'

'But don't you understand…?'

'My older brother died. I understand. It was hard, but he did not come back. People like you. They don't exist.'

'But I do exist,' she murmurs, close to tears. 'I'm here.'

'You shouldn't be.' Leena hears their chairs scraping. Time to go.

They wait for the rain to send her on her way. In the deafening sound of the downpour, her footsteps might as well be silent.

Kathmandu Guest House empties, one day at a time. When the time comes, Anuj wants to cut her hair himself. Insists on it, lip trembling like a sulky child. So she props him up on pillows until he can sit upright, and crouches in between his knees. Outside, the roads are like rivers; the dust turned liquid, licking at their doorstep. Their room absorbs the thick, hot damp of August.

Leena listens to the *scraaape, scrrraaaape* of the scissors with a sense that Anuj is shearing someone else. Dark tufts tumble to rest on the pale bedspread. She turns to him, eyes bright, resisting the mirror.

'How do I look, Anuj?'

'Very sweet, *bhai*,' he tells her. *Little brother.* His teasing smile is almost able to reach his eyes. 'Come here, babu.'

They make love tentatively, him clumsy with the new shape of her. She wonders where he finds the energy. Beneath her, his ribcage feels fragile as a bird's. She dips her tongue into the space between his collarbones and thinks, *Remember this.*

'Don't get sick,' he says, half-hopeful.

She still smells of him as she pulls on his shirt, his trousers, his narrow-waisted belt. The shoes she had to buy, pretending they were for her nephew, gleam like hair oil. He catches her by the wrist, his grip like a moth-wing, and she fights the urge to brush him off.

'Are you ready, Leena?'

She nods. The upward-only jerk of her head, like he does, like his older brother used to.

'Because he's never met me,' he says, 'there's no reason for him to think anything is wrong.'

'I'm not afraid.'

'I'm afraid for you.'

She plants a rough kiss on his forehead, her eyes darting to the clock.

'I've got to go.'

'Show me the signature again,' he says, clawing at the moment. 'Practise. Here, on my arm.'

He rolls up his sleeve. His wasted flesh is tinged with yellow. Even through his shirt, she can feel him burning.

'No,' she says. 'There isn't time.'

She tries to pull away from him, but he clings to her arm. With painful effort, he rolls himself half over, reaching for his watch; his fine gold watch, with his initials etched onto the flipside of its face. It fits her wrist better than his own.

The rain has stopped by the time Leena steps outside, but her trousers are quickly hemmed in crimson mud. It's only a short walk across the city but she takes a taxi, thrilled by the freedom of it, her bare arm out of the window to shoo away the boys that come to tap against the windscreen. She rests the rucksack loosely on her lap, and shrugs it on again when they reach the shop: no big deal. In it, the details of a new story, a man who found religion here, gave up his name and all his worldly goods, became a monk and died a natural death. An easy fix, no passport needed. A nice, round tale. A Ghost created.

Two beggars crouch at the side of the road, a few metres apart; a man with no shirt and deep-set eyes that linger on her, and a woman in a pale yellow sari with a tiny baby strapped against her chest. The air conditioning hisses at her as she approaches. The man has a look of her husband about him, she realises. Something familiar, something haunted in the shadows of his face. He crouches with his elbows on his knees, the way that Anuj does, the way his older brother used to. Leena lets her spine relax. Inhales. The beggars watch her.

The shopkeeper is talking to a Tourist in the doorway, looking strained. It is a souvenir shop, he explains, with fixed prices. The Tourist haggles anyway. He is the man from the internet cafés, the large, pink man with short fair hair, his chin protruding. The Tour Guide is always the last one to go, and the deal is always done in person.

'How much for this?' he asks. American accent. He is shown the price tag, marked in euros and dollars.

'Alright. How much for three?'

The shopkeeper holds his hands up in front of him, despairing.

'It is the same,' he says. The Tourist frowns, his pale eyes disappearing in his rosy face. He points at Leena.

'How much if he was buying, eh?'

'The same, the same.'

'Like hell it would be.'

'Sir, I cannot change the prices. Do you want to pay now?' The Tourist shrugs.

'I think I'll look around a little longer.'

The shopkeeper grimaces and backs away. He looks past Leena to the street outside, where the beggars look on with interest.

'Again!' he shouts at Leena. 'You see them? Every day I move them on, and here they are again!'

Furious, he marches off, to return a moment later with a bucket of water. He tips the entirety of it over the woman's head, soaking her. Her baby screams.

'Hey!' The Tourist thunders over. 'What the fuck do you think you're doing?'

On the doorstep, Leena puts down her rucksack. No big deal. The Tourist has his big red hand on the shopkeeper's chest; the man looks terrified.

'I told her!' he says, his voice shaking. 'I told her yesterday, come back here and I'll beat you. She brings the child so I cannot beat her!'

The Tourist looks about to hit him, and Leena digs her nails into the palms of her hands. A man on the brink of vanishing might be unpredictable, she guesses. But instead, he pulls out his wallet and waves a handful of notes in the shopkeeper's face.

'This is your apology,' he says.

He picks up Leena's rucksack like it is his own and throws it over one large shoulder. He gives the money to the beggar woman, who takes it silently. She staggers another metre down the street, and crouches again. The Tourist walks away, and does not look back.

The shopkeeper rolls his eyes towards the heavens.

'You see, brother?' he says to Leena. 'You see what I have to put up with?'

He goes inside. Leena takes the money from the beggar woman and signs the receipt, quick and easy, just like her husband. She hails a taxi home. The shirtless man watches her leave, his gaze bold. She feels as though his eyes are burning through her clothes.

When she returns, she takes the money up to Anuj and she sees that he is dead.

She makes ready. She lays out his best clothes for him, and in between her letters she keeps vigil.

My wife has passed away. I will be staying with my family in Pokhara. Please send all future correspondence there.

The disappearances continue at the same steady rate. Outside the city, the air is fat and fragrant. She sits at the table with the windows flung wide open while she works. In the mornings, she plans the Tourists' journeys. When a destination fails, she tears the map. The world shrinks under her hands as the letters keep arriving.

The partners visit her, of course, to see that the business is in safe hands after another family tragedy. She remembers the death of her brother-in-law eight years earlier. The sudden change of authority, the new lines on her husband's face. But he handled it. He kept the people moving, as his family always had. The journeys were plotted, the stories delivered, the fees collected. Ghosts had rarely reappeared, and they posed no major threats.

There was a rhythm to this work and it had suited him. The partners and their families relaxed. Stopped eyeing up their own sons, readying.

'My story is going to outlive me,' Anuj had said to her the week before he died.

She commands the household now, and her mother-in-law, who knows, but will not notice, is stiff and silent. Leena shrouds herself inside his second-best suit. She feels bigger in it than she's felt for months; no more shrinking inside the glowing silk of her own clothes. Her waist opens. Her walk loosens. The arches of her feet relax.

Below, the murmur of her guests gathering. She goes down and plays the grieving husband. She wears Anuj like a coat in winter, his wedding ring warm and loose on her right thumb, his initials listening to her fierce pulse. Flesh of my flesh.

'So sad,' she hears Amar say. 'She nursed him and she died so quickly. She was a good wife to him, but she must not have had his strength.'

The men nod, their faces grave. They are dressed expensively; they eat Amar's cooking with sombre enthusiasm.

She does not think of his small body, quiet now where hers should be. She does not think of the alternative, of the shirtless man whose face was like his brother's; she does not hope.

She shakes the hands of all these men and looks them in the eye. She smiles, and they say:

'It is so good to see you looking so well.'

Greenwood Tree

Sarah Dale

When I was a child, I used to lie under the huge conker trees that edged the caravan park. I watched the dark, dense mass of leaves stir and lift. I breathed deeply. As the sun set, the light caught on the upper branches – so far up, touching the sky – filling me with ideas and possibilities for where my life might lead.

'Oh, there you are, you daydreamer,' my mum would say, smiling, coming to ask me to help her prepare the dinner, or to say we were about to go out. I'd go with her, a piece of me storing the images, the precise shades of green, of dark and light, for recalling in times when I felt lonely or frightened.

Time passed. At school I read Shakespeare and learned by heart a poem about lying under a greenwood tree. I learned about biology, about phloem and xylem, about the placement of leaves being perfectly adapted to catch maximum sunlight, about the power shade produced by the absorption of the sun's energy. I learned about the constant hidden motion, about the cycle of carbon and oxygen. I learned how long such trees could live – centuries – and I collected conkers each autumn. I never drilled holes in them, never used them to fight or destroy or win or lose, but held them secretly in my coat pocket, fingers curled around the glossy surface as they fitted into my palm.

I grew up. I learnt a job, a profession; I took responsibility. I learnt to be ambitious and driven. I was rewarded. I married, bought a house, had a child. We moved to be near the sea. It was agreed to be idyllic, enviable. I valued success, I was promoted, I became senior partner. I had everything my friends and family wanted for me.

We all aged. My parents moved to be near me. My daughter grew up too. My husband retired. We held parties with champagne on the lawn overlooking the harbour. We didn't talk about how thin our daughter was to start with. We threw money at our parents' frailty, at my mother's worsening dementia. We kept busy. So busy. We had a boat now, as well as the house, to maintain. We had our daughter's A levels to navigate. Her Oxbridge entrance exams. My pension to think about and the firm's succession strategy. That awkward business with the bungled merger. Such a series of misunderstandings. I knew I could steer us through it.

I was tired.

And then Rosa's anorexia – we had to face it – became a full-time job in itself. I left no stone unturned to find her world-class help. I argued her case whenever I needed to; I got her into the best treatment centre around. It didn't mean university had to be shelved. Not indefinitely. I worked hard to present a cheerful and positive attitude, especially when I couldn't avoid the subject coming up. What mother wouldn't?

We kept going. There was no alternative.

I'd forgotten about trees, apart from managing those in our garden, which in truth were taken care of by our gem of a gardener.

But one hot Saturday in May, I'd arranged to meet a friend for coffee. Well, a potential client more than a friend. She'd recommended this place, a garden near a spring with a vegan café. Cool running water, dappled green shade. Trees in their prime.

In the end, she didn't turn up. She texted, to be fair, but it was too late. I was already there. Irritated – I had plenty to do – I was about to turn round and leave, but I realised, with a pain like a splinter driving deep under my skin, that I was empty. Drained. No energy, no power. My limbs felt weak. A blast of suffocating heat passed through me.

I needed to sit down, lie down. I moved away from the people, the tables, to the edge of the garden. To a grassy area in the shade of a mature horse chestnut tree. It was in flower, and coming into full leaf. I glanced around. No one was looking. I lay down and stared up at it.

I felt the years piling up and falling over, falling away. I felt twenty, fourteen, seven. I thought of the lives lived while this tree had grown from conker to sapling to majestic great-grandmother. My own life. I felt the pressure of doubt in my chest, in my stomach. Vertigo. I had never felt like this. My terror grew; I couldn't breathe. Was my heart giving out? Was I losing my sanity, having a breakdown?

Come, come. The leaves stirred. I heard my name. I crawled to the trunk and pressed my hands into it. It felt soft, cool, surprising. I watched. I couldn't see my hands anymore. They had taken on the pattern of the bark. I tried to pull them away but they were stuck, fixed. My heart raced; I felt silent tears cascade. *Come, come.* And then, complete, sudden release. I fell forward against the tree. *Enough, enough, enough.* Surrender. Relinquish. Let go.

Bliss ran through each vein, each nerve. A sense of completeness. Wholeness. Of putting everything down. Weightless. Pleased with what is. *Enough.*

This was many seasons ago. Unmeasured. I wait, I stay.

I watch the little girl lying beneath our branches. I see her look up at us intently. There are so many of us here, each flower bearing witness. Witness to the little girl's sadness, her wonder, her trust and fear. I hear her parents call. I watch her start, push something of herself into the background. She jumps up and runs off to meet them, smiling.

I will wait for her. I have all the time in the world.

The Midwinter Marriage

Margaret Crompton

Four men asked me to marry them. I said yes to them all.

Vernon March whisked me to the altar in the month which matched his name. His courtship had soothed me like a breeze, flattered me into a flutter. I wore a green gown with a wreath of violets and primroses. They wilted nearly as fast as the marriage.

First of my friends to be seduced, I boasted about my man. Ah, that Spring. What bliss to be young and alive and married to— but who was I married to? Vernon March might have come in like a lamb, winsome and winning, cuddling and gambolling. But gambolling metamorphosed into gambling, winning into losing. The Spring-like charm, warm as an April sunbeam, dissolved into an April shower, which shivered into a freezing deluge. No more cuddles. Rough winds would definitely shake such darling buds of May as dared to show their chilly pink noses. Mr March was elsewhere when I marched away.

Sonny Summers found me shivering on the beach. My Springtime was long gone. I was alone, unwanted and past caring. Almost. But not yet ready to paddle into the sea with a pocket full of rocks. Not quite. Sonny offered what I most wanted from him: his name. Absurd and warming. A long way from chilly Mr March. We married on a different beach, beside a gleaming ocean. I wore a yellow bikini with orange polka dots, under a transparent mantle of gold-flecked silk.

Home. Safe. Beautiful again. To be forever warm. Beach after beach, sea after sea, ocean after ocean. My eternal summer was beginning to fade, baked by relentless suns, scoured by swirling sand. Sonny treated me to boatloads of creams and treatments, lotions and masks. He treated himself to shiploads of ladies whose skin retained a Spring-like glow without, it seemed, artificial aid. He was always generous, but unremitting warmth became oppressive. I was burning out with the effort of showing enthusiasm for eternal life on interminable shores. Basking and volleyball, bathing, sailing, drinking. Taking my turn in the ever-lengthening rota of bed visitations. It wasn't hard not to care about rivals. I simply didn't. Have the energy. To care

Sonny's beams failed to fade when I asked for a ticket to ride. Anywhere. Preferably sandless. His attention was already bestowed on another shivering refugee. We parted with a hug. Warm. Naturally.

I fell for Mr Leif by mistake. Too old for marriage now. Too late for love – whatever that might be. Half my life gone. Nothing left. I gave up all thought of men. No more hope meant no more disappointment. No one had ever given me what I most wanted – whatever that might be. I must fill my remaining days with useful activity. Become productive. I went to work. In a wood. In a country populated by trees. To be safe from people. From men and marriage. From longings.

My work was hands-on, hypnotic, hard. I grew to understand the growing trees, to recognise tiny changes, to care when a tree had been injured, to rejoice when a wound healed. One afternoon, I rested on a moss-covered rock with my back against a strong brown trunk. I stroked the bark, noticing its unusual texture, like velvet. I leaned my head against the tree and drifted into a doze. I woke when the tree shifted. My head nodded forward. The tree had... moved? I looked round. The tree had disappeared altogether. Or rather, had been transformed into a tall man in brown corduroy trousers and a camouflage jacket. He apologised for disturbing me but after an hour as my backrest, his leg had begun to cramp.

Mr Leif was the Wood Warden. He took me to his log cabin in a glade. We married without the aid of registrar or priest, holding hands in the grove where we had met. Gentle sunlight penetrated our canopy of leaves: scarlet, gold, cinnamon, nut brown.

My wedding outfit was everyday woodswoman's gear – tough trousers, steel-tipped boots, triple-knit jumper, thick protective gloves. Birds sang our epithalamium. Deer and squirrels served as witnesses.

Perfect. I had everything I could want. Nearly everything. In the Autumn of my days, I felt mellow, quiet. Complete. Nearly. Except. I was sometimes lonely. Mr Leif was a very peaceful person. Not very talkative. Very entire unto himself. The wood was his perfect place. He was completely connected with every tree (every other tree, I'd catch myself thinking). And completely self-contained. He often disappeared for days, even weeks. I had company, of course. Loved our neighbours. Birds, insects, animals. Delightful. But conversation rather limited. And on misty mornings, cloudy afternoons, dark evenings, I could feel melancholy.

One day I set off early for a walk. A long walk. To the edge of the wood. Away from trees. Towards people. Perhaps.

I don't remember much after that. Until I was sitting in a snowdrift. Singing. The man who pulled me out was older than me. And somehow younger. He had a look of Vernon March, fresh and bright but warmed by Sonny Summers' smiles, yet shielded from burning intensity by the cool mystery of Mr Leif. This man had a great curly beard and long hair. He wore the colours of ivy and pine needles, broccoli and the young spears of winter wheat. He wrapped me in a crimson blanket, drove me in a scarlet-painted sleigh, welcomed me to his comfortable chalet. I loved the glowing warmth inside and the sparkling cold outside. Winter fires within. Winter sunshine without.

We married on Midwinter's Midnight, lit by Northern Lights. I wore my husband's gift. It fitted me perfectly. It was – is – who I am. The colours of holly berries and mulled wine. The texture of comfort and romance. The clothing of love. Red velvet. He brought me a posy of snowdrops, aconites and Christmas roses set amidst delicate carrot fronds. My ice-white veil was held by a cap of purple-flowered rosemary and sage, interwoven with golden winter jasmine. My feet were warm in soft boots of green velvet and my hands were caressed by gloves the shade of frosty winter evenings.

At last I am fully alive. Vernon, Sonny and Leif have led me to my maturity, to the coming together of all my lives. To the Year Turner whom I know as Adam Wintergreen. I remember my past with pleasure. I live my present with delight. And I have a future. A daughter. She is to be married soon. Her husband is a young man, fresh, bright, like a Spring breeze. She will wear a green gown, with a wreath of violets and primroses.

Mariette

Sophie van Llewyn

Each evening, my ladies-in-waiting dress me for the daily ordeal: the *Grand Couvert* of Versailles, where my father-in-law the King, my husband the Dauphin and I have to eat in front of a standing crowd of rustling silks, bejewelled necks. There are no ovations – just mouths curling in evil smiles as they utter their gossip. 'Behold, Marie Antoinette has blundered again.'

Tonight, the Queen's antechambers, where the servants set the royal table, are more packed than usual: ample silk skirts are squashed and crumpled; sculpted canes land on innocent toes. There is hardly enough air for so many to breathe. Even Madame du Barry is here. I can see her three-foot-tall pouf rising above the other powdered wigs, the lazy movements of her signature black lace fan. I can hear her shrill staccato voice.

'Hate me? No, nobody hates me, my dear,' she says to one of the honourable ladies her patron, the King, pays to keep her company. 'They all simply want my place.'

My husband asks, 'Why do you not eat?' with a cackle, as if he has made a good joke.

I mean to tell him how I cannot stomach the smell of the violet water the cooks sprinkle on all our food.

I mean to ask him, 'What is so particular in the way that I, an Austrian-born Dauphine of France, cut my food into tiny morsels, impale them upon my jewel-encrusted fork, and then proceed to chew them? What makes counts and dukes of France wish to stand in front of me every single evening while I am having my dinner?'

I mean to tell him about the hole that opens in my stomach as my ladies-in-waiting dress me for dinner. It is the opposite of hunger, a hollow that claws itself into my belly. A chasm that casts a long shadow over my mind, making me forget even my good manners. Tonight, for instance, I have forgotten yet again to unfold my napkin – which shall cost me a good scolding from Madame de Noailles, my ruthless Madame Etiquette, as she prepares me for my bed.

I mean to tell my husband, 'How cumbersome these rules you have at Versailles are. Life was much more pleasant in Vienna for the lack of them.'

There is so much I mean to tell him, but I do not know the words. Instead of speaking, I part a crumb of pickled cucumber from the slice of stuffed pheasant on my plate.

'Why do you not eat?' my husband asks again, the beams of dozens of eyes upon us, hungry for my mistakes.

My father-in-law, the King, stays the hand cutting his meat and looks at me, frowning.

'Marie Antoinette, indeed, why do you not eat?'

I wish to toss my fork away and scream that my name is *not* Marie Antoinette. Nor Mariette. But this is what they call me, smirking, as if I am an untrained monkey that has yet to learn its name.

'*Mange, mange*,' my husband continues. 'Or do you prefer to gobble your food in the solitude of our bedroom, as you do every night?'

It is as if an invisible conductor has fluttered his baton, released a wave of collective laughter from the crowd of dukes and counts. I would like to pinch my husband's boil-covered cheeks, to squeeze and twist. I would like to say, 'Because that is all that happens in our bedroom, when night comes. I suspect that sleeping on opposite corners of our bed, twice a week, is not how one makes babies.'

But then, how *she* would laugh, Madame du Barry, this sewer cat who has slithered into the Royal Palace.

When I arrived in France, I was so vexed upon finding out what she did for my father-in-law, and that she was called the *maitresse-en-titre*. The King's mistress! Not even the King can be his own master – he requires a *mistress*. All men, no more than dogs on their backs, waiting to be kicked or scratched. How abject, how abhorrent! Such creatures as Madame du Barry do not even deserve to be frowned upon. It would have been far beneath my station – that is why I pretended not to see her. And how my indifference stung her! She took such pains to get rid of my only friend amongst my ladies-in-waiting, the Countess of Grammont: she had her removed from court. Then she proceeded to orchestrate the fall of the Countess's brother: the minister of Foreign Affairs, the very man who arranged my wedding to the Dauphin.

I wonder, how can this be a fair world when a godless wretch can gain so much power as to remove a minister. I *shall not* add anything for her amusement, so I remain silent about what happens in my bedchamber. How ear-piercing would Madame du Barry's laughter be if she knew that my husband, her lover's son, would do well to take a few lessons from her.

The King finally stands, and the ordeal of the dinner is over.

As we make our way towards the Hall of Mirrors, I hear the skirts of my ladies-in-waiting swishing behind me.

In the Hall, there is no hiding from the ceiling-high mirrors, reflecting the golden light of countless candles held by bronzed, bare-shouldered Graces. This burden of having to see my own reflection, a scrawny sixteen-year-old with long fingers like spider's legs, pale cheeks and a flat bosom underneath the silvery white dress with its golden brocade. I find refuge near a marble statue in a niche: the delicate cloaked figure of a woman with a covered head, tilted, eyes cast downwards. I can't tell if she is a Juno or a Mary, though I should know. Mother used tenderly to call me her 'little halfwit'. And yet she has never ceased to ask of me much more than I can give. For instance, last year she insisted: 'Henceforth, we shall correspond in French, because I am now writing to the Dauphine of France and not to my own daughter,' even though she knew my French was poor. Now, not even Mother calls me by my true name. Its metallic Austrian inflexions forever lost to me.

The Count of Mercy-Argenteau, the Austrian ambassador, finds me in front of the statue.

'Madame la Dauphine,' he says, 'a word!'

I dismiss my ladies-in-waiting with a flutter of my hand. Madame de Noailles wrinkles her sharp, witchy nose, then bows her head and retreats.

'Perhaps asking for a bit of discretion might have been more tactful, Your Royal Highness,' says the ambassador.

I sigh. The Count has mistaken my poor French for coldness – and he will surely report this little gaffe to Mother. I cannot excuse myself, for he shall not believe me.

'The Empress writes to me,' he says.

'Oh.'

I fiddle with my fan, hurt. She has not written to *me* in more than three weeks.

'She wishes that... No, she entreats you... But not as her daughter,' he babbles.

I study the faces of the noble ladies painted on my fan. They appear to be having a garden party.

'Your Royal Highness, I am unable to find the words,' he says, chuckling.

'Ambassador, this is as unpleasant to me as it is to you. Do go on.'

The Count coughs, looks at the marble statue that stands in its marble niche.

'The Empress says she prefers not to write to you, because she might be tempted to command you like a disobedient child in this particular matter. Instead, Her Imperial Majesty prefers that I speak for her to you, the Dauphine of France, in this matter that could endanger the peace—'

I shut my fan, its snap like a blade falling on an extended neck.

'Is this about the whore du Barry?' I say.

'Madame la Dauphine,' he says, his eyes now drooping like those of a beaten dog. 'The woman has so much power with the King. I understand you must be furious after she exiled your friend, but she can... She could do so much more.

So much more harm. Her Imperial Highness entreats you to think of all the orphans, and the widows, and the bodies of young men rotting on battlefields should war break out again. All because of a matter of pride.'

I turn and stare at the marble statue myself. I decide it must be a Mary – a Juno's eyes would never so meekly search the floor.

'Should I allow myself to be intimidated, then?' I whisper. 'Is this what my mother wishes?'

'The Empress, Madame, wishes for long-lasting peace between France and the Habsburg Empire,' says the Count de Mercy.

Madame de Noailles approaches, nods towards a small dais erected in the middle of the Hall, and the elegant harp placed upon it.

'They are ready for you, Your Royal Highness,' she says.

I forgot that this is the night when I extend the court my olive branch: if we cannot find common ground in French, I shall try to speak the universal language of music. I shall sing – for the whole of Versailles.

While I am taking my leave, the ambassador says, 'A few words – that is all Madame du Barry needs.'

As I take my seat behind the harp, my thoughts boil like a sea in a storm, almost spilling over and drowning me in tears. When I caress the first notes from the strings, I am still shaking on the inside. I am amazed that silence settles over the courtiers like a heavy cloak. Only Madame du Barry still speaks in her shrill magpie tone. But soon she is defeated. The whisper of satin feels loud in this still chamber.

I lock my eyes with *hers*. She is a few feet from my stage, her fan raised, hand stopped mid-motion, fearful of making a single move. The trills of my harp fill the room like a flock of heavenly birds, while the crowd rocks and sways. I am Orpheus and I have tamed them.

I too am no longer here. I am at Hofburg, and I hear Joseph and Leopold teaching my sisters to play Hazard in a corner of the room, while Mother's stately silhouette is seated in a chair in front of me, eyes closed as her mind is swept away by my music. I close my eyes, too, and sing, sing, sing for her.

But soon the crowd begins fidgeting and rustling and striking canes on polished wood. The courtiers turn towards each other in groups, whispering. By the time I end my song, no one is listening. I let my hands hang at my sides, wish to disappear. I have disgraced myself. Just three people cheer for me: the King in his high chair, the ambassador and Madame du Barry. She can barely applaud because of her fan, so she drops it to the floor. Only a girl who was raised on the streets can make noise like she does. Her claps are tiny thunderbolts. Powdered heads turn. Madame du Barry has caught the court's ears, and the courtiers pick up the sound. Applause rises, at first like a soft summer rain, then turning into a proper deluge. Madame du Barry claps even harder, and I can see her silver satin dress trembling with the effort. The court answers. I rise from my seat and, bathing in a downpour of applause, take my bow.

When I lift my head, I see that lonely statue of Mary standing in her niche. I think, *This is why Mother gave me and my sisters this name. So we would always remember humility.*

As I descend from the dais, I steer towards Madame du Barry.

'There are a lot of people today at Versailles,' I say.

She smiles, bends to pick up her fan and twitches it open. She gives a despicable little laugh.

'Madame la Dauphine,' she says in her unbearably shrill voice. 'Come, will you join me in the King's apartments?'

In spite of myself, I follow her. The crowd parts to let us pass. An icicle expands in my chest, preventing me from breathing, and I wish to turn and flee.

The doors to the King's apartments are thrown open, but the ladies and gentlemen at the tables take no notice of us. They are far too absorbed, watching as their fortunes are made and unmade. My heart beats faster as I remember my mother's words. 'A princess who plays poorly is quick to be parted with her fortune.' My brothers saw to it that I learned how to play, and they were proud of their little gambling prodigy – until I began taking everything from them.

I walk around the chamber, listening to the shuffling of cards, the whispering of dice calling me by my rightful name.

Madame du Barry stops by the Trictrac table. As the game advances, the movements of her black lace fan become erratic, while her hand throws increasing mounds of gold livres onto the table. As the dice fall, so do fortunes in the hand of the King's mistress. As my circles around the table draw closer and closer, her laugh is at its shrillest. My prey is finally at bay, so I stop to face her. She points at the table, and I nod.

The chamber stills. The stakes are even higher than the heaps of gold on the table.

The game begins.

Soda Jerk

Lee Wright

Everyone is out doing something else.

Shrimp calls to me. He's going in back, to hide among the potions, prescriptions and nostalgia. He can do that. As he reminds me often, 'I'm the boss around here. You're just the soda jerk.'

Here comes Sapphire Sam. Waddling along the sidewalk, looking like the prize hog at the county fair. Rolling in money. Wearing it badly.

He opens our door. Doesn't quite fit through. I wonder, if someone shot him in the gut, would he even feel the bullet?

'Shrimp in back?' he asks.

'In back,' I confirm.

Shrimp peeks his head around the corner.

'What time is it, Shrimp?'

Shrimp reaches under the counter with the caution of a Christian sneaking past a sleeping lion. Out comes an envelope. Sapphire takes it gladly, opens it up and counts the dollar bills. He looks at me. Then at Shrimp. The face of a man who hasn't had a bowel movement in weeks.

I press forward and wait.

Snapping his fingers, Sapphire points at Shrimp.

'Next month. Double or down, you hear?'

Sapphire sneers at me, at everything.

It is true. The ugly only get uglier.

Sapphire doesn't look like much, but he plays cards with people who do.

Shrimp is running out of time. This place is to him what a beer is to a barfly. There is nothing I can do, except tip soda. And right now, that's about as useful as throwing seed into an empty birdcage.

I look back – Shrimp is away to his remedies and dust. No courage.

Jimmy pedals past. Waving as he goes by. Giving me a big smile. A smile and a man's attitude can go a long way.

Some guy drags his kid into the store.

'Where's your payphone, soda man?'

That thing I was saying about a man's attitude. Well, there you have it.

I point to the other side of the store.

'Okay, Harry Junior. Sit and stay,' he commands.

The kid climbs up onto a stool, keeping his eyes busy counting the buttons on his shirt.

'How old are you?'

His eyes go wide with fear. His neck retreats into his shoulders, reminding me of when you poke a snail in the eye.

'Speak up, I don't bite.'

'Six.'

The number falls to the floor.

'You and your pop from out of town?'

I get a nod.

'You hungry?'

Sure does look a sad one.

'What's your favourite flavour ice cream?'

A glance and I catch him with my warmest smile.

'Vanilla,' he squeaks.

'Right you are. How about some chocolate with that?'

His face turns from ashes to roses. I get to work with all the enthusiasm of a doctor fresh out of med school.

A tall glass, chocolate syrup, and two scoops of vanilla. I add the carbonated water until the foam is an inch from spilling over, then I top it off with whipped cream and throw on a cherry for good measure.

I slide it over the counter, along with a soda spoon and drinking straw.

'One black and white, made to order.'

He looks at me head-on for the first time. I have to give him the nod before he dares begin.

I comb my hair back.

Some of us live for the booze, some for skirt, and some for drag racing along the main strip at 2am on a Saturday. But when you're six…

The job is done with the phone and the father comes back, clicking his fingers in earnest.

'Okay, let's scoot, come on. Come on.'

The kid looks as though he's about to swallow his tongue in panic. He spins his seat round to his old man. Vanilla lipstick and all.

The guy makes a fist.

'Did you ask for that?'

Soda Jerk

Harry Junior shakes his head while pointing at me. If I were six years old, I would wet my pants.

'I ain't paying for that, buddy.'

'It's on me,' I say.

He stops. Waits. The injustice drifts on past. Intrigue. That's what washes in with the tide.

'Man, oh man. Well, I don't have time to wait. You'll have to leave it, Harry.'

'No sweat,' I tell the kid. 'Take it with you.'

I can feel the weight of the guy's entire soul on me.

'Thank the man, Harry.'

The softest thank you. A fly crawling along a wall would have made more noise. The kid takes his black and white and follows his father.

I give an outward sigh. As if all the pain has been removed.

'They pay for that soda?'

A reasonable question. But Shrimp knows that I've let him down. Don't matter what you do, you'll always let somebody down.

I expect to be asked to leave at any moment.

'It's okay,' I say. 'I've got it.'

Shrimp shakes his head with the saddest of looks.

'You know what you are?' he asks.

I know. I know.

I'm a jerk.

Bird Brains

Maggie Ling

It's their highly responsive MHV! Aurelia said, adopting that high-flown tone of hers.

They were discussing the intelligence of birds. Aurelia had edged the conversation in that direction, maybe as a way of proving, if proof was needed, how very clever she was. Her PhD had been on avian cognition: *Thinking Psittacinae-fashion*. She had spent two years in close communication with a rather bright parrot, for a while student and 'guinea pig' becoming almost inseparable. Well, until Aurelia's dissertation was complete. She dumped the poor bugger when she met me! her husband, Frazer, had joked on more than one occasion, before going on to do his *Who's a pretty girl then?* party-piece parrot impersonation. But then, beneath those sleek Sloane Street clothes, that expensive salon-blonded hair, that purring cut-glass accent, there had always been a cut-throat masculinity about Aurie.

Their *what*? Andrew questioned.

Mediorostral hyper striatum ventrale! (Said as if any fool with half a brain would know that.)

Well, torture me with a turkey baster for not knowing. Can't birds just have brains like you and me?

Forgive me, Andrew, Aurelia said, a hand drawing back her lustrous hair to expose the forehead within which all that grey matter resided, but *my* brain and *your* brain are two quite different kettles of fish.

Ah! Andrew said, topping up his wine glass. Explains those wretched seagulls dive-bombing me in Whitstable last summer then, left forefinger tapping his temple. Must've completely emptied my rusty old kettle.

There was a ripple of amused laughter around the table, though not, Helen noted as she slid the sautéed courgettes into a dish, from Aurie herself. Aurelia had always taken herself far too seriously. But then, to get where she was in the competitive world of neurosurgery – a world dominated by preening men who took themselves very seriously indeed – she'd had to.

If as you say, Frazer, Duncan said while transferring the penultimate duck breast from pan to plate, parrots can only count to six, how come they can say *Pieces of eight*?

Duncan had suggested it: A little dinner party come *le weekend*? *Ça va*? A rare weekday morning, husband and wife together at the breakfast table, neither in a rush. Christen the kitchen!

After a decade of aimless discussion, the dining room wall had at last been demolished, creating, according to Duncan, *an extremely convivial space*. I'll call a few (Please don't say it, Helen had silently pleaded) chums, shall I? And then, Howsabout my signature dish for mains? Don't worry. I'll take charge of the duck!

Duncan was the sort of man who took charge of things. Helen, it transpired, had become the sort of woman who did the vegetables, the sort, her husband informed their assembled guests over an aperitif of champagne on the postage-stamp patio of their pocket-sized Georgian terrace, who *rustled up a very yummy pud*.

Public school boys had *chums*. Little boys brought up on Janet and John Readers had *chums*. And Duncan, though he would have liked to have been the former – and had worked hard to give the impression he had been – was neither of these.

Right then! he'd said. I'll give the usual suspects a buzz.

And although a closet fan of Gabriel Byrne, Helen wished that film had never been made, the number of times Duncan, and a whole line-up of men like Duncan, had hijacked the title. And *buzz*? Whoever said buzz these days? Beekeepers, maybe? Except, if bees were on the decline, then beekeepers would surely follow – not to mention the manufacturers of their peculiar garb. Unless of course, seeing a gap in the market, with a slight revamp, they were made available to far-right racist groups. Now *they* were most likely on the up.

Don't forget the ducks! Duncan shouted as he flew downstairs that Friday morning. After all, a man who led an *über-busy* life as a cardiothoracic surgeon (a job offering up a steady supply of subordinated handmaidens) could not be expected to take charge of the shopping as well as the ducks – his live-in handmaiden thus deployed to wade through a Waitrose awash with frustrated Friday evening shoppers to source the dead, denuded birds.

And had not the ducks in question already been made oven-ready, Helen imagined, prior to quacking their last quack, the once feathered trio might, at first sight of Duncan in masterful Master Chef mode, have plucked out their own feathers, performed their own ritual mastectomies, flipping the tender breasts into the pan to lie, breastlessly, down to die before Mr D J Threvithick BS FRCS (Eng). Duncan sometimes had that effect on people: a way of subordinating them just by being Duncan.

Sometimes, Helen had thought – sometimes fondly, sometimes not – Duncan has that effect on me.

Whole ducks, Helen! had been Duncan's parting shot before slamming the front door.

It had become a habit: this surfeit of duck. One begun by the Senior House Officer out to impress the young Art Therapist who would become his wife. Impress her not only with his cooking skills, but also with the surgical precision of his dissecting skills – not to mention, back in those single days, his shopping skills. Duncan wielding the knife that afternoon with ever-greater expertise, while commanding his wife check all the ingredients for his special-recipe marinade were available to him. Helen, searching the larder cupboard for runny honey, wishing her husband would sometimes 'take charge' of the ravioli or the risotto, or could occasionally 'rustle up' some sub-Eton-mess of a pud, resenting the gender-specific pigeon-holing her husband's carnivorous nature had forced upon her.

Cormorants can count to eight, Frazer responded, ducking the parrot question. Some fishermen... China, I think it was – isn't it always China – allegedly offered up every eighth fish as a reward and, do you know—

Bollocks! Andrew interjected. Don't believe a word of it. Not a single digit. Bloody birds were just hanging around for the damn fish. Who says they were *counting*?

But what about crows? Duncan stepped in. I imagine a crow, should it need to, could count *way* beyond eight. Crows, jackdaws, all the corvids, are as bright as their gimlet eyes. And they've pretty meaty forebrains, I believe. Isn't that so, Aurie?

Aurelia nodded.

Reckon, given the chance, they could run the whole damn country. At least get the economy moving.

Then, Frazer said, slathering a roll with a similar volume of butter, at last we'd have something to *crow* about.

Hurry up with those potatoes, darling! Duncan commanded, his knife incisively lacerating the final duck breast, I've just finished slicing Andrew's breast.

Ooh-er, Frazer's large, square hands protectively clamping his pink-shirted chest. That's the trouble with you surgeons: you don't know when to stop.

Listen you lot, I may be a tad porky, but I do *not* have boobs! Well, not on a par with yours, Aurie.

Reaching for the vegetable dish, Aurelia raised a disdainful eyebrow.

Watch it, Andrew! Frazer instructed. Not your territory. Thought you would've learned by now.

Just comparing and contrasting. No offence, Aurie.

Leaning back in her chair, the fingers of her left hand checking the whereabouts of her plunging neckline, Aurelia remained silent.

Jesus, Andrew! Helen put the dish of creamed potato down on the table before sitting down herself. You've got through half that bottle already. I hope you're not driving home?

Dunno. Thought I might boot old Dunc out and stay with you, Hel.

It was happening again. That was the trouble with chums. Chums sometimes took advantage. Chums had a habit of pushing the boundaries of friendship.

How could she, Hel? You wouldn't kick a gorgeous fella like me out, would you? I mean, that woman... you *know* how

I love that woman. Love her to bits. Tell her that next time you see her, eh. To bloody bits.

Please, Andrew, Helen said, filling his empty water glass with water. Do *try* to hold off until dessert or we'll all be in tears, and you will definitely be cabbing it home.

Last time he had drained their whiskey bottle dry in the night. Last time he had puked all over the stair carpet as they were hauling him upstairs. Last time Helen's bare feet had experienced an overly intimate encounter with her husband's oldest chum's urine, a large quantity of which was puddled about the bathroom floor.

Remember last time? said more sharply than she'd intended. Andrew's vacant, bloated face gazed blankly back at her across the table. Well, you may have forgotten, but *I* most certainly have not.

His puffy eyes brightening, he said, *Do* remember you reminding me of it a couple of weeks later, though.

Just remembered, Aurelia said, brightening herself, I was once quite close to a *Jack Dawe*. Briefly. Way back when. At med school.

Two-timing the parrot, were you? Andrew chipped in.

A morsel of duck hovering near his mouth, Duncan said, Didn't realise your wife was such a bird fancier, Frazer.

Nice body, Aurelia continued, so-so brain. Made it through, somehow. Couldn't count for toffee though. Three months into his proper job, the idiot left a clamp in a patient.

Just the one? Andrew's familiar boozy-woozy smile spreading across his face.

Apprehensively eyeing his loaded fork, Farid wondered why so many middle-class Brits and, come to that, almost all the carnivorous French, were so fond of undercooked meat. A love of bloody juices apparently adding a soupçon of sophistication. You see! he said. Now a cormorant would *not* have made that mistake.

Everyone smiled. Including Helen.

Helen has such a lovely smile, he thought, admiring the glossy redness of her hair as it brushed the plum-coloured silk covering her shoulders.

Is this duck *sushi*, Duncan? Helen asked her husband. Thought you'd seen enough blood for one week.

Big ops? Frazer asked.

Knackering! Three of the buggers. Then turning to his wife: And I assure you, my sweet, this duck is perfectly cooked.

Just right, Andrew, between glugs of wine, professed of the meat he'd yet to taste. Something to get your teeth into.

Finally doing just that.

Watching him masticating the undercooked flesh, Helen pictured Andrew collapsed on a flattened box, legs splayed, cardboard soaked in urine, spidery rivulets of pee meandering across the pavement. Still chewing, he was already topping up the half-drained wine glass, his glass of water left untouched.

Shouldn't you hold off a bit on that, Andy? Aurelia suggested.

Give me one good reason why.

I'll give you three: Jules, Franci and George.

His big, empty eyes welling, Andrew put down the glass.

Helen flashed Aurelia a piercing glance. OK. It was a good answer. It was the right answer to give. But Helen did not want Andrew sobbing at her dinner table again. Did not want his salty tears on her shoulder again, his winey drool on her new silk shirt. Did not want to mop his urine, wipe up his puke ever again. Did not care for, or about, a man who would do one stupid arsehole thing and then, when he was found out, proceed to do an even more stupid arsehole thing, while still expecting his friends to feel sorry for *him*.

As she reached across for the water jug, Helen's eyes met Farid's. How kind they are, she thought. How feminine. His lashes are twice the length of mine. And then, It must be strange to wake up beside such a beautiful man.

Turning to Andrew, Farid said, You know, there is life beyond alcohol, Andrew.

Beyond? Frazer questioned. Since, Fari, you've never jumped on that particular wagon in order to get off it again, how the hell would *you* know?

True. But I have lived for forty-three years, thirty of them knowingly without the stuff, and twenty of them in this country – with all the alcoholic temptations implicit in that fact – without feeling I'm *missing out* on anything.

But you *are*, Fari, old man, Duncan insisted. You decidedly are.

But he's not, Duncan, Helen felt forced to say. He *decidedly* is not. And you know it. Booze is a trap. A prop. Dinner-party drinking around a table like this? Winos on a street corner? What's the difference? It's all addiction. It's all weakness.

Hey there, folks! Can we change the subject, please? I was just beginning to enjoy myself.

No you weren't, Andrew. You bloody weren't!

And overcome with anger, Helen whisked the glass en route to Andrew's mouth from his hand, Shiraz splashing over his plate to mix with the pinky-red juices of the duck.

You're just burying yourself. Drowning yourself in the damn stuff. It's so, *so fucking stupid*! And standing up, her chair almost toppling as she did so, Helen grabbed the three bottles on the table, rushed over to the newly installed Butler's sink, the assembled diners, including Farid, watching in stunned silence as what remained of the rather expensive wine was poured down the drain.

Returning to the table, she raised her topped-up water glass in the air.

There were several seconds of silence, then, raising his glass of elderflower, Farid said, Cheers! Here's to Helen!

That was *quite* a performance you gave us last night, Duncan got around to saying on Sunday morning. Not like you at all.

No?

They were clearing up the kitchen. Or rather, Helen was clearing up the kitchen. Duncan, who had suggested they had 'better get up and tackle the bloody mess down there', was sitting at a table awash with unwashed glasses and stained coffee cups, the sports section of the newspaper in one hand, the mug he had just filled with coffee in the other. As if I was a paid helper, Helen thought as she loaded the dishwasher. Was Her-Wot-Does. Was his skivvy. Was not the other half of this relationship, the other name on the deeds of this fine Georgian three-up, two-down box of a house, this money-pot of a property which, she had recently found herself calculating, for some reason, if split down the middle could purchase two very decent flats in perfectly decent parts of London. Not *this* part, you understand, but still... a change was as good as a rest.

The rest of my life. The words wandering in and out of her head. I will be forty-five come November. The rest of my life?

Suddenly irritated by the back of her husband's neck, she said, Could you pour *me* one of those, please? A small ridge of fat had collected there. Duncan had become a little fleshier of late. *Bulk* was how he'd described it – apparently with some pride. Too much duck, Helen thought.

Duncan had not spoken of her 'performance' until now. Frosty in the bathroom, he had managed a perfunctory peck on the cheek before putting out the light, and a cold Good Morning on waking. Although immediately after that performance of hers, pulling a sub-standard bottle of red from the wine rack, he had managed to crack a joke at Helen's expense. Not that anyone, other than Helen or Farid (should they have sampled it), would have noticed the wine's inferior quality. Even Aurelia, the designated driver – she who regularly operated on battered brains, on lives shattered by the idiocy of drink-driving – felt the need to accept another 'teensy-weensy glass'.

Helen, Duncan declared, had spoiled the evening. Had ruined his mood. All their moods. Had, in his opinion, made a molehill into a mountain: thus demeaning her recognition of the pile of trouble Andrew was in. Perhaps they were all in? All except for Farid. Farid who had neither drink problem nor spouse problem – or child problem, Helen supposed.

It was often that way round: often Helen who made too much of something. Helen who took life too seriously. Lighten up, Hel! Duncan would say, unconcerned as to why she might be feeling heavy.

For heaven's sake, Duncan. It *happened*, OK? I couldn't stop myself. You and Frazer are his oldest friends. Aren't friends supposed to support each other? To *care* about each other? Surely friendship's about challenging actions, not simply accepting them. Friends don't just stand by and watch their best *chum* crash his entire life. A friend's got to be more than the good guy with deep pockets who buys the next round of drinks!

Quite a performance, Duncan repeated, looking vaguely in her direction, but not looking her in the eye – and not really listening.

He was pretending to read the sports section. Folding the newspaper so aggressively it made sharp crackling sounds as she spoke. Then, tossing it on top of the mess on the table, he stood up. Helen did not turn around, but continued emptying the dishwasher, filling it from the dirty pile on the worktop.

Goddammit, Helen! There are places and times for challenging my friends...

So they were *his* friends now, were they? Was that the way it would go? This sofa's mine. That chair's yours.

...and a civilised meal on a Saturday evening is *not* one of them. As if Andy hasn't got enough on his plate. What good did it do? Putting him in the spotlight like that.

Pressing the start button, she turned to look at him: Christ almighty, Duncan. Hasn't Andrew been putting himself there for quite long enough?

He was standing by their newly installed French doors, looking out into the garden. His back to her, he exuded resistance. Looked solid, impenetrable, but, at the same time, weak.

I could mend this, she thought, mend you. Could bridge this widening fissure simply by walking up behind you and wrapping my arms around your broadening girth. I could take responsibility for spoiling *your* evening. Could say, There, there. Promise I won't do it again. We're OK now, aren't we,

Duncan? He would like that. Would like to feel her close, yet below him – beneath him – his overly paternal hand stroking the hair of his submissive little wife, tamed once more.

He was still standing there, sipping his coffee, staring out.

Taking in the clipped box 'clouds', the ubiquitous ivy, the darkness of the jasmine foliage, no longer lightened by its starry mass of flowers, Helen wished she had not given in to Duncan's desire for professional garden designers. How empty it looked. How colourless. How sterile. Not a garden for children. Just as well. How could it have worked? Her eyes drawn to the back of her husband's neck, she felt tears welling.

At twenty-five, his body spooned into hers, it had been the first thing she saw on waking: his soft, sandy hair, longer then, curling into his neck, tickling her nose as she willed him to wake, to make love to her.

For heaven's sake, Duncan, breaking the poisonous silence, don't you *want* to save Andrew's life?

There you go again! *Over*-dramatising. A few drinks, for fuck's sake!

A few *months'* drinks. A bender that's lasted precisely... she paused, counting the weeks, the months, nineteen months! Christ knows how he holds down his job. And you're prepared to let him continue in this way?

Putting his coffee mug down on the draining board, Duncan turned to look back at his wife. Helen searched for the kindness in her husband's face, the love she wanted to see there, hoping it might osmotically draw out her own, but saw only Farid's soft-eyed gaze. Pathetic. Juvenile. Grow up, Helen.

Andy'll pull himself together, given time, Duncan was saying, still waiting for her to go to him.

Come *on*. Do you really think that? Can't men mother their friends as well as be their best Budweiser buddies? Can't men *grow up*!

He looked a tad hurt by that. She did not want to hurt him. But what else could she do?

In fact, on the contrary, you seem happy being his supplier. Because that doesn't deprive *you* of anything, does it. Because *your* preferred tipple comes in bottles with chateaus on the labels, you can all be chums together. Which must be all right, since posh people live in chateaus. Posh people spend a fortune soaking those they love in expensive booze. It's low-life scumbags who use dirty syringes and bits of foil, and get high in back alleys, or purchase their preferred tipple from a hardware store who are the problem, not a six-pack of classy consultants sipping claret from crystal glassware!

Did she love him or hate him? It had become as woolly, as uncertain as that.

She could see he'd had enough. He'd never liked her raising her voice. It was not what *nice* women did. Nice men? Well, that was a different matter. Nice men had to stand up for themselves. Nice men *should* stand up for their chums, for their women, too – if they were nice. Nice men should stand a round of drinks.

The fingers of his left hand combing angrily through his sandy-brown hair, Duncan said, Of course, when it comes right down to it, your performance was really for Farid's benefit. A way of *currying* favour, you could say.

What!

She hated his use of that word. Hated the way his lip curled when he said it. Hated the whiff of racism attached to it. At that moment, hated Duncan.

Yes. You were putting yourself in the spotlight. You were playing to an audience of one.

I was *what?*

Your number one fan.

Jesus Christ!

She was so angry, she thought she might hit him. There were a few seconds of silence. Then the telephone rang.

Helen agreed to meet Jules in Cream Teaz. Countless Sunday afternoons had been whiled away there: first, the two of them, the midwife and the art therapist, then, coupled up with their high-profile specialist partners, came the romantic foursome, then five come Georgiana, and six come Francine. Will it soon be we two again? Helen wondered, watching Jules ordering cakes at the counter. Maybe Duncan and Andy see us as safe bets, she'd suggested to Jules, on a similarly grey Sunday twenty years before. As good, supportive wife material. They know we're not quite in their league.

Franci at a sleepover, and George sleeping in with Maxxi, Jules was free all afternoon.

Don't you mind? Helen asked her. I mean, George is barely fifteen.

Fifteen and a half now! Well, y'know, better the devil, and all that.

And is Maxxi a bit of a devil?

Far from it! Picture the cutest choirboy, put him on the rack, stretch him to six foot one, add a smattering of pimples, dress him in black, and there you have it! Not the greatest catch, in my opinion – not that I've said as such. More than my life's worth.

Still, Jules sighed as she topped up their teacups, George dotes on her Maxxi.

And precautions?

Sorted! Bed 'n' breakfast 'n' pill. All part of the parental service.

Jules was amazing. A natural mother. No. It would never have worked.

Y'know, Jules was saying, I've even found myself wondering what it'd be like to start over myself.

Jules professed to having turned a corner, to have seen the future and found herself intrigued, not frightened by it.

But sex? she went on. Sex with a stranger? Exposing this! hands searching for her waistline. Then, fingers returning to break off another piece of cake, Perhaps I should stick to the book club for company and slices of lemon drizzle for comfort. Wiping the crumbs from her lips, she said, How is he?

Not bad, Helen said, not wanting to dampen her friend's spirits. Then, picturing Andrew staggering to Farid's car, Well, not so good, actually. It'll take time, Jules. Anyway, I'm to tell you, he still loves you.

Lemony fingers scraping back her straw-coloured hair, Jules sighed: Trouble is, he's a *helluva* lot of work. The girls... well, at least they behave more or less like adults. And they've been so supportive, so sensible through this. I need a grown-up for a partner, not a stressed-out boy-dad in need of a mum. I can't, Hel, I *won't* allow him back the way he is. Andy's gotta do the work. And do it fast! Then, maybe... looking down at her plate. Oh, I don't know. She crumbled off another mouthful. So! How's the lovely Farid, these days? I do miss him dropping by. Such a sweet guy. He and Annie still going strong?

Afraid not.

What a lie. When Duncan told her there were to be six, not seven, diners on Saturday night she'd felt a rush of pleasure, had not been in the least bit afraid – or was she?

Gosh! Annie doesn't know when she's well off.

Actually, I think it was Farid who did the dumping.

Why? They looked so good together: the Beautiful People.

Farid Manduri! he'd announced.

Not Doctor Manduri, but *Farid* Manduri. And then, when he'd called the department to ask how his patient was progressing, simply, It's Farid from Haematology, as if he were some lowly technician.

Eight years ago, Helen thought. My chum then. *Mine*.

They kept bumping into each other at lunchtimes. That third time (by then, their patients overlapping, Farid had also met Duncan) he had talked of his childhood in Pakistan, of visits to his cousins in the once beautiful, *still beautiful*, Swat valley. Helen had pointed out the bitter irony of its name, imagining it crammed with children, swotting for their exams. Boys *and* girls! And Farid had spoken of benevolent rulers who had developed a network of libraries and educational institutions there. Maybe, he'd said, hoping for just that. And then, My favourite cousin's daughter was shot while walking to her school. They missed Salma's brain – one assumes they were aiming at that. Scary things, where I come from, women's brains.

She knew then. Just knew.

But they got her in the neck. Miraculously, the bullets – there was more than one – missed her spine. She has a voice, of sorts. But will never sing as she used to.

Tears brimming, he had produced a tissue from his pocket. I'm so sorry to have upset you, he'd said, holding it out to her.

What pampered lives we lead, Helen finally managed to say. What selfish, pampered lives.

Nonsense! We are born where we are born. If, as I believe, we have but one life, better to be comfortable and content in it than miserable. Do *not* feel guilty for your good life, Helen. And do not let my sad stories ruin your good life.

But my life is already ruined, she'd thought.

Returning home, she found Duncan in their newly painted kitchen-diner salting the duck legs: confit of duck was, understandably, his second signature dish. He did not look up, but did say, Hello, You, in a friendly tone. Hello, she replied, a hand brushing his shoulder as she squeezed past him to open the window – did men need less oxygen than women?

I'll just go up and put on something sloppy.

How's dear old Jules? he asked, sprinkling the rest of the salt, pressing down the lid of the container and shaking it as he turned to her.

Very good, actually. Best I've seen in a long while.

She won't want him back then?

Probably not. Maybe. Who knows?

He slipped the salted duck into the fridge and pulled out a carton of eggs.

By the way, Farid called an hour or so ago.

Oh.

Said to say thanks for your contributions to the *delicious* meal. Turns out Andy stayed with him last night. Well, Fari insisted he stay. Says he hadn't the heart to leave him at the flat in that state.

Helen said Farid had almost too much heart. Duncan agreed.

Did Andrew puke on Fari's carpet? Piss on Fari's bath-room floor?

Duncan said he didn't think so. Or if he had, Farid had been courteous enough not to mention it.

But Andrew *did* cry on his shoulder. Last night and this morning. In a terrible state, apparently. Rock bottom. So rock bottom that, thanks to Fari's gentle, persuasive tongue, Andy's agreed to go to AA. Even checked online. Found his nearest group. What's more, his teetotal mentor has volunteered to get him there on Thursday evening. So, my Princess, your wish has come true!

Wasn't it your wish too?

I guess. Yep. Course it was.

She was right, he said. But then, she was almost always right. Which could be *particularly* annoying, particularly for a man.

Putting the carton of eggs on the table, he slipped an arm around her waist. She felt his hand stroking her hair in that paternal way.

Howsabout I whip up a cheese soufflé omelette for a light supper?

He hadn't done one of those for months and months.

That, a spot of salad, and a glass of apple juice should do us, eh?

Lovely, and releasing herself from his grasp, she walked into the hall.

Frazer had once told them how Aurie's grieving 'guinea pig' had mourned the loss of his mistress. Poor bugger called her name every morning for weeks, he'd said: *Aurie! Aurie! Aurie!* reprising his parrot impersonation. For fuck's sake, Frazer,

Aurelia had snapped. Then, more softly, The *poor bugger*'s name, as you well know, was Ton-ton. Dear Ton-ton, repeated in barely a whisper. Helen thought there had been a glint of moisture in Aurelia's faraway gaze back then.

Would I be like Ton-ton? Helen asked herself. Would I mourn my loss?

Omelette in fifteen! Duncan called up to her.

Great! she called back, pulling on her comfy velour loungers.

She could hear him down there, whistling while he worked: a clear, melodious tune, if a tad high-pitched for a man, and a little too wavering for the sort of man Duncan was, the sort who took charge of things.

Winter, 1963

Judith Wilson

A well-aimed kick winds her; gasping, she bends double.

Late afternoon, deep-dark February, and on the snaking branches of the common limes outside, snow sits tight, a vanilla crust ready to drop.

She knows it won't fall. There's not a breath of winter wind. The air – it's freezing.

Another insistent kick, a dense heel to her soft stomach, and now her belly is a Wurlitzer, the baby zealous for thrills and spills.

She spreads the slim fingers of her left hand, square-tipped, across her sweater – knit one, purl one, she made it herself. She hasn't lit the side lamps in the front room, barely registers the scarlet of the wool stretched tight these last few weeks. The street lamp casts sodium-yellow tints, but she only sees the sails of the ship billowing across the window, emerald and navy glass turning red to rusty blood.

Blood. She won't think of that. She's been fretting all afternoon. At lunchtime, she pressed the contours of the telephone too hard against her pale cheek. A mark remained. She saw it in the crescent hall mirror.

'You've two weeks still to go. I'll be back.' Her husband was matter-of-fact.

'I don't want it to...' She couldn't tell him about that smear on the toilet paper.

'I'll be there. Pack your bag. Just in case.'

That was no comfort.

All afternoon she's moved so slowly around the chill house, her right hand gripping the ebony bannister tight, belly heavy as sand. Upstairs, she dragged a turquoise vinyl vanity case from under the bed. No need to pack. It was already filled – two nightdresses, pink-sprigged, a new hairbrush, a scarlet lipstick. 'Don't let yourself go,' her mother had whispered, standing shoulder-to-shoulder with her at the department store. 'He'll be off if he can't, you know...'

In her armchair, she winces. The mayhem of the baby fills her with terror. She thinks of the narrow, silky channel her husband enjoys week in, week out, even now. How it may stretch a little, when she pushes her wedding-ring finger inside, in secret moments alone. How can it gape wide enough for a baby? Nausea rises, sweet and sour. She's hoping for a tiny infant, six pounds or less. But perhaps she'll get a bruiser, a boy, a male...

'You've still two weeks to go.'

His voice, it's in her head. He's so sure and she must believe him. He's mature, he'll know. The baby won't come this teatime, nor interfere with supper, won't gatecrash past midnight with the worst manners. She'll still be able to make his meal, warm the front room on his return, after he's handed her the key to the shed where the coal scuttle lives. No panic. Her husband will come home. He only has to catch the tram, his mackintosh buttoned against the rapping cold, one restless hand on his Brylcreem flop of hair.

'I'll walk if the trams are stopped.'

Now his words float across the ceiling, patterns above her head. She shuts her eyes, listens. That snow. It's been a noiseless threat all day, but she's seen it, showering, piling high, slipping and tipping, in the streetlight a creamy ripple. Even the rose bush on the front lawn has disappeared, though it was frilly and succulent in early autumn – after the honeymoon.

She pulls a shawl from the back of the grey armchair, wraps it tight. Her hands press lightly on her belly. 'Hush, baby.' She breathes in and out. Hears the vanilla crust give up its fight outside, splintering in a powdery rush.

*

'You're getting fat. Too much sitting around, all that revising for O levels. Get outside, play tennis. Go swimming.'

She sits motionless at the kitchen table, watching her mother's back, the way her floral dress digs in at the waist and splays out, one flimsy layer above her girdle. Like a lampshade, but not so elegant.

The glass of strawberry milk circled in her hands tastes like soap. She runs her tongue around her lips, dry throat, tongue clicking.

'Mother, I...'

'Fruit for pudding, my girl, no more ice cream.'

'Mother, can you listen – I...'

'There's temporary work going on the factory shop floor. Vera says...'

She doesn't know how to tell her mother what she's done.

What happened in the bushes behind school, the day the exams were over and they were cock-a-hoop, every one of them.

'You can't get pregnant the first time. Virgins can't.'

She smelled his lemon-pop breath in her face. She believed him before, during and after, but not later. Now sickness arrives every morning of every day. In her bedroom mirror, her stomach strains above her white cotton pants.

'You'll stop being sick now exams are over. It was nerves, that's all.'

Her mother turns, gazes at her with a smile. Her lips are the colour of cherries, but her eyes, they don't smile. The daughter sees fear, and a question, but she needs to ask one herself.

'Mother, can't we... I only want...'

There's a bang as her mother slams the door.

*

So it was a swift wedding, family only: her mother and father, and an aunt as witness. Her parents picked a church in another parish, in case of nosy thoughts and clicking tongues. In the August heat, she was trussed up in white lace, married by 11am. ('You're only sixteen. I think *He* will forgive, now we're doing the right thing,' her mother had whispered in the shop, fingering snowy nylon.) She'd already screamed, one Tuesday night at home, that she would not, could not, abide 'Cream lace! Dear God, the look of it, the meaning of it!'

Finding a willing husband hadn't taken long. After she'd blurted, been spied head over the toilet, her mother fuming at the open bathroom door, her parents had gone quiet, too quiet. Then it was over.

'David is coming for dinner. You'll be married late August. He's a good man.'

A good man?

'Mother. I'm sixteen.'

'He's a respectable bachelor who doesn't mind taking on a young wife.'

'He's as old as Father.'

Her mother had rubbed her lips together so hard the cherry stain slipped to flesh. They'd faced one another over the walnut coffee table. Her mother held her chin with hard fingertips.

'Should have thought of that before. You need to be married. That's all.'

The bells pealed after their vows, and she looked down at her tiny dome, encrusted with lacy flowers. Her husband – 'David darling', her mother called him – took her hand. His skin was moist; he only looked at her sideways. At that first dinner party, he'd dabbed his lips after each mouthful. She'd tried to smile nicely. Instead, tears had plopped onto the chicken chasseur and pear upside-down tart, swimming in custard. No cheeseboard.

There were no photos outside the church; the vicar had been briefed, slipping away, a flash of monochrome robes. She didn't mind. 'David darling' opened the door of his car, tucked up her point-toed shoes. He revved the engine loudly, staring straight ahead. She strained forward, gasping at thick, warm air, to catch her mother's eye. She saw only her father's face, flushed and crumpled.

'He's a good man, your dad,' David said, foot on the gas, out of the church gate, hitting open road. Pressing a warm hand on her knee. A squeeze.

'Stop the car!'

She retched on the grass, peat brown from too much sun.

'You'll be a good wife. I want a baby; I'll be a good dad, good husband.'

Staring straight ahead again as he drove faster.

'Yes,' she said.

She was perspiring hard; her body was drowning in sweat and shame.

*

Now she stands at the window and presses her cheek against the leaded lights. Exhales one jagged sigh after another. It is eight o'clock and he's not home. She has eaten nothing all day and inside the front room, with no fire to kindle, coal locked in the shed, it's freezing. Imperceptible frost melts beneath her fingertips. Her belly is on fire.

Pain is circling; the baby's in a frenzy.

Outside, she fixes her eyes on the suburban street. The common limes are a whiteout; there's a blizzard. She's rung his work telephone, but no one picked up. She shut her lids then, picturing his teak desk, the plump secretary in lemon-yellow crêpe, a large clock on the panelled wall. No chance of missing the correct hour, his home time.

'I'll walk if the trams are stopped.'

She exhales slowly onto the windowpane. A month has passed since the temperature plummeted below zero. In the local paper, photos of tiny icebergs on the river, the park lake frozen and children skating on it, precarious.

David has bought snow galoshes; he carried them into work in a carpetbag.

'One night, they may stop the trams and I'll have to walk home.'

Perhaps it's tonight. But she needs to go to the hospital, she's sure the baby is coming.

She won't telephone her mother; can't.

'Now you're a married woman, you've a house to run. Your father and I, we're busy with the church, with work. Come for Sunday lunch every third month.'

That was all.

'You've made your bed – now lie in it!' She'd screamed it once, before the wedding, after too many G and Ts, and those little blue pills.

Even so, her mother wouldn't want her first grandchild arriving in a panic. *Would she?*

She picks up the phone, dials slowly. Her stomach rigid, a sharp ripple searing, someone pulling a belt too tight. Surely the baby can't breathe?

'It's me, mother.'

'Is it a quickie? How's David?'

'He's not home. The snow… he's delayed. The baby's coming.'

'He'll be back. Babies arrive late, so have hot milk, go to bed.'

Her mother's voice recedes, straining away. She waits.

'You're a woman now: a wife, a mother almost. No good running to me, not after…'

She replaces the receiver with a click.

Out, she needs to get out, down the path, through the gate, knock on a neighbour's door. But there's a sharp kick now, bending her double, felling her to the hall floor. She repeats to herself: 'David is a good man. He'll be home soon.'

She retrieves her coat from the peg, eases it over rigid shoulders. Sinks to the step, pulls on her school wellingtons, black rubber. Her ankles are swollen, they barely fit, pain swooping down to her calves. She puts her hands on her knees.

When she opens the front door, the snow flares into her face. She pockets her keys and one hand grasps the vanity case. The vinyl is grey now against the silvery snow. It's so heavy. She puts one foot forward, then the next; snow flings into her boots. It's so deep, too slippery. Nearly there, down the path, almost at the gate.

Above, all bleached and silky, multitude of flakes career down, disorientating her.

Pain unleashes in her belly; she loses her balance. Slips, cracks her head.

*

David has been unable to make it home. The trams have indeed shut down. His snow galoshes sit in the carpetbag beneath his desk. It was so much more convenient to walk to the hotel in town; in its bar, the whisky slips down a treat. Later, he'll call his wife.

'You've still two weeks to go.'

He'll remind her when she mentions it all over again.

He stands, moist hands cradling his tumbler.

'Top up?' he leans forward to ask his secretary. She's splendid in purple wool and a slippery smile.

At ten o'clock, he telephones the house. It rings over and over, no reply. David is puzzled, then relieved.

'She's gone to bed, good girl. Probably had hot milk.'

He smiles at his whisky, conscience salved.

On the path outside his house, the blizzard gently covers a new mound, lying motionless. There's a trickle of scarlet. The baby shifts and pushes, desperate to be born.

Winter, 1963 *won second prize at the Colm Tóibín International Short Story Award 2016.*

An Experience

Sam Reese

And you're happy to work? she asked, repeating my phrase back to me. Yes, I said. I'll be coming from a competition and just want to take a week somewhere quiet before classes start again. What kind of competition? I hoped my impatience didn't carry down the line. Freediving, I said. She gave something like a snort. Isn't that like drowning, slowly? I did not know the woman's name or anything about her save that she was not the owner of the homestead and macadamia orchard. Just taking care of the place, she said.

My sister had passed on the details – an email address and phone number – after I mentioned that I'd like to do some WWOOFing following my next freediving competition. It fell in the holidays between uni terms, and my part-time job at the language resource centre wouldn't need me until classes started either.

Mum took me there one summer when you were with Dad, my sister said. I think the guy who owned the place used to be her shrink. It's half falling down, and they always struggle to get anyone to pick the nuts.

Somehow, I could not picture a macadamia orchard. We used to go berry picking with our dad when we were small, and last year, when I went to Thailand for my first international competition, our club captain had arranged a trip to a Buddhist temple; afterwards, the driver stopped off at a cashew processing plant. Placards showed the terrible conditions the workers endured – deadly spikes, toxic oils – before we were shepherded through to a neon-lit store.

When I asked my sister, though, she said that she had picked a few. Not dangerous. Just boring.

I could take the bus from Tauranga towards the Coromandel. It stopped at the local beach, the woman told me down the line. It was easy to walk up to the homestead from there. She could have driven to meet me, she added, but... She trailed off. I called her once again, halfway through the competition. One of my fellow club members, Lee, had asked if he could tag along. It makes no difference to me, she said, and hung up.

It took us half an hour and a pathway ending in a marsh to tell us her directions were amiss. I suggested we retrace our steps and ask somebody local, so we left the township twice – the second time with coffee beans and several blocks of chocolate. I'm not taking any chances, Lee said.

I had to admit that the shops along the beachside strip where the bus had dropped us off offered better choice than their salt-eaten frontages would suggest. At first, my eyes practically glided past them; the beach itself was a dreamy curve of creamy sand. Each end rose in a bluff, the grey stone sprouting dark green leaves and red pohutakawa tufts. The shops, though, were fascinating – some from the days when the railway was built – and Lee had to tug me away from one bungalow I got caught up in admiring.

This felt a little out of character for Lee. From the first time we'd met, I had loved his calm. There's a danger, when you're getting ready for a long dive, that you'll get yourself too excited. If you hype yourself too much, your heartbeat starts to rise, your fat blood-bodies crave fresh air, and you find your throat contracting thirty seconds down. But Lee has tranquillity. His face radiates this glow of peace. It's a kind of emptiness you can lose yourself inside.

The second path we took led us around the outskirts of the wetlands on a wooden walkway overlooking reeds and grass. As we had been instructed, we crossed the lawns in front of the old railway station and slipped down a grassy bank to the sunken, overgrown remainder of the lines. On either side, the ground rose up in grassy slopes topped with harakeke. The tui song distracted us from our mosquito bites. A dash across a highway and another twenty minutes up a driveway that curved around the edges of a hill – then I saw the letterbox I'd been told would be our sign.

The sun was on the brink of sinking down behind the hill, casting the pathway we'd followed in a dampened shroud. But the homestead – a wide-decked old house, with a newer second tier in the same cream and red – caught the last thick wash of gold. I knocked while Lee rested on the deck, eyes closed, face alight. No one answered. I knocked again, then tried the handle. The door swung ajar.

I turned back to Lee for a nod or word of restraint, but he was distracted by a skinny cat on the path. He clicked his tongue, rubbed his fingers. I sighed and stepped inside, calling out, Hello? As the façade had suggested, there was an old-fashioned cleanness to the wide sweep of the kitchen and the large living room with its iron fireplace.

I was halfway down the corridor when I heard voices outside. At first, I thought it was Lee talking to the cat. Then I caught the same voice that had given me such misleading directions.

She looked a few years older than us – maybe twenty-five? – and her fringe fell across one eyebrow, making her look permanently sceptical. She squinted at me, hands on hips. Make yourselves at home, why don't you?

Lee stood, introduced me: This is Ace – he's the one who called you up. She nodded. Naomi. She did not offer her hand.

We followed her inside. Take any room along there, she said, pointing down the corridor. But never go upstairs. Lee had turned back to the deck, beckoning the cat. And the macadamias? I asked. Now she sounded irritated. They can wait.

The macadamia orchard overlooked the house. Past the slope, you could see the old railway tracks we'd followed, the marshland, and in the morning light a green-blue line of sea. Originally, the trees had been planted ten rows by ten, but at some point two rows had been taken out – or at least that's what Lee said, pointing out the ground along the far edge of the field.

For my part, I noticed the dew, still heavy on the grass in the shade of the orchard. The trees were all at least twice my height, and some branches ended in a couple of large, green husks the tapered shape of a fig; soon we saw that other branches held clusters of five or six.

The curtains in the room we'd chosen turned out to be quite worn through, so we both woke early with the sun. While I took a shower outside, Lee ground down some coffee beans and made a thick, black brew. The old coffee pot was just one of his discoveries. Large boxes in the cupboard held staples like flour, dried pasta and rice, and eventually we found an old loaf of bread, hard but not yet mouldy. There was no sign of Naomi. Still upstairs, I guessed.

Through the leaves that masked the outdoor shower from the pathway to the house, I had spotted the old shed. It looked promising, so after toast and coffee, we decided to explore. Inside was a wooden hopper with instructions for husking the macadamias. A set of wide drawers at the far end of the room turned out to have half a dozen lonely brown nuts inside. This is where we'll put them to dry out once they're husked, Lee said. I trusted him on this.

In the end, we decided not to wait for Naomi to show. Splitting the nets and two long sets of clippers between us, we took a large wheelbarrow each, crushing the occasional green husk as we went. These should have been picked by now, Lee said, and gestured to the nuts scattered through the grass. Several had large gouges in them. Rats? I asked. Must be, Lee said. We nudged the fallen shells aside – at least the ones that looked spoiled – and set up the netting around one tree's base.

By eleven, both our wheelbarrows were heaving with nuts. I had shimmied up the first tree, reaching for the highest clusters while Lee worked the lower boughs, and we'd alternated like this until we were sweating and several trees were bare.

I took off my top, and Lee paused before doing the same. Though the sun was high, the grass still felt damp against my back. When he caught the light, Lee's face was smooth and glowed like he was fresh from a dive, taking in that first deep breath. I was surprised at just how close I felt to him then. He asked, Can we stay here just a little longer? I said, Sure, and for a moment I wanted to say more.

Later, we'd both say we felt her presence on the edges of our sight wherever we went. But we couldn't see her when we brought our loads back to the shed. I suggested I start feeding nuts into the hopper while Lee made up some lunch. Though he was studying at the same uni as me, it did not take much of a conversation to work out that it was food Lee was interested in – though he didn't seem prepared to admit it to himself.

Lunch was large mugs of black coffee and a salad of chopped fruit, dark leaves, and crumbled macadamias. Something glistened on the top. I made a dressing with some honey, Lee explained. We ate on the deck. By day, we could see out to the ocean over the treetops here, too. Is that an island in the bay? Lee asked. I was distracted by some movement further down the path. Naomi emerged, walking the same way she had before. Like she owned the space.

Hard at work I see, she said. We've been at it all morning, Lee replied. I don't know if he'd missed the sarcasm in her voice, or was just being polite. Nice morning, I said. What have you been up to? She folded her arms, defensive. What is it to you? Then, spotting the few nuts left over in the salad bowl, she asked, Do you like the macadamias?

She led us through the kitchen. Lee had already found the vast tub of nuts between the flour and the rice, but she shook her head and opened up a tall standing freezer. It was packed with Tupperware, each box filled with macadamias. There's more than that, she said, more than I know how to handle. Use as many as you like. Go nuts.

By the time we reached the beach, it was past mid-afternoon. We walked the length of the bay, turning now and then to watch a group of surfers waiting for the right wave to break. Beyond them, off to one side, we saw the island more clearly. It rose bluntly from the water into a domed curve of green, dark leaves bursting from its crown.

The water was cold at first, but the trick is not to gasp, to bypass the body's hungry clench. I went further out than normal for my first fresh dive. Showing off, I guess. I turned back to look at Lee. Even through the murky thickness of the ocean water, he had this clarity, this lightness to his face. The first time I'd really noticed him, during a training session at our local pool, he'd had that same look about him: like he was aglow.

Later, as we dried out in the sun, one of the surfers clambered past us up the beach. I propped myself on my elbows. Good surf? She nodded, eyes half-closed. Lee turned on his side. What is that place out there? Donut island, the surfer replied. She paused, planted her board in the sand. 'Cause it's hollow in the middle. Round one side, there's a channel through the rock that people kayak to, scoot underneath the rock. Then suddenly, you're there. A calm pool. An emerald lagoon. Silence, green. Trees and flowers all around.

It was a long moment before she blinked, hoisted up her board, and added, But it's *tapu*. You're not meant to set foot on the land. You can look, but you can't touch. She clambered away across the dunes. Lee turned to me. Do you think we could swim there? How far is it, really? I wonder, I replied. I was thinking the same thing.

Earlier, after lunch, we'd managed to clear a few trees more. At this rate, now we had improved our tempo, I thought we might manage half the trees by the end of the week. But our new challenge made me feel a little anxious.

Like Lee, I wanted desperately to reach the island. It was all that we could talk about as we walked back. We would need plenty of time if we wanted to be sure that we could make it out there – and I began to worry that half of the orchard might not be enough. Naomi had been insistent on the phone that we should work. I tried to pin her down more precisely over dinner, hoping I could gauge her expectations. But she quickly became impatient and changed the subject.

Later, she grew energetic. Standing up, she pointed out the rows of records on the shelves above the fireplace. Together we walked along pulling sleeves out, collecting a pile that looked interesting. Only later did I wonder about her excitement as I discovered the wide range of jazz. Oh, who's that? Sun Ra?

From the couches we could listen to the rolling waves of saxophone and still see into the kitchen. Lee made dough with the flour, salt and honey he'd discovered in the cupboards, and some yeast he had bought before our long walk back.

Naomi wandered over when he started pulverising nuts in a blender, watching as the shards turned into crumbs, then a gritty paste, clumping in a ball before suddenly expanding into smooth, cream-coloured butter. Once he'd switched the blender off, she dipped in a finger and licked it as she walked away. She disappeared upstairs.

After that, she started joining us for breakfast. I was curious about Lee's reactions: his face, normally alive, went solemn when she talked to him. He'd nod and look down at his toast, or answer, Yes. That's right. But then I would add a detail – describe someone in our club, or a rival from Australia – and I'd catch his eye and see him break into a grin.

While we cleared the next row of trees, we dissected the story she had told us between mouthfuls of toast spread thick with macadamia butter. This was all before I moved here, she began. A while ago, but don't ask me for dates or anything. I went to some café friends had recommended. Nothing special, but not bad. When I went up to order another coffee, this old man called out hello to me. I replied without noticing that we weren't speaking English.

He must have been old. In his seventies at least. He had thin, white chicken-scratch hair, and the wrinkles down his cheeks were so deep you could fit a pencil inside them. But his eyes were young. And he looked so pleased that I had spoken back in the same language that I stopped and asked him how he was. I never get to talk to anybody here, he said. Are you – No, I said. But my father was. Ahh, he said, I remember fathers.

Now, I'll be honest, the man smelled like piss. And, looking him up and down, I noticed his hands were stained black with ink. I guess he noticed I was staring, 'cause he started telling me about his work. Turned out he delivered flyers into letterboxes. But his scumbag boss – that's my word, not his – had changed up his route. He had spent the whole night wandering these unfamiliar streets delivering leaflets.

But I get to have a tuna sandwich now, he said. I like tuna best. I nodded: Tuna's good, I said. I was still a bit distracted. You see, underneath the ink, his hands were super young. Like the hands of a teenager. By comparison, my hands looked middle-aged. And his sleeves were rolled up, so I could see his arms, and they were smooth and hairless. Not a wrinkle, no sagging skin. Like the arms of a boy.

We wound up talking for a while, and I'm not sure the waitress liked that. Probably didn't help their business having old men smelling of urine hanging out beside the counter. But I didn't care. One thing he said stuck with me more than anything else. He asked me if I was religious. Did I believe in God, or in some higher power? Well, I hedged my answer. Sometimes it's not good to rile up old folks. But he said, Don't worry. I was brought up as a communist. I've never believed in God. But the other day, I had an experience.

That's the best word I can use in English to get at it, but imagine it written down in italics, like it's not just any old experience. He meant something special. My mother got sick, he said, and I had to work a lot to get her medicine. I used to read to her in bed. I cleaned the house for her. I think about her often, but once you're dead, you're dead.

I nodded. That is how it goes. But he looked at me, and I knew whatever he'd say next was the most important part of our conversation. He put two blackened fingers on my wrist like this – and she turned first my hands over, then Lee's, placing her own fingers on the soft spot between palm and arm, as if taking a pulse – and he said, The other day, while I was getting ready to go to sleep, I heard my mother's voice. You're a good boy, she said, you took care of me. And now, he finished, I'm not sure.

Lee was dubious about the way she'd finished off the story. Do you think she really spent several nights out delivering pamphlets with the old guy after that, he asked from the boughs above me, when she hasn't lifted a finger since we both arrived? I'm not sure, I said. But that feeling she described, of a thin barrier between this world and another, I think I get that.

I looked up. Lee was nodding. Yeah. It's like that moment when you've been underwater too long and the feeling in your fingers has begun to go. I sometimes hear the softest music, like there's another space just beyond the edges of where I can reach.

Exactly, I said. I knew the feeling Lee described; I think every diver does. It's the place that sirens come from, the allure of the ocean, the suggestion of release. Besides, I added, I liked the way that the old man read to his mother when she was ill. I'd want someone to do that for me. Lee snorted. Don't be morbid! But I thought I heard a catch. I tried to bring the conversation back to earth. How are you going up there?

That's it. He jumped down, dropping one last handful of green husks into the wheelbarrow, and took off his top to wipe his brow. I was sweating too. We had found a better rhythm now we understood the process, but somehow it felt like harder work today. I noticed his swimmer's chest. He was leaner than me, but that only seemed to make the swell of his pecs look sharper. He breathed out a sigh. Chest rose and fell.

A rumble carried down the hill. We turned and saw a quad bike coming along the slope, towing a trailer. I waved, while Lee shaded his eyes. The man slowed the bike and pulled up close to the fence. Standing in the saddle, waving back, he seemed to want us to join him. Lee shrugged, and we walked up the slope.

His name was Peter. He must have been in his fifties, but his thick, tanned skin gave his light blue eyes a brilliant, icy glow. I own the next property along, he said. Do you grow things too? He laughed. It was deep, melodic. No, I raise sheep – a breed I bought from Switzerland – and keep bees around the hills here. He nodded to our heaving barrows.

I'm glad they've got someone in to clear the nuts. Lee nodded and said, I noticed the signs. Rats? Peter looked grave. I was worried about what would happen to the property in the interim. I'm glad they've made a move.

His phrasing sounded odd. What interim did he mean? I wanted to ask him more, pry a little for some details, but he looked away. Then we all caught the flashes of light coming from a distant slope. What were they? A torch? A signal? He grinned. Sorry – time to go. He revved up the bike. Swing past sometime, he called, I'll trade you honey for some of the dried nuts.

That night, neither of us had the energy to ask Naomi anything about her mother. In the afternoon, we had gone back to the beach, thinking we could try to swim partway to the island. To get a sense of the distance, I had said. But the ocean was against us. Even with long stretches underwater, when the surface noise went silent and it was just murky water and the sight of Lee's wide breaststroke pull, every time we breached the surface the island still looked just as far away.

On the walk back, I tried to stay optimistic. I'm sure we'll hit the right weather. Think about reaching that spring! But we could not shake our silence. It filled out the kitchen as Lee made some egg-fried rice, buzzed against the sound of Miles, Dizzy, Bird. It drove Naomi upstairs before she had finished eating. It kept me awake long enough to hear the morepork cry.

Right from my first exploration of the house, I had noticed that the space set out for a laundry room had been cleared of white goods. Gaps for piping and ducts remained, with a faint outline in the paint showing where the sun had bleached the walls. But this didn't seem so strange, given there was also just a single old-fashioned toilet downstairs, and no shower except the one fixed to the exterior on the far side of the house. As far as we could tell, this would only come out cold, so our mornings always started briskly – a few minutes of furious scrubbing, then relief and clothes warmed by the sun. I knew Lee did not mind this any more than me; we were used to similar rituals after training at our local pool, where the freezing showers were set out like a prison. We were more than comfortable to share our nakedness.

But we had to wonder about her. Neither of us dared to break her taboo and climb the stairs. We both wondered daily whether she had her own shower there. Heated water, too? And it didn't help that she'd appear with unexpected swiftness, like a cloud across the sun. Lee asked if I had the feeling she was watching us, even when it was clear that she was not around.

The third day of harvesting, she surprised us in the shed as we brought our final load of nuts back down to de-husk. Is that all you've done, she asked? Lee shook his head, but otherwise ignored her, instead loading up the hopper. For my part, I opened up the drying drawers at random, gesturing to rows of brown spheres clunking now against each other, now against the wood. She made a noise that could have indicated contempt or satisfaction, and stalked off.

We'd left the subject of the island in the realm of yesterday, working until almost the last light of afternoon. But for some reason, while I dished up the pasta Lee had cooked, I decided I would ask her about donut island. She twirled spaghetti on her fork, looking serious. That island's no joke, she said. I went there – a while ago. Lee said, I didn't think you'd been here that long? She just shook her head. It's empty inside.

In the night I stumbled. I was still half wrapped in dreams, and when the light switch in the bathroom didn't light the room it threw me off course. In the morning, Lee noticed the bruising on my cheek. I shivered when he brushed it with his thumb, the flicker of pad against the surface of my face.

I thought it was just the bulb, but when we tried the toaster and the record player neither would respond. We could get the stovetop going – the gas still worked at least – but none of the lights or electronics seemed to work. I left Lee to take care of coffee while I tried to find a fuse box. I did not have any luck. Lee pointed his chin upstairs. I called out Naomi's name, but there was no response.

We still half-expected her to join us on the deck. The cat was back, belly open to the sky. Lee scratched him while I finished off my coffee and, when she still didn't show, began to drink hers as well. In the shed, we found that the de-husker wasn't working either. No point harvesting until the power's sorted, Lee said. I think he had noticed the foul smell coming from the deep standing freezers in the corner, but neither of us made a move to look inside.

What about— I started asking, once we'd stepped outside. Lee looked serious. I second-guessed myself. Then I said it anyway. What about we try swimming to the island again? Lee did not speak. Then he smiled.

I suggested that we take a different route, once we'd finished the long slog down the trainlines to the station. Hoisting bags and towels over our shoulders, we plunged into the long grass and made for the bluff. In the sunlight, his face was alight, ringed with a corona, and I thought that maybe I could hold this moment, somehow make everything stop.

As we'd left the property (note addressed to Naomi sitting on the table), we had spotted Peter in the distance, on his bike again. He had waved one paw-like hand at us in a wide arc. Now, climbing up the bluff, I started wondering again if he'd wanted to talk. Perhaps he knew what was happening with the power? But that was something Naomi could figure out.

Lee's eyesight was perfect and I trusted him to gauge the distance to the island better than me. But even I could tell, once we'd pushed our way past thick pohutakawa branches, that the island was much further out than we had thought from on the beach. Up high, and at this angle, we could make out the dark gap in the rocky ring.

I met Lee's eye and knew he was imagining the same deep breath as me – the long, silent swim along the rocky channel, and the moment when our heartbeats would pulse inside our throats, when we could wait no longer and would breach the surface in a secret place all of our own.

Lee nudged me in the ribs. There was Naomi on the beach. Around her it was busy: a family walked a dog; several surfers stood and watched the ocean for a sign of life. But it was impossible to miss her ponytail and severe fringe, or the way she stood with her arms akimbo, challenging the world. We scrambled down the slope, thinking we'd surprise her. By the time we cleared the scrub, though, she had disappeared.

According to Lee, the tide would be lowest an hour or so from then. I suggested we grab coffee; normally we would avoid caffeine so close to a dive. But today was not about escaping to a space where the rhythm of our hearts was as steady as the ocean. We would need as much energy as we could harness if we wanted to make it out to the island this time.

We heard a rap on the window of the old café. Peter waved and came inside. With him was a quiet woman dressed in silk trousers and shirt. I was hoping to catch you, Peter said. This is Diana, she's the estate agent for the family. She's been trying to tie down a buyer for the property. Diana interrupted: The thing is, she said, no one in the family knew that there were people staying on the property.

Lee looked pale. I said, I'm sorry, I think there must have been a lapse in communication. My sister put us in contact. She knows the owner. But we've only dealt with Naomi.

The woman looked puzzled, Peter concerned. The owner died three months ago. I've been working with his family, but none of them are called Naomi. Peter blinked, and said, I'm sure they're not squatters. What kind of squatters harvest trees? Unless, and he looked meaningfully at our bags. Lee scowled and unzipped them both. Towels, sandwiches, and a change of clothes. No black market nuts.

Look, I said, she's been staying upstairs the whole time, but we saw her maybe twenty minutes ago, just standing on the beach. She must have gone back to the house. Either way, check her room. Talk to her. I'm sure there's a simple explanation for it all. Diana said, Hmm. Well. Peter said, Yes, let's go have a look. He fixed us with glacial eyes. Don't go anywhere.

On the beach, I closed my eyes against the sun. Somewhere in my bag were bus tickets back to the city, a pair of headphones we would share, heads resting against one another as we journeyed home, rough, salt-tufted hair matting with kind. Somewhere close by was a palm waiting for my grip. Lee murmured, It would have been an experience.

The Miner

Yvonne Dykes

'I'm writing a play for my end-of-year exam,' Chloe announces.

I throw my coat and bag on a chair. I got caught in an almighty shower on the way home from the office; me, the coat and my oversized bag create a little puddle on the floor.

'Do you have to write in the kitchen? I've got to get the tea on.'

'It's warm in here, and anyway, it's a kitchen sink drama.'

'What's it about?' I ask, pulling clothes out of the tumble dryer. I'm glad of the warmth on my hands.

'A woman mourning her lost love.' She writes in her notebook, head down, her shoulders moving to the rhythm of her pen.

'She won't find a lost love in the kitchen – she needs social media. Or a detective agency.' I'm thinking of this kitchen. It has barely enough space for the table and two chairs. I bend down to fetch a reticent pair of drawers out of the machine and my behind gets a slap from the wet coat.

'I'm thinking of giving her a visitor. Or she can have a party.'

'Shove over while I get the wash sorted.'

She brushes away pens, a tube of sweets and her mobile. We exchange a tut or two.

'What's she like, this woman in your play?'

'Cool, sophisticated. She's like... Helen Mirren.'

'What's *she* doing in the kitchen?'

'It's a character, it's not Helen Mirren herself.'

My fingers ignite sparks as I shake out our tights and bedsocks. 'She probably doesn't do much cooking.' I imagine Ms Mirren eating oysters with other celebrities. 'Is there a part in your play for Stephen Fry? I do like him. I can see him pairing socks on the kitchen table, but not her majesty there.'

Chloe ignores me. She leans her elbow on the table and lands a flat palm on her head. It works for a few seconds and I am silent. But it doesn't last, I'm not one for dramatic pauses. 'What does she do for a living, this character?'

'I'm not sure yet. An adviser to the UN or a top barrister, something like that.'

'You don't find barristers in kitchen sink dramas. She'd have someone who does for her.'

'What do you mean, does for her?'

'The woman who does the cleaning, fetches a bit of shopping, does the washing and ironing. Like what I do for you, but she gets paid for it.' I fold three crackling T-shirts and place them by her notebook in the vain hope she will take them to her room.

'That's irrelevant. I'm thinking of opening the first act with her having to cook a dish. It was one she ate on her travels around Europe when she was young. But she doesn't have all the ingredients.'

'So she goes out to the supermarket to get them and meets the bloke she lost years before?'

'No. She has a nervous breakdown.'

'Why?'

'It's an existential play about loss.'

'You've completely lost me now. I was alright up until the missing ingredients, but existentials? I've got to peel the spuds.'

'The missing ingredients upset her because they remind her of her first love, who died. She met him when she was travelling, and she hasn't got over his death.'

'Well, don't make the missing ingredients fish, whatever you do. You won't connect with your audience if she's thinking her lad is a mackerel fillet.' But Chloe's not listening. I snatch up the vegetables for a shepherd's pie and start peeling.

'How does the lad die, then?' I ask.

'Skiing. No,' she holds her forehead with probing fingers, searching for her muse, 'how about, he drowns in a tragic boating accident in the Aegean?' Her pen catches the words from the air before they disappear.

'Ooh, very dramatic. Is she with him when he dies?'

'Erm. No, that's the point. Act Two is a flashback. She's young again – I'll need a different actress for that.' She makes a note in the margin. 'Anyway, they meet at the harbour, have a terrible row and he goes off on the boat without her. She never sees him again.'

'So you could make mackerel the missing ingredient.'

She scowls, and I imagine she's writing Act Three – the moment when Ms Mirren is having a panic attack because she's got six guests coming to dinner, one of whom is Stephen Fry, and she has neglected to order the fish starter from Ocado.

I peel an onion, then fetch the foil-covered leftovers from our Sunday lunch.

As the meat hits the oil and nestles in among the onions, it sends a fug of charred fragrance swirling around Chloe's head. She responds with an involuntary sniff. She lifts her arms to tie up her hair and throws the shadow of a horse's pert tail on the kitchen wall.

'What does she do then? Old Helen, when she finds the cupboard bare? Does she whizz out to the corner shop to buy a tin of tuna?' I ask, picking meat from my teeth.

'Now you're being facetious. I can't work like this,' she huffs. It's a drama school-induced teenage huff. I squeeze round her chair to search for the potato masher.

'When I find it difficult to work because someone is making my dinner, I have a nice cup of tea and relax.' I raise my eyebrows and she closes her notebook.

The shepherd's pie is covered with cheddar and bubbling away in the oven. We are opposite each other, blowing concentric circles on the surface of our hot drinks. I've changed out of my work clothes and I spread out. The kitchen is moist from recently boiled veg and the notebook is open again. It's a recycled, organic job with gritty pages that make it impossible to read from here.

'What happens then? In the play?' I ask.

'So, the main character...'

'What's her name?'

'Diana. Diana invites her neighbours to supper, but she's manic and it's really awkward. She can't stop apologising because she's done a fig dessert and forgotten the pistachios and honey.'

'She'd need some yoghurt with that. Did she remember the yoghurt?'

'Mum!' She gives me the look. It's not one I've seen on my side of her family tree, and I wouldn't know about the other side.

'Diana just gets more and more crazy. Then she finds out

that one of her guests knows the island where Diana had her passionate affair.'

'How?'

'What?'

'How does she find out that one of them knows the island?'

'Erm.'

My daughter chews the button on her pen while I scan the walls, looking for inspiration. A witch has visited while I was at work. There is the imprint of a hand accompanied by the mark of a cat's paw visible on the steamed-up window. This explains the fact that the milk bottle sprung up almost weightless when I pulled it out of the fridge.

'Diana could have a fridge magnet. A souvenir from Greece,' I say.

'She's not the type to buy fridge magnets on holiday. She'd have a painting by a local artist.'

'Yes, I suppose she would. Do you want baked beans? I fancy beans tonight.'

'Do we have any?'

'I'd better check – I don't want to get all existential about missing beans.' I open the cupboard, sliding tins about as if I'm playing the three cups and a ball trick. 'Oh dear.'

'Life imitating art,' she says. 'Don't throw a wobbly.'

I listen for the tone, the rise and fall of my voice in her words.

'No, I'm not having any of that existential angst in this kitchen – life's too short. We'll have peas instead. Go on, then, what happens to Diana?'

'She learns from her dinner guest that her lover didn't die on the boat trip after all. That he already had a wife and kids on the island and was just using her.'

'That would make you go bonkers.'

'Yeah, that's the point. She's been upset over her supposedly dead lover all these years and it feels like a lifetime of wasted emotion. And. And...' She bends her head over her notebook to write and long strokes zip across the page.

I glance over the contours of her nose and cheek. At this angle it stirs a memory, but I brush it aside and wait.

'And although she kind of used the supposed tragedy to become successful in her career, she couldn't sustain a loving relationship.' The writing on the page slopes forward and when she looks up I see in her black pupils the figure of a young woman standing alone on a quay.

'I feel quite sorry for her,' I say. I pour water into the same saucepan I used for the potatoes and set it to boil for the peas.

'Oh, she comes to terms with it all in the end. She sees her life as fulfilled despite the wasted years mourning the man who lied to her.'

She sits back and stares into the middle distance; she's searching for the point, the theme of the play.

'That's it, isn't it?'

I know this is a rhetorical question, so I carry on straining the peas.

'In the end, Diana will forgive herself for being fooled by a scumbag – she'll find someone who cares, probably one of the dinner party guests.' The pen taps the edge of the table. 'The bad that happens, whether it's our fault or not, shouldn't be allowed to ruin our future. We need to be wiser and learn from the hurt, find the positive, however long it takes. Find a bridge. Get over it.'

'That's very profound. Ketchup or brown sauce?'

The pen runs boundless across the page.

The Miner

I smile at Chloe's back as she becomes a study for a portrait: at the dark slick of ponytail falling luxuriantly over her shoulders and the fine hairs at her nape, black against olive skin. So different from my own northern paleness.

Standing by the stove, I think back to a time when she could fit on my knee so entirely that no limb dangled outside the hull of my lap. One night, as her head began to dip, I told her our story. I described a seascape of bleached sand, boats lifted and lowered by somnolent waves and the languid charms of a fisher-king. I sang her the songs we shared while our faces were lit by the bonfire on your beach. I spoke of the scent of jasmine that drifted on warm thermals above us and I told her that once, for a brief moment in time, I thought I was in love. I didn't tell her how my letters to you over the years remain unanswered, or how much I pity you for never knowing her.

I placed a photograph under her pillow as I tucked her into bed that night. In it, there is an outline of a lean young man, face hidden by the white glare of the camera's flash. Sitting in front of you is me with my blonde eyelashes and salty, sun-kissed cheeks. I'm so gloriously happy that the camera in my hand is out of control. When I left her sleeping the photo was curled up in her hand, and yet I've never seen it since. And what I told her as she lay on my lap must have slipped into her ear and disappeared; the scene buried deep, hidden away among the overwhelming experiences of childhood. It appears that it takes a pen, not a pickaxe, to free gold from a seam.

My eyes sting when I open the oven door and smoky air fills the kitchen. Our daughter closes her notebook and lays the table for two.

The Fragility of Goodness

Omar Sabbagh

Amr was cogitating on Time – or to be more precise, timing. Like most gamblers he had a very large and capacious mind, and could think his way round to the latest cutting-edge research, say, on unicorns and UFOs. The way he figured it, standing there in the small, square, white-walled kitchen, was as follows...

The roulette table was spinning, spinning continuously, if periodically. So that the exact time he left his flat, caught a cab for the short ride to the casino, and arrived at the roulette table – made all the difference! If the small cream-coloured ball (that god on his pyre!) was at this moment landing on, let us say, '3', then '31', and so on – then the exact time he left and arrived would entail a wholly different scurrying run of numbers. The pattern would change, for better or worse, depending. However, by the end of these ruminations, he realised the paradox, that it all came to the same thing – if all was well with the world and if God indeed was in His heaven.

And yet his cogitation hadn't been pointless. It had made him a touch warier about going to try his luck, whether to be serenaded or whipped by fate and fortune.

The quick mind-scouring had made him more self-aware, which was a devil to the devil of gambling. He turned to his wife and said:

'Right. I'm off. What was it, again, you needed from the pharmacy?'

'Anti-bacterial handwipes. Two new toothbrushes. Some shaving cream for you. A razor, or two; for you again.'

It wasn't that she knew he might be headed, surreptitiously, to the casino; no. She didn't know. But there was this charmed twinkling in his eye which she never failed to recognise as an indication that he was excited – about something.

They'd arrived in London earlier that morning, in the chilly dawn hours. She knew of course that it was his tradition to go to the casino this one time each year, on the first day of their arrival in London, where they were wont to travel over the summer. But for close to the whole of the plane ride there, they'd scuffled over it, and she, to all intents and purposes, had won. He'd promised, with a battered brow, that he'd forgo his totemic tradition this year.

For a few more moments, squaring off in that white-walled kitchen, husband and wife eyed each other. Both seemed pregnant with thoughts that needed, seethed to be articulated. But both kept silent, a deuce of two sets of almond and thyme-mottled eyes. Amr now smiled, amorously, leant in to kiss his wife on the cheek. And she accepted it with due grace, for now at least.

*

On the way back from the casino, two hours later, Amr was deep in avid discourse with the cab driver. The latter's son, as it happened, had just graduated with a stellar result in a degree in some hard science that was a far cry from Amr's softer skillset. After bathing the driver's quite evident pride in his son with all the balm and charm he could muster, Amr began to discuss a topical matter. He had no detailed or textured knowledge about AI – but liked to think he had some broad conceptual grasp that might permit the inkling of some kind of insight, for or against, or somewhere, perhaps, in between.

'They say,' the cab driver continued, 'they say that in twenty years computers will be able to think, like us, like humans, I mean.'

It hurt him to think of this being the case, so Amr tried to explain his stance on the matter.

'That's the difference between the mind of a scientist, a hard scientist, and the mind of someone like me.'

'Ah. What is it you do, sir?'

'I'm a professor.'

'Well, then, you should be the right person.'

'Not really. I teach subjects in the liberal arts. You know: literature, philosophy...'

'Ah! So you're a philosopher, then?'

'I try to be. Listen. A hard scientist – and I've met and spoken with many – will tell you that we, they, or whoever, *really don't know* what the future will look like, how it'll be rigged. But I, I can't do that. I'm the kind of person who sees and feels the way things are, and clings to that, and if I'm asked to speak of the future, I project from what we have, what we are, what I clutch at...'

'Sorry sir, I don't quite follow?'

'I mean, I suppose, that I don't think a computer, or an indefinite set of them, will ever really think like a human being.'

'They say—'

'I know what they say, but thinking, like us I mean, just isn't a computation. Our minds are interwoven with our bodily instincts, our feelings, emotions, perceptions, in a way that just is a mystery, and, being a mystery, I just don't see the science of duplicating it – artificially, I mean.'

'Fair enough. But won't they be able to duplicate the human body soon as well? And then couldn't they just – oh, what's the word?'

'Graft?'

'Yes, graft the two together?'

Amr pondered. Then he said: 'OK. But will a computer, or a system of them, or a system of them grafted, even seamlessly, onto a duplicated human body – will that, whatever it is, will that ever *suffer*?'

The cab driver hesitated now.

'I don't quite follow you, sir.'

'What I mean is, when we understand something, whatever, a tree or a car, it's one thing. But there's a different kind of knowing and thinking, or thinking through, which is just more real and lived and felt for us. Take this cab, say, ok?'

'Alright.'

'It's a black cab.'

'It is indeed, sir.'

'Well, you know it's black, right?'

'I do.'

'So, what if when you drop me off in a few minutes, there's a bloke waiting with a bucket of bright white paint? What if, once I've left, he chucks the whole lot onto your black cab? Then, I think it's fair to say, your knowledge of the blackness of your cab will be of a different sort. At some level that knowledge will be combined with a new and deeper and richer way in which *it is felt*, as well as just logically or computationally understood. Right?'

The cab driver was nodding.

'Yes, I do take your point.'

Amr gave the man a five quid tip. Not because of the entertaining conversation, but because though he'd lost a lot at first, he'd recouped it all, with a couple of hundred quid's profit, and felt like he might appease the vengeful god of gambling by spreading some of that extra wealth, as though to say to the fickle, unchivalrous deity that he was playing fair – and not to be too angered by his minor, his *oh so minor* win...

*

From one house, now, to another – where the house (*and the house*), in both cases, always wins...

*

Amr entered the flat to find Farah curled up on one of the sofas in the living room, cradling a book. This made him nervous, because, though a highly literate woman, his wife, at least since their marriage a couple of years back, rarely read anymore – books, that is. The omen was either dire or propitious; he couldn't tell. Thankfully, he'd managed to get the requested stuff from the pharmacy on the way back from the casino. So, with a gait close to tiptoeing, he placed the bag of goods by her side. She looked up.

'It says here that an apple is eaten for reasons other than mere nourishment. Which is true, I think.'

He looked at her searchingly, with a teetering, unstable gaze. There was the whiff of something in the air that certainly didn't bode well.

Having walked over to kiss his now seemingly sedate wife, having placed the requested shopping on the round mahogany table, as per a second request, he peered at the book in which she seemed to be knee-deep. It was a book of philosophy – clearly picked, whether with prior thought or at random, from his abundant library. The title on the cover ran: *The Fragility of Goodness*.

He racked his mind while unpacking the goods and putting them away. Yes, as it happened, with all the sour sauce of serendipity, he actually recalled the passage she must have been alluding to; though why the allusion, as yet, he couldn't quite fathom.

The philosopher in question, a doyen and a classicist, had been discussing the fallacy at the heart of a puritanical mind-body split, whether it was in Plato or in Descartes or in whomever. The puritans of the mind, she'd averred, relegated the bodily, the strictly speaking 'aesthetic' life, and saw the mental life as infinitely superior – because, *mistakenly, in her view* (the modern philosopher in question that is), they parsed all bodily life as bound up, well-nigh bestially, with mere survival and nothing more noble or admirable than that. And then... well, she'd given the example of how the bodily life was not – *seen rightly* – merely a survival mechanism. One ate an apple, as a human being at least, not only because of some biologically geared search for some sweet vitamin or what have you; no. The apple eaten also had a nice green-looking sheen to it, dappled with small light-grey dots; it had a texture on the tongue, peel or flesh, which was also relished. It was associated, perhaps, with a long train of cherished, storied memories from youth. And so on, and so on... It had quiddity, that is to say, quality.

On tenterhooks, Amr said: 'Yes, I recall the passage.'

'And what do you make of it?' queried his wife.

'Insightful, fresh, definitely. The life of the flesh has more to it than flesh, no doubt. The soul, the formative mystery between, *through* mind and body, well...'

Farah now closed the chunky tome in question and placed it on the table next to the sofa on which she was reclining.

'So: *casino?*'

'No,' Amr lied.

'Because I've just spent the last two hours trying to come up with an excuse for you. You – my dear, dear husband: *the infinite dreamer* – you always believe the best in people, never the worst. That neat optimism comes from your utopic childhood and youth, no doubt. And so I've been trying to find a way of making sense of this gambling business. Because *I know* it's not about the money. Like the apple, eaten for its taste or texture? Or, let me put it this way: is gambling for you a thing of beauty and a joy forever?'

This was a very difficult situation. Was he being tested? Was it, in some deep and Byzantine way, some kind of trick question, trick statement? Again, Amr racked his mind. It seemed, presently, that the only thing for it was to change the subject.

'I didn't go, by the way; and Keats? Why Keats?'

'Oh? You didn't?'

'No.'

'Because the house always wins?'

'Just so,' and Amr nodded his head, vigorously. It was the somewhat-confused closing of a heroic simile. And now he ducked his head, smiled with a desperate attempt at grace; but failed, coming off, no doubt, as creepy – even to his wife.

She pursed her lips and squinted her eyes at him, searing, sere – two green and chestnut daggers.

But a godsend, now. A ping pinged on Farah's mobile. She looked away, down.

Briefly, she checked the new entry in her junk mail inbox. It was, it seemed, from a certain Reverend Noland, basking in some Catholic hospital in upstate New York. As it turned out, by all the ludicrous and ludic fates, he'd just gifted Farah approximately five point seven million dollars in his will, asking her in his well-worded email – in what was clearly a gallant effort at seeming genuine and on the level – to spend the money, following his departure, on the poor and the needy. She guffawed, then deleted the message.

'I get them all the time,' Amr said, on the verge of being grateful to Fortune. So, he continued: 'Junk mail like that reminds me...'

'Of what?'

He was entering into his element now; on safer, more sacred ground.

'A little of poetry, too.'

'Yes?'

'Well, there's a major poet who seems to think that *this* millennial generation – with its use of emoticons and contractions, in emails and tweets and so on, like 'lol', or 'btw', or 'wtf' – that these new developments in the way the young express themselves are a form of flexing the poetic muscle. But I agree with her nemesis, a very different, statelier poet – who recently passed away as it happens—'

'Explain...'

'Well, there's condensation – and then there's *condensation*. Yes, sometimes to curtly contract one's means of expression *can* amplify meanings, reach into bigger worlds. But I don't think this virtual onanism is doing anything substantially poetic. It's just poverty of spirit, meanness of it, too – and laziness.'

'I'll think on it,' Farah replied. Presently she folded her body upwards like a rising cobra and went for a late afternoon nap. The way she strolled through the apartment seemed to thrum with a certain queenly authority.

The house always wins.

Yes: it does, *of course it does.*

Amr stayed riveted at his computer screen. He had the inch of an inkling to write something: the urge was tart and sweetly venomous in his veins. Each page penned, he always felt, was like a tiny dose of poison – in some slow, imperial effort to render himself immune; or to render himself, somehow, tragically victorious...

*

Meanwhile, in upstate New York, a certain Reverend Noland, imminently dying of some fatal bout of cancer, felt gratified that he'd gifted his wealth – nearly all of it inherited many, many decades ago – to the one random recipient he'd gambled on.

He'd picked her name and email address virtually out of a hat. Had googled her to the best of his ability, checked her Facebook account – among other small, sundry searches. He didn't know her, of course, had never met her. But it was as if – decrepit and on his deathbed now – he wished to emulate the fortuitous, fragile goodness of Christ.

Dry County

David Lewis

Frustrating times. Glenn had worked as a junior caretaker at Whittaker Park since he was twenty. That meant lawn-mower or leaf-raker, depending on the season. After ten years he'd persuaded his boss to promote him to caretaker. That meant lawn-mower or leaf-raker, depending on the season.

Frustrating times.

Frustrating in all ways. It was no surprise when the most eventful month of Glenn's life started with other people having sex. Even better, while he was at work. Better yet, having to work late on a Friday.

The evenings were cooler and people had stopped lingering in the park after sunset. He thought he was alone as he finished clearing the leaves around the pond, but then he heard a couple moaning behind the thorn bushes at the water's edge. He should leave them to it. But it was Friday, he didn't have anyone important to see and, come on, who wouldn't want a peek? This was a good one. Walter, his boss, was having sex with the new girl. He'd never seen Walter naked. So, even though the bushes had particularly nasty thorns, he crouched between two leafy ones and watched.

There was a splash in the pond. A fish. They'd just stocked it. That was one of the reasons they'd hired the new girl – or so Walter said. Another splash. It had to be a fish. The pond was still safe, wasn't it? It wasn't deep enough for a mermaid. He'd taken down a few unauthorised 'No Virgins in the Water' signs. Nobody, virgin or not, was supposed to swim in the park pond. And who said that mermaids only took virgins? There had been no official warning. As usual, when nobody knew anything, everybody had an opinion.

Walter grunted. Remember, he was having sex with the new girl. Sex, not mermaids, was the reason Glenn was hiding in the thorn bushes. Okay, that's not completely true. His naked boss was the reason. Now, Walter wasn't a fixation of his, but if he had to be honest, he'd admit that the view was worth the scratches. His boss put a hand on the new girl's neck.

'Shit, Darleen.'

She stopped him. 'It's Dorothy.'

That confused everybody. Glenn heard a loud splash. If that was a fish, they'd stocked the pond with great whites. He looked at the water then back at his boss, who was still thrusting away.

'Are you close?' the new girl said.

Walter groaned. 'Sure as holy fuck, no. Not now.'

He pulled away from her. He could be a real asshole – one that bought Glenn's drinks on beer pitcher Mondays, but in all other contexts, an asshole. The asshole started dressing, unfortunately.

'Mood's dead anyway. Put your clothes on, Darleen. I'll drive you home.'

The new girl didn't respond. She was looking at the pond.

'What if something's out there watching us?'

Walter smirked. 'Don't be ignorant. Now I'm not saying we're degenerates, but they've never gone for park-side fornicators before. We've got nothing to fear.'

A thorn wormed its barb through Glenn's sleeve. He flinched. The branches shook. Did they hear it? Walter turned to the new girl.

'Get dressed. Someone might come.'

She hugged her legs. 'You're the first man who's ever been in a hurry to put my clothes on.'

Walter tossed her a pair of underwear. 'First time for everything. Now let's move.'

Glenn tried to remove the thorn from his arm and two others stuck him. He bit his lip. What was the expression? *Thorns for patience*. The new girl turned to the pond.

'What's the hurry if they've never gone for, what was it you said, park-side fornicators?'

Walter looked annoyed. 'Someone, a person, might come.'

'Not this person, that's for sure.' She huffed. 'If you always finish so quickly with women, maybe you need something else.'

Walter slapped her legs. 'Sure, whatever. Stop talking shit and start dressing.'

'Maybe Mr Walter needs a man.'

Impossible. Glenn blushed even though the new girl wasn't talking about him. Walter looked towards the parking lot.

'I'm going in ten seconds.'

The new girl stepped out of the bushes, into the shallow water. 'How about a swim?'

Glenn surveyed Walter's face. Was he attracted to her? He didn't look it now.

The new girl challenged him. 'We've got nothing to fear, right?'

She walked to where the pond floor dropped and dove in. Glenn's legs ached. When he tried to shift his weight, another thorn pierced through his clothes. *Patience*. Walter cursed, left the thorn bushes' cover and walked towards the parking lot. He didn't turn around. He really was leaving. The new girl wouldn't catch up with him unless she ran to his car naked. That was probably what he wanted. *He needs a man*. Bullshit. Gay? There was and there wasn't, and Walter wasn't.

Frustrating times.

After Walter's car drove off, there was nothing more to see except the new girl skinny-dipping. Crickets yawned out their chirps from the shadows. Time to go home. He took a last look at the spot where the couple had been. Next to the new girl's clothes, he saw a pair of socks. Walter's? They looked male. Maybe he'd take a souvenir. He parted the bushes, inched forward, picked them up and sniffed. How else could he check? He thought about Walter's legs.

The new girl had reached the centre. Her head was bobbing in and out of the water. She probably wasn't used to swimming. Then she slowly turned to face him. He dropped the dirty socks from his nose and fell back into the bushes. Thorns needled deep into his back. He swallowed a curse. *Patience*. Lots of *patience*. He didn't move. Everything was quiet. The new girl was staring at him. Something was wrong. She wasn't moving. The pond was still. After a silent minute, Glenn crawled out of the bushes. He stared back at her and she held his gaze.

A chill travelled from Glenn's feet up his body and through each vein. It trickled out of the thorn pricks and down his skin. Everything slowed down. The park was still.

The water was motionless. It had solidified to flat ground, holding the new girl rooted in place. Her eyes – he wasn't sure – no, he was; they were growing round and black, turning into glittering orbs of pitch. He had to do something.

But – no, he couldn't budge. His muscles had forgotten the habits of motion. In the pond, the girl's dark eyes widened. She started sinking. Was she doing it deliberately? He couldn't tell. Why couldn't he move?

Glenn directed thoughts of action to his legs. Nothing. Determined hands had gripped his limbs tight. He tried to yell. Impossible. He couldn't open his mouth. He watched the new girl sink. Her eyes didn't flinch from him. They didn't blink. Then her lips moved – as if a dark thread was pulling them, they twitched into a smile. Glenn had to stop this. It had to stop. He couldn't stop it. He couldn't move. He couldn't even shiver as cold air crept over him. She dropped underwater quietly, grinning at him. In the bushes, the crickets were screaming. The smooth pond glistened, unperturbed.

Then, with the pop of a bubble, he collapsed. He could move again. The crickets' call rattled out of the bushes in warning. *Leave. Leave.* Then a splash. He jumped. Was it her? He shouted: 'Are you there?'

Leave. Leave. No, just a second. God, what was her name again? He had just heard it. What had Walter said? What was the wrong one? Darleen. Yes. That wasn't it. Was it? Or not? No.

'Dorothy?' he whispered. As though pronouncing her name was a miracle that could pull her from the water. Of course it didn't. *Leave. Leave.* He yelled. Nothing. Again. Nothing. A splash. He couldn't see the ripples in the water. Maybe it was her, or a fish, or a shark. Something round, like a smooth rock, broke the surface in the pond's centre. It gleamed in the jaundiced park lights. *Leave. Leave.*

'Oh God, let it be a shark. Not a mermaid.'

He didn't leave. The cricket shrill ceased and a low note vibrated out of the pond, making little breaths of air tremble around him. He thought of Walter in the bushes. A soft wind, or something like it, fumbled against him clumsily like a married man. It cupped his face and licked the hairs on his arm. He felt dark eyes watching. They drew him – no, invited him into the water, promising something different, something that he wouldn't be ashamed of. This wasn't a wasted hope; it was real, whatever it was. Without questioning, he stepped forward into the pond.

Then it stopped. Glenn gasped. He hadn't been breathing. Ripples spread from the centre of the empty pond. It was gone. Dorothy was gone. Dead? Maybe. He ran.

Glenn told the police everything. When he talked about Dorothy, he felt an awful jealousy.

*

It was beer pitcher Monday, a football night. But Glenn and Walter were the only regulars at the bar, so the bartender let them watch the report on the disappearances. Walter emptied their pitcher. The bartender smiled.

'Tackle another one?'

Glenn nodded. It was good to be out. All weekend he'd heard the pond's note droning in his mind. So he'd stayed at home thinking about dark underwater eyes.

Walter was watching the TV. The show's host reappeared.

'Welcome back to *Your State Debates*. Today: are mermaids an argument for more sex education in Oklahoma schools?'

None of those Channel 23 pricks had a clue. Nobody, not even the police, believed Glenn's story. Nobody listened. The first guest on the debate was a woman: a red-headed doctor representing HI-SEAS (Health Institutions for Sexual Education Against Sirens). She looked at the host.

'Since the first sirenian attack, our state government has issued no official warning. But we have to face the facts. Rumour travels. Kids aren't stupid—'

'Teenage pregnancies have tripled,' the host interrupted.

'Exactly. And if you look at the most recent victims, the reason is—'

'Same old saw. Don't you liberals watch the news anymore?' A reedy man in a suit jumped into the discussion. He was the chief minister of the Oklahoma Gospel Organisation for Democracy (OK-GOD). He turned directly to the camera and winked, like he was sharing a joke with the audience. It made Glenn feel helpless.

The preacher continued: 'I hate to cut in on such a lovely lady, but this past week has shown – pardon the expression – a sea change in mermaid behaviour. Look at the most recent victim, a Miss Darleen Gautier—'

'Dorothy,' the doctor interrupted. The host held out a hand.

'Yes, ma'am, let the reverend finish.'

Walter slapped the bar top and cursed. Glenn slapped the bar top in agreement. Was Walter angry or sad? Either way, Glenn agreed. On the TV, Reverend OK-GOD beamed.

'As I was saying, this Miss Gautier, a virgin? The lady doth undress too much, methinks.'

He smiled at the doctor. 'That's Shakespeare. You remember Shakespeare, don't you, doc?'

Walter called the bartender. 'Turn that shit off. I've had enough.'

He turned to Glenn. 'Seriously, here in America. Fucking mermaids. Thanks, Obama.'

Glenn patted Walter's shoulder, letting his hand rest there for an extra second. No reaction. The bartender put the game on and brought them a fresh pitcher. Walter raised his glass.

'Drink up. Drink the county dry. Those underwater witches can swim in our piss.'

He took a long drink, then thumped Glenn's arm when he saw him sipping his beer.

'Don't stunt your thirst today, buddy. Down it. We deserve it after that weekend.'

The police had interrogated Walter too. They'd questioned him for a long time. He must have figured out that Glenn had watched him with Dorothy. But he hadn't mentioned it.

'I'm fine, boss.'

'I'd sure be drinking if I'd seen her go.'

'I'll drink,' Glenn raised his glass, 'to us keeping safe. At least we're okay.'

Glenn didn't feel safe, but he had to say something. Walter snorted.

'I'm not okay, sure as shit. I'm losing a hell of an egg, what with damage payments to our girl's family. So the next pitcher's on you, buddy. If we drain the bank, I'll have to hire illegals.'

Walter's eyes squinted like he was looking at a floating idea, or a mosquito.

'What do you reckon those mermaids come from Mexico?'

Another idea, or mosquito.

'And why are they calling them sirens?'

Glenn answered seriously. 'Have you ever seen one? What if they're men?'

His boss cocked an eyebrow.

'Buddy, I understand you. Really. But the name says it. Mer*maids* are maids, women. Ugly ones. Bunch of old crones with trout tails. You can't homo that shit up. Trust me, you don't want to.'

That was the final word. Mermaids weren't gay. Glenn considered that as he watched a bubble break the smooth surface of his beer. He remembered the sound it had made at the pond, like a long note from a heavy guitar. He imagined plucking a string, dark eyes snapping open. He felt a chill.

'Don't you think they'd look pure?'

Where did that come from?

'Pure?' Walter said. 'First queer, now pure. Do you even know what you mean? Fuck pure. Trust me, they're hags. Everyone can ditch the dreams about a school of tasty fish bitches.'

He took another drink.

'Or fellas.'

Glenn looked at him, imagining that his eyes were dark and round. He hummed softly and thought about water. No, stop. He had to stop. He finished his drink. Walter shook his head.

'Do you know what I think, buddy?' He patted Glenn's leg. 'You need to get laid.'

His hand rested long enough to mean something. But it didn't. There was and there wasn't, and this wasn't. The bartender took their pitcher.

'Tackle another one?'

*

Crime scene tape had quivered around the pond for two weeks. Two weeks of leaves to rake. When the police abandoned the search for Dorothy's body, they called it a typical sirenian abduction. A memorial service was to be held on Saturday, probably a mannequin in a coffin. That was how they did it now. Unsurprisingly, nobody came to the pond anymore. Especially at night. Nobody except Glenn; he'd given in and returned. For two weeks he'd tried to mute the note that Dorothy or the pond or a mermaid or siren or whatever – the fucking crickets maybe – had strung into his mind. It was becoming more insistent daily. If he concentrated, he could silence it. But eventually he'd relax and a dark-eyed demon would pluck the string again, bringing his thoughts back to the water's edge. So he'd come back. He had to. He didn't know how far he'd have to go, but he wasn't leaving until he could quiet the music in his head. He stood on the bank and stared. It had to be there. How could he bring it out?

'Dorothy?'

Nothing. Like he'd expected. He'd known that calling from the bank like some fairy-tale princess wouldn't work. It wouldn't release him that easily. Fine, he'd go to it.

He kept his clothes on and stepped into the shallow water. His shoes would protect him from broken bottles. He waded to the point where the pond floor dropped. He heard nothing. He had to go in. No, he'd stay here a few more minutes. Typical. Instead of sitting and waiting for nothing to happen, why couldn't he just go in? Walter would just go for it. Okay, okay, he'd swim to it.

He felt a shard of glass in the silt underfoot. It had been smart to wear shoes. Safety first. For Christ's sake, would he dive in or not?

He kicked his shoes off. His clothes made swimming almost impossible. They pulled him back to the bank as he struggled to the centre. Fish nipped his socks and darted away. They'd overstocked the pond. Fish were everywhere, sliding along him then escaping. He reached the place where Dorothy had drowned. No, he couldn't say drowned. Disappeared. She was fine. She'd even smiled. He imagined her on the pond floor, her arms reaching for the surface, algae growing in her lungs, tiny fish slipping in and out of her smiling mouth – no. No. She wasn't there. She'd gone somewhere else, become something else – he'd seen her eyes – something better.

So where was this stupid mermaid? What else did it want him to do? His jeans made it difficult to tread water. Nothing was happening. Was it ignoring him now? His arms ached. The night was so silent, it seemed like nothing could shake the quiet. Except him; he could. He knew what to do. He imagined tightening a string and plucking a horrid note. The sound came from his throat.

He felt it.

From behind, a chill caressed him; a breath cooled his neck then slid like ice down his back. What was that? He couldn't turn. He opened his mouth to speak. Nothing. He couldn't move, but he didn't sink. The pond held him up. But for how long? Something touched his legs. Some things. He would drown, drown like Dorothy, Dorothy grinning on the pond floor, on the pond floor with her arms reaching up, reaching up to trap him. It would happen to him too. His heartbeat rose.

No. A finger – what else could it be? – a finger touched his chest and slowed his pulse to an even tempo. This was how Dorothy had died. It was, wasn't it? Her mind panicking as her heart tapped the beats to a dull tune. He'd been an idiot to come here. Typical. Stupid. Stupid. Tears formed in his eyes, but he couldn't blink. He gave up.

The pond turned warm. Was this it? If it could just be painless. Under him, bubbles rose. His clothes slid off him, down into the muck. If it could just be painless. Underwater fingers drew ticklish lines down his arms. What was it doing? Why wouldn't it just finish? Then a hand against his back. A warm surge rose to his head. This wasn't what he'd thought. Black, unblinking eyes were watching him underwater. A note vibrated off the water's surface, off his skin, around his skin, unrestrained. He closed his eyes. He could close them now. He had been wrong to worry. Everyone had been wrong. Something warm slid up to his waist then down his leg. It didn't stop. Walter had been wrong too. Wrong about this. Wrong about Dorothy, with Dorothy. Wrong about him, in the bar, the bushes – naked. This was better. Warm. Right. Glenn's heartbeat spiked. He doubled over and spasmed.

When it finished, the pond was still. Back on the shore, Glenn found his clothes, soaked and neatly folded. There were no abductions, just escapes. His foot stung. It was bleeding.

*

Glenn was alone at the bar. Walter had said to meet him half an hour ago. First his boss was desperate for company, now he was late. He was probably still at Dorothy's funeral service.

Hell, the whole town was there. Hopefully one of them would remember her name. Glenn thought about the pond. He'd admit it, he was fixated. He didn't want to be. Whatever was in there was too good to be good. But it wanted him and, good or too good, he wanted it too. He might go underwater next time. What was down there? He imagined what they looked like – variations of Walter. Go figure.

'Tackle another one?'

The bartender woke him from his daydream.

'Yeah, another.'

What was he thinking? He wouldn't risk drowning for some underwater Walter. Dry-land Walter was bad enough. On cue, the doors opened and his boss came in. Glenn signalled to the bartender.

'Make that two.'

It looked like Walter had been running. He was flushed and had scuff marks on his suit. His suit! Glenn had never seen him in one. He wore it like a kid in an itchy Halloween costume.

'What a steaming, solid fuck of a day.'

A sweary kid. The bartender set their beers down. Glenn smiled.

'That should help, boss.'

Walter pushed the glass aside and nodded to the bartender.

'Double whiskey.' He scratched his chest. 'I'm not fuckin' around with kiddie drinks today. And stop calling me boss.'

Glenn shrugged. He'd keep cool. What an asshole. Why had he even come? He shrugged again. Walter watched him and muttered.

'Jesus Christ. Fine.'

Had Glenn said anything out loud? Walter took the beer.

'First, it's a shittier funeral than my grandma's. Then my

car breaks down. Now you look like your dick'll fall off if I don't take your drink.'

The service must have made him extra sensitive. Glenn fought back another shrug and reached for the beer. 'If you don't want it then I'll drink it.'

Walter shook his head and held the glass to his chest. 'Tell you what, after that funeral—' He finished his sentence by draining half the glass. Glenn felt bad.

'Was it really worse than your grandma's?'

'Nah, she's alive.'

'What?'

'My grandma.'

Asshole. They drank for a moment, then Glenn had a curious thought. 'Did they use a mannequin?'

Walter finished his beer. 'Jesus, I wish.'

His whiskey arrived. He downed it and ordered another.

'They hired an actress. An actual live person in the coffin. They had her all made up like our girl with her lipsticks and a special-made wig. Only they greyed her face so she'd look dead. Turned it into a goddamn zombie show.'

Did the actress hold her breath for the viewing? A swimmer could do the job better. Walter's second whiskey arrived. He sipped this one. He was starting to look relaxed. He'd even grown into the suit.

'Then, in the middle of the mother's speech, the rent-a-corpse sneezes.'

Glenn was watching him turn his glass. A spot of engine oil had stained his hand.

'No shocker there. They had her so painted up, it's a wonder she didn't suffocate.'

Glenn chuckled. 'It doesn't sound too bad.'

Walter eyed him darkly. 'The mother didn't take it very well.'

She wouldn't, would she.

'What'd she say?'

'Nothing. After the sneeze, the old lady stops her speech, walks over to the coffin and slams it shut.'

Another sip of whiskey. Walter's throat moved slowly as he swallowed.

'Turns out the actress is a claustrophobe. Yeah, a claustrophobe tucked and fucked inside a closed coffin. So she knocks on the lid, keeping cool for all of two seconds. Then she's yelling, then screaming.'

'Nobody let her out?'

'Can't. There's some fancy lock on the lid, God knows why. So when we try to force it open, we almost flip the whole box. Man, then the wailing really comes, the kind that freezes the hairs on your arm. Gets so bad the mother faints. Then out of the blue, here comes the brother who's been sitting in his pew all this time like a broken tool. Useless cocksucker remembers that he has the key.'

Walter turned, waiting for a response. Glenn spoke automatically.

'Nothing sadder than a useless cocksucker.'

A grin twitched onto Walter's face. He sipped his whiskey. Glenn blushed. The silence was embarrassing.

'Did you stay?'

Walter scoffed. 'Hell no. Once that coffin was open, I was out of there. No body, no funeral. That's my rule now.'

A pause. He reached over and squeezed Glenn's arm. Glenn flinched.

'Thanks for waiting for me, buddy. I'm hardly worth it.'

Glenn wanted to touch his hand. He almost did, but the bartender snuck up on them.

'Tackle another one?'

They ordered another round. Glenn felt he should say something.

'If I wasn't here, you'd always have the barman.'

Walter shook his head. 'I'm a baseball man.'

Did that mean something? Glenn thought about it until their drinks came. He gave up. 'What about your car?'

'It broke down by the park.'

They'd drink until the bar closed. It wouldn't be hard.

*

To the park, the park. No, they weren't done drinking. It was just down the road and Walter had a bottle in his car. A bottle of what? Who cared? Glenn had booze at home but Walter was set on the park. To tell the truth, his boss wasn't such an asshole. And he kept draping his arm, a heavy arm, over Glenn's shoulders and talking really close to his face, saying things like, 'We'll drink in that hiding place in the bushes.' Quickly, to the park. He smelled like whiskey. When he spoke, really close, the words vibrated through that arm of his, and Glenn thought about the bushes and other things they could do. And then walking was uncomfortable because he had an erection. Of course he did. He was thinking about sex in the thorn bushes. *Thorns for patience.* No, it wouldn't be good or anything. There was and there wasn't, and we all know Walter wasn't. But one thing he was was really drunk. And that arm was still draped over Glenn's shoulder – and surely that meant something, something Walter wouldn't say out loud – God, he had heavy arms... And his breath was on Glenn's face when he talked, and he kept talking about something, but Glenn was thinking about that arm and sex and the whiskey on his breath and sex and the bushes and – *patience* – sex. And as they settled down in the hiding place, Walter kept his arm, the heavy one, around him. *There was and there wasn't* be damned. Much more of this and Glenn's crotch would pounce from his lap and all over Walter, Walter, Walter, Walter.

Then Walter let go to take a swig from the bottle. The place where his arm had been cooled immediately. Glenn deflated. He had to sober up. Walter was staring at the pond. Had he heard the mermaids singing?

'You know what I'd like, buddy?'

He needs a man. Dorothy's words bubbled out of the water.

'What, boss?'

'Stop calling me boss.'

Well, what was he then? Walter pointed at the pond.

'I'd like to drain that hole and harpoon every merbitch flopping in the mud.'

The pond went silent, still. Glenn hoped they weren't listening. Walter swayed onto him. He was having trouble sitting up.

'Murdermaids.'

That was definitely too loud. Walter didn't seem to care.

'Help me up.'

He calmed as quickly as he'd raged. That arm, still heavy, returned to its place on Glenn's shoulders. He held it. Why wouldn't he? He was helping. The hairs on Walter's hand were softer than he'd imagined. Well, hello erection number two. Or was it twenty? At least they were sitting. Stop. He was helping. Walter took a long swig from the bottle and swayed. One of his feet splashed into the edge of the water. He didn't notice. Glenn's heart doubled its pace. They should call it a night. They could take the bottle to his place. It wasn't far.

'You know, boss—'

'Hey, boss, sure, boss, you know, boss – buddy, you sound like a mobster's sidekick.'

What the hell? He was trying to help. He let go of that arm.

'Fine, how does asshole sound instead?'

Walter jerked back. Glenn could see his eyes refocusing. What was he doing?

'So how about it? Asshole? You like it? Asshole.'

Walter had been looking at him like he was a puzzle. His mouth was twitching. Then, as if a thread had snapped, a smile bounced up on his face.

'Uh-oh. I got buddy-boy mad.'

He started to snigger. This was ridiculous.

'Bosshole – boss, we should go.'

Walter squeezed Glenn's shoulder and lifted the bottle with his other hand.

'Sure, buddy. Let's just finish what we started.'

A splash in the water. Glenn looked at the pond. It was flat.

'Boss, did you hear that? Look at—'

He stopped. Walter wasn't listening. He was drinking. He'd black out if he didn't slow down. Glenn took the bottle and helped him sit up, humming a deep note. The sound might help. Help what? He wasn't sure. He could feel each breath rise and fall in Walter's chest. It was too much. Glenn slipped an almost imperceptible finger under Walter's belt. No reaction. Did that mean something?

No. Walter jolted up and spoke.

'Wait. What are we looking at?'

He reached for the bottle and missed. His hand fell inside Glenn's thigh, Glenn's now very tense thigh. Was it going to happen? It was so close. Walter smirked, rubbed Glenn's leg – so close – and leaned in.

'Sorry, buddy, must be the whiskey.'

His lips touched Glenn's ear. It was going to happen. The whiskey fumes numbed his mind in a warm fog. He slid a hand under Walter's shirt. It was happening. He turned. They were so close.

No. Walter laughed, right in his face. His breath was saccharine from the whiskey. He slapped the thigh he'd been rubbing and pushed away. Glenn gasped. Gasped? How ridiculous. This, no, *he* was ridiculous. He felt like he should apologise, but Walter was still chuckling. It was all a big joke, wasn't it? Was it? Walter had known what he was doing. He didn't look annoyed.

'Oh buddy, buddy.'

What did that mean? Glenn reached over to touch his leg. Walter batted his hand away and snorted.

'You can't— You can't— You—'

Spasms of laughter killed each sentence he tried to make. Glenn wanted to punch him. He couldn't. He felt like apologising again. He blushed. He wanted to vomit.

Enough.

That was enough. He stood up. Fuck this. He knew what to do. He'd give Walter just what he wanted: the merbitches he hadn't shut up about for weeks. Would he be laughing then?

'Let me show you something, boss.'

Walter looked up at him and chortled.

'Bud, if you're talking about your dick, then no.'

No, he was being stupid. They should go. Forget it or apologise tomorrow. Walter had a vicious smile.

'But you want to see mine, I'll bet.'

He had the arrogance of an armed poacher.

'You do, don't you? Maybe I'll show you.'

Glenn's heart skipped like a bruised animal. Walter unbuttoned his trousers. He stretched his face into a parody of seduction.

'Sit down, buddy. Maybe I'll let you touch it.'

This wasn't what Glenn wanted.

'How bad do you want it, faggot?'

Glenn's throat twisted. He heard a note. Was he making it? It sounded like a long fingernail scratching a guitar string. It swelled from his throat to his head. He turned. The pond was trembling. Air throbbed out from it. It was calling, hard. It wanted them. No. Him. Glenn. Was that what he wanted? He knew the answer. He whispered, 'Yes.'

How much time passed before Walter's hand touched his shoulder?

'Look, bud, I'm—'

Glenn didn't let him finish. He walked into the shallow bank. The water was already warm. Walter fell into the bushes.

'Shit – buddy, wait. It was – fuck – it was a joke. I'm sorry. I was just playing. Really, I'm sorry. Fuck.'

Glenn turned.

'We've got nothing to fear.'

He dove into the water and swam. The vibrations increased,

filling the whole pond. He heard a splash. Walter had dived in after him. His boss, even drunk, was a faster swimmer. He reached Glenn before they arrived at the centre. It was waiting. They could both tell. Walter looked panicked.

'Glenn, we've got to get out of here.'

'Boss, I don't—'

Walter's eyes rolled up and he gasped. He thrust his arms into the water, trying to push himself into the air and out of the pond. But just once. Then his eyes closed and he quieted. Glenn's mouth was half-open from the unfinished sentence. He watched Walter's muscles go still. His face emptied of tension. What was happening? His eyelids were quivering. Were his eyes spinning behind them?

'Walter?'

The lids snapped open. The whites and irises had darkened and shone like black pearls, still wet. Without making a sound, he swam towards Glenn and slid his arms around him. Then other arms slid around them. Then others. They felt strong – dangerous, perhaps. His heart thumped wildly. He felt powerful. Walter stared silently at him with round, black eyes. Glenn wasn't afraid. He was in control. He held Walter tightly. No reaction. He could feel Walter's hands pressing though his shirt. No, their shirts dissolved. Then their shoes, their pants, their underwear. This was happening. It was. Their clothes weren't folded in neat piles by the thorn bushes this time. *Thorns for –* bullshit. He was done with patience. This was why he'd come here. No, why they'd both come here. They'd started this long before tonight: in the bar, in the bushes, in secret spots, with secret gestures. This wasn't going to stop. It wasn't.

Glenn kissed Walter. No response.

The vibrations doubled. A hundred hands pressed them together. Gentle strokes guided them underwater. This was why he'd come here. Their hold tightened. It was fine. He'd be fine. He was here for this. He'd wanted this. A splash sent water into his mouth. He coughed before the pond swallowed them. Walter's eyes didn't blink. Their heads were submerged. He was here for this. He was. He couldn't have doubts now.

Clouds of grey silt drifted around them. Through the murk, Walter's face was still. A bubble was forming at the side of his lips. It didn't rise. He wasn't breathing. Glenn's lungs ached, but he'd stay. This was why he'd come.

Walter moved. His head dropped, then bounced back into place. There was a slant to his mouth. It was new, unfamiliar. He jerked. His lips stretched wide into a sharpened, mischievous rictus.

Glenn hiccupped water into his nose. It dripped into his throat and chest, burning. He could hardly keep from coughing more water into his lungs. He'd die here. He would.

Walter's smile cut long, mocking creases along his face. This wasn't. No, it wasn't. He hadn't. No.

Glenn kicked. It was awful how quickly the hands darted away when he pushed free, like frightened minnows. Walter didn't react. He hung suspended just under the surface. Glenn could grab him and pull him out of the water. He could. He just had to do it.

Walter looked up, raised his arms and sank to the pond floor.

This time the police held Glenn longer for questioning. When he thought of Walter, he felt a horrible jealousy.

Parma Violets for Breakfast

Chloë Ashby

I hadn't heard from my mother for a month. Normally
she left a voicemail once a week, informing me of her and
Stanley's whereabouts, occasionally asking how I was and
even more occasionally asking after my own husband. Then,
all of a sudden, she announced she was in London. Could
we meet for breakfast? I wanted to say no, I didn't have
time. I'd love to, I said. Can't be too picky when you're one
parent down.

I left the flat in a rush, winter coat unbuttoned, wet-dog
hair. I mostly bathed in the evening, but the night before Jamie
had surprised me with sex. We were flagging back then: he
at the beginning of a new book, me mentally exhausted by
boundless research. It was nice, even if it didn't last long; the
soggy hair was a souvenir.

My keys jingled as I locked the front door, the (ever-so-slightly
soppy) wooden heart keyring he'd given me as a stocking filler
that Christmas bouncing against the cracked skin of my knuckles.
Slowly down the steep stone steps because of the slippery surface.
Faster on the pavement, where the ice had become slush, gritted
with salt. The sound of half-melted snow crunching beneath

my rubber soles made me wince. A warm-up for the prickly encounter ahead.

We were living in our first flat – the split-level off Caledonian Road – and my mother was staying at the St Pancras Renaissance Hotel. We didn't have a spare bed, and even if we had I wouldn't have offered and she wouldn't have accepted. I suggested a coffee shop around the corner from me that sold lots of pastries. She suggested another around the corner from her. I'd have been on time if she'd listened.

Anyway, I decided to walk down Caledonian Road rather than catch the bus. A huddle of middle-aged Ethiopian men were sitting outside Costa smoking cigarettes and sipping sweetened coffee from paper cups. A postman trundled by, mailbag in hand, and gave them a knowing wink. I narrowed my eyes at him. A stale whiff of the ocean as I passed the Asian supermarket, barely alive fish bobbing in a murky tank.

As I walked, I applied the finishing touches required in the rare event of an IRL mother-daughter meet-up. I hooked a simple chain out of my purse and fixed the clasp at the back of my neck. Dragged my fingers through my damp hair, shaking any loose strands onto the chewing gum-pocked pavement. Would he want me again this evening? We hadn't done it two nights in a row since our honeymoon. I wondered whether my mother would be able to tell, and applied some peachy lipstick.

Beep!

A Lycra-clad cyclist swerved towards the curb.

'Watch it, fuckwit!' yelled a man through the cracked window of his off-white van.

'Yeah?' The cyclist craned his neck to look back for a brief moment before spitting on the tarmac and pedalling fast. 'Fuck you!'

Another beep. A prudish father covered his son's ears.

I plugged into my iPhone. Everyone moved to the music: some kind of symphony.

Down by the canal I paused to look at the houseboats, even though I was six minutes late by now and my mother would be wondering where I was. Not because she was concerned about my wellbeing, but because she was hungry and having to wait was hell on earth for her. Parked top to toe in the mossy water, the floating homes reminded me of salty sardines in an oily can. Beside them, men and women were talking, texting, hand-holding, pram-pushing. A dog was barking so low and loud I could hear it over the tinkling piano in my ears. I pulled out one earbud and spotted the hound, its leg cocked against a rubber ring.

Round the bend and down the slope to King's Cross, past grand and grotty terraced houses, the majority divided into flats. At the traffic lights, I waited beside a pale-faced man whose nose was the same shade of crab-apple red as the signal. Together we strolled across the faux piazza in front of the station, weaving our way between strangers like two pieces of thread. He sneezed into his sleeve and I glanced up at the clock: ten past. When I looked back, he'd unravelled. I shrugged. It happened.

My mother's choice of coffee shop was more of a restaurant, with white tablecloths and waiters and waitresses all in black. Against this monochrome backdrop I located her immediately: there, wrapped in a cashmere coat the colour of her favourite confectionery, Parma Violets. A silk scarf wound around her neck once, then twice; enough slack for each end to drape limply over her chest. Pinkish-red beads dangling from her lobes like freshly shucked pomegranate seeds. A matching bracelet.

She looked different. Older, obviously, though instead of going grey her hair, once auburn like mine, had magically turned a brilliant shade of white-blonde – funny how that happens to so many women her age. It looked quite natural until I compared it to her wrinkled forehead (no Botox yet). She was in full make-up as always, but she looked tired, her eyes ferrying big bags. What about her eyesight? She didn't notice me until I was standing next to her, and even then I had to give her a poke.

'Camilla!'

No one calls me Camilla. I'm Milla to most, Mils to Jamie. I felt the corners of my mouth rise on cue. A well-versed smile.

Her chair legs scraped against the parquet floor as she rose abruptly and gripped me by the shoulders. 'What's that?' She squinted at my face as though it were scrawled with my spidery script, leaning me backwards into the light to get a better look.

'Hello, Mother.'

She licked her thumb and spread a swab of warm saliva across my cheek. 'Did I never tell you the clue to lipstick is in the name?' She laughed. My smile waned. Her eggy breath told me she'd already eaten.

'Must have slipped your mind.' I swiped a napkin from the table and dragged it across my cheek without unfolding it.

'Sit, sit.' No need for a hug, let alone a kiss. She gestured to the chair opposite with a flick of her bony wrist.

I unfurled my fingers from the back of the chair beside her and edged around the table. Pushed off to the side was a china plate streaked with gooey orange. 'Isn't this lovely?' I said.

She clawed an adolescent boy with a silver tray. 'Another coffee.'

He didn't raise an eyebrow at her even tone. No rising note at the end.

'Actually, I'll take a fresh mint tea if you have it?' I over-compensated and sounded strange.

He looked a tad nervous, tugging at his apron. Still, he didn't waver. 'Yes, of course.'

'Thank you.'

My mother was gaping, eyes glistening.

My choice of tea or the pleasantries? 'What is it, Mother?'

'Are you finally pregnant?'

I sucked in my tummy as she lowered her gaze. 'No, just off caffeine.'

'Why?'

'Why what?' I rolled my shoulders back and down.

'Why are you off caffeine?'

'I don't know, it makes me anxious.'

'Oh, Camilla, if only it were that simple.'

'What's that supposed to mean?'

'I'm just saying, you can't go blaming all your problems on caffeine.'

'All my problems?'

'One fresh mint tea?'

'Thank you.' I decanted some boiling water from teapot to cup. It had barely brewed, but I needed something to focus on other than my mother's sour face.

'You should have left it longer,' she said, wiggling her fingers at the pallid water. My father's engagement ring relegated to her right hand and dwarfed by Stanley's rock. 'Look, it's very weak.'

I took a sip, too soon, scorching my taste buds. 'That's how I like it.'

'Naturally.'

'Excuse me?'

'How's Jamie?'

Nice segue. 'Busy researching his next book: historical fiction.'

Her phone dinged.

'He's at the British Library. Shall I tell him to join us?' I asked.

Now she was hard of hearing.

She'd never liked him: Scottish, a writer, the only child of highly educated and happily married parents. Never read a single word he wrote. Met his mother and father only twice: once at our engagement party, a second time at what she called our 'little registry office wedding'. When we started dating, she asked how I expected to give my children a decent education when my future husband would never be able to afford school fees. When I told her we didn't plan on having children, she didn't speak to me for weeks. What did she expect? I wasn't exactly inspired by my own upbringing. Dead dad and a boarding school better known for its bad food than its exam results. Not exactly a childhood filled with warm and fuzzy feelings.

I looked up and found her texting. I wonder where she learned that. Okay, mouth corners up. 'So, Mother, to what do I owe the pleasure?'

'Hm?' Still prodding at her screen. Maybe still learning.

My cheeks began to ache but I held the smile steady. 'MOTH-ER,' I said, loud and clear, pronouncing each syllable, 'WHY DID YOU WANT TO SEE ME?'

She exhaled noisily, as though she'd been holding her breath for the past minute and had plenty of saved-up carbon dioxide to share. 'Does a mother need a reason to want to see her daughter?'

'This one does.'

'Tsk.'

I drank some more tea, which was admittedly lacking in flavour. Or maybe that was due to the defunct taste buds. It smelled minty. As I gulped it down I kept hold of my cup, observing her over its rim. She and Stanley spent their days flitting between Kent, the South of France and, when the ski season began, Austria (she'd laze around in the spa while he skied – or rather tried to remain upright on skis). My mother wouldn't embark on a journey to London for nothing.

'Well, actually, there is something.'

Aha. 'Which is?'

'You see, darling—'

'Darling? Shit, must be serious.' Had Stanley done a runner?

'Camilla, would you please let me finish.'

Again, no inflection, but at least she managed a please.

'Right. As I was saying. The thing is, I'm unwell.'

'Unwell how?'

'Unwell unwell.'

'You mean you're—'

'That's right. I'm dying.' As she said it, she pulled a plastic tub from her handbag, cracked the lid and shook two pills into the palm of her hand. A pair of lilac pills to match her lilac coat. The real thing?

'Mother, are those Parma Violets?'

She paused, mouth open wide. Or perhaps I imagined the

disc-shaped sweets lolling on her pink tongue. She threw her head back, stretching taut the slack skin on her neck, and dry-swallowed. 'You heartless creature.'

'Mother, I'm terribly sorry if you *are* dying.'

'*If* I'm dying? How could you doubt me?'

'Well, we've sort of been here before, haven't we? The life-threatening common cold, the deadly stomach bug—'

'Look, Camilla, I'm dying. I caught it too late.'

Caught it. My throat tightened, making it hard to breathe.

'And my dying wish is to see my grandchildren.'

There it was. I exhaled and went back to my tea.

'It isn't much to ask, is it.'

No inflection, no please.

'Stanley thinks it might even help. That it could extend my lifespan, spending time with youngsters. He read an article on the internet.'

'Well, have you ever thought about volunteering in a school? How about a nursery? Maybe you could try your hand at midwifery?'

She guzzled some water, presumably to dislodge the sweets stuck in her throat. *Not suitable for children under thirty-six months.*

'Are you going to ask how I am, Mother?' Corners up.

'Camilla, I just told you I'm dying.'

Again, my throat tightened – involuntarily. 'I'm well, thank you. Almost there with my thesis.' To make up for my croaky voice, I wiped my forehead melodramatically with the back of my hand.

'I don't know how you can stand it,' she said, rolling her eyes. 'Working with those filthy rats.'

I relaxed into my chair. 'You never know, my work with those filthy rats might just cure one of your fatal diseases.'

'This isn't a joke, Camilla.'

'And how's Stanley?'

'Stanley's concerned about me. As should you be.'

'Well, do send him my regards.' My love, however, he did not deserve. How eager he was to replace my father, one of his oldest friends, slipping into her bed while Dad's side was still toasty warm. My stomach flopped at the thought that I used to call her new husband Uncle Stan. I downed the dregs of my tea, now tepid, and picked up the menu. 'Shall we order?'

'I've already eaten. You were late and my blood sugar was low.'

'Of course it was. You don't mind if I get something, though, do you?' I waved to the waiter and asked for the Dartmouth crab and avocado on toast, please. 'Oh, and a freshly squeezed orange juice, thank you.'

'Anything else for you, Madame?' He looked at my mother, pen poised.

'Grapefruit juice.'

'Right away.'

I handed him the menu, followed by my mother's yolk-stained plate.

She scrunched up her nose. More wrinkles.

'So, Mother, how long are you in London?'

'I leave straight after breakfast.'

'Flying visit.'

'Hm.'

'Where next?'

'Austria.'

'Hitting the slopes?'

'My doctor says I need to rest.'

'Well, you know what they say, you can sleep when you're dead.' I winced as the last word left my lips, wondering whether I'd taken it too far.

She played along and closed her eyes, giving me a preview.

Our juices arrived.

'I hate grapefruit juice, too bitter.'

She took a swig. 'Only to some people.'

When she picked up her phone again, I excused myself and went in search of the loos. The restaurant was full, which was unsurprising since it was a Sunday morning and brunch was now a thing. As I passed the open kitchen, I caught the scent of fried bacon. It made me nauseous, which was weird because I love bacon.

Waiting outside the loos, I overheard the chatter of a mother and her young daughter. The mother was explaining why we all have to wash our hands with soapy water even if they don't come into direct contact with our wee.

The sound of a dryer, then the sliding of a bolt. The little girl trotted by on an invisible pony, clicking her tongue.

'Apologies,' said the mother, smiling with her eyes as well as her mouth.

'No need.' I don't normally like children, but this one was sort of sweet.

I didn't really need the loo, only some respite, but I sat down and sure enough there was a short stream. I washed my own hands with soapy water, and tore off some loo roll to dry them with. Then I looked at myself in the mirror.

What if my mother really was dying? What if this was the last time I'd see her, and my final words to her turned out to be cruel? Still, I felt nothing, desensitised, numb. Even tried to picture her lying in a hospital bed, little tubes tunnelling into her nostrils, to summon a tear or two. I laughed at myself, falling for her hypochondria, then arched one eyebrow at my laughter: who's the crazy lady cracking jokes in the loo? I tossed the loo roll into the bin, and that's when I saw it: a crinkled wrapper, translucent in the middle, purple at the ends. In pink capital letters: PARMA VIOLETS.

Now I know my final words to her *were* cruel. I walked back to the table and called her a liar. When she told me I was in denial, that I'd never learned how to grieve, I held the wrapper up in front of her eyes. Ha, I said, I have proof.

She told me it was her fault. That she'd carried on after my father's death as if nothing had changed. She'd thought it was the right thing to do: I was only a child.

I handed her the wrapper and she ironed it out with her thumb. Folded it once, twice, and put it in her handbag, a memento of our morning. She left just as my breakfast arrived. The crab was good, the avocado bruised.

A month later, my mother died. I learned at the funeral that she'd been diagnosed stage four in the autumn.

She Picks Up The Cat

Hannah Stevens

She picks up the cat, climbs the stairs and closes the bathroom door softly behind her. She puts him down and slides the lock into place. He pads about on the lino and looks at her. She knows he doesn't like the coolness beneath his paws but, for now, he will have to be patient. She runs the hot tap and steam begins to cloud the mirror above the sink.

The website says: pack an emergency bag for yourself and hide it somewhere safe. She wiggles the bath panel loose, slides it out enough to fit her arm inside the gap and searches for the material of the bag. There, it's in her hand and she pulls it out.

Be prepared to leave the house in an emergency. She isn't sure exactly what this means, though she has money on her at all times, like it says. Change for the phone, for bus fares. It's inside her bra.

She can hear the banging downstairs, the crockery smashing. She imagines the shards of blue plates joining the broken glass dish, the teapot, the coffee cups.

If you suspect that your partner is about to attack you, go to a lower risk area of the house, go somewhere you can find a way out. Avoid the kitchen or garage where there will be knives and other weapons.

She thinks of the knife block, how he knocked it over, chose the one with the serrated blade, brushed her face with its point. How close; how easy it would've been for him to press harder, to pull it slowly across her skin. She avoided his eyes, watched as he turned and threw the knife across the kitchen, watched as its handle hit the cat and felt lucky it wasn't the blade.

The bath is half full now. She pushes the bathroom window wide, looks down to the flat roof below and the back gate that is slightly ajar.

Avoid rooms where you might be trapped, such as the bathroom, or where you might be shut into a cupboard or other small spaces. She quietly clicks the bath panel back into place, thinks of the darkness behind, the space like a coffin.

The bag is on her back now, the cat in her arms. She hears his footsteps on the stairs, looks at the door and hopes that the lock will hold.

'She Picks Up the Cat' was first published in the collection In Their Absence *by Hannah Stevens, published by ROMAN Books in 2020. Reproduced with permission.*

Funreality

Anna Appleby

MONDAY

Carol is so sad. She hasn't gone downstairs to make the pasta bake
and she hasn't put her trousers on and she hasn't replied to her
boyfriend and she hasn't called her brother and she hasn't made a
doctor's appointment and she hasn't fixed her skin and she hasn't
started her tax return and she hasn't taken up pilates and she
hasn't done anything about capitalism or systemic inequality or
global warming or burgeoning fascism or state-authorised torture
or dwindling orangutan populations or political corruption or
her mum's voicemail. She is angry with the world for expecting
too little of her and too much of her so she should write about
this and sell it and become infuriatingly rich.

She must channel the anger into something productive and
collective and historic but she can't even channel the energy
from a sandwich into going downstairs and making some pasta
bake in order to have some more energy to channel into doing
god knows what until it's way past the time she's supposed
to go to sleep and then she'll get up hungry in the night and
burgle the kitchen and wake up with peanut butter breath and
there we go all over again.

She googles herself. At least yes freelance journalist Carol has achieved lots of interesting things in twenty-four months and where is that Carol right now hmm can she please report to the bridge immediately but no here she is sitting at her small desk in her grey pants trying to be fascinating and instead taking another twenty-seven photographs of herself all of which are horrible.

Carol hides her phone in the bottom drawer so that she won't be bothered by anyone then takes her phone out of the drawer again and sends her brother seven gifs and internet stalks her boyfriend instead of replying to his messages.

*

She has made a beautiful pasta bake. It is radiant. It is the best thing she has created in days. And he is late home. Maybe he is dead. She starts thinking about how inconsolable she will be for months no years no decades and then she messages him. His meeting has just finished. She puts some sliced tomato on two plates.

TUESDAY
She feels like she has entered the parallel universe where she is happy but she keeps picking at it in case it disintegrates into one of the billions where she isn't. She can't see it from any other angle so she must live in it.

Carol decides that she is going to write the Great British Novel of Her Era.

WEDNESDAY

She has learned from reading that she is supposed to learn something when she reads but she can't think of anything of general interest to put in the Great British Novel. She has the kind of memory where she can pass exams and recite TV episodes and direct London cab drivers but as soon as she's at the pub quiz she forgets everything in the stress of it all.

THURSDAY

Carol has got up and put on clean clothes and eaten cold porridge and opened the blinds and made the bed and emptied the sanitary bin and washed up and removed the dead flowers from their vase and put them in the compost bin with the eggshells and banana skins and mouldy teabags and texted her boyfriend to tell him that she is now vertical although all of those miraculous tasks have been carried out by a different part of her brain like an invisible carer who picks her up and washes and dresses her without her noticing. All hail the arrival of household assistance robots except that she is already morphing into one with less personality.

She realises that now is a good time to begin writing the Great British Novel but instead she spends twelve minutes putting things in her online shopping cart then three minutes taking them all out again and by the time she starts typing all useful emotions cease to be present in whichever lobe it is in which these things occur. She lies down and tries to achieve the Great British Orgasm but her phone rings halfway through and it's a compensation scam and his voice isn't even remotely sexy.

Carol knows that today is a good day to go out and do the things she has been wanting to do for weeks and weeks and weeks but now that the world is her shellfish all desire has fallen away from the surface and she doesn't want anything at all.

Carol knows that she should go and buy some new flowers like Mrs Dalloway and some toilet roll and something nice to cheer herself up and she should cook something healthy for lunch as gut flora have a real influence on mood disorders. Carol knows that she should answer some of her emails and she should also shun these menial tasks and realise her creative potential as an empowered woman. Carol knows that as an empowered enfranchised woman she should walk around the corner to the polling station and cast her vote in the local elections.

Carol feels like a disempowered disenfranchised blob. She feels emptier than the vase and the sanitary bin and her savings account. She writes that down. She writes *The blob feels so strange that it can't quite believe it is a blob at all.*

*

Carol feels unstrange. She has voted for normal candidates in the normal local elections and bumped into her normal postman as normal and had a normal thirty-second conversation about normal weather and has got the normal bus with normal clothes on and has sat with her normal friend in a normal café and eaten a normal jacket potato and has got the bus back as normal and here she is looking at her very peculiar hobby i.e. writing.

The blob looks in the mirror and realises it is not a monstrous blob at all but rather a friendly-looking potato. The good thing about catastrophising is that when the potato discovers that life is as normal the normalness is suddenly bliss. When it has fallen into the deepest horriblest sweatiest brain chasm the pavement is a glorious meadow.

Carol deletes the Crap British Paragraph then lies down. There is an unread article sitting on her bedside table called HOW TO UTILISE YOUR TIME TO ACHIEVE YOUR GOALS and instead of reading it she thinks about time and what it is for fifty-five minutes before she notices that underneath the magazine there are dusty invitations to a wedding and a cervical screening test and a networking event no not at the same venue and a letter from her Gran all of which she really should respond to but she doesn't know how.

FRIDAY
Carol decides to join a writing group in order to utilise her time and achieve her goals but also so that she can write the Novel and become a better freelance journalist and write better articles that make people briefly miserable but long-term happy and she will make heaps and heaps and heaps of money although maybe people only pay heaps of money to make themselves briefly happy and long-term miserable otherwise magazines and tanning and sex wouldn't be so popular but then again not everyone is a heroin addict.

She looks through her inbox and there is a bright scary tantalising notification from her old boss but oh no just his out-of-office reply to an email she sent him that morning ugh well then again it is January and here Carol is slobbing around in her pyjamas eating noodles so who is she to expect everyone else to be in their offices and she did send exactly the same boring email to every editor who had ever commissioned her or given in to her relentless cajoling at the time when she was a very busy successful ruthless important serious journalist.

SATURDAY

The man at the library tells Carol that there is a writing group at the local hipster coffee shop if you turn up out-of-hours and wait for it to mysteriously appear. He winks at her and she imagines that he wears knitted vests and watches *Countdown* but has a surprisingly attractive cat and several older girlfriends to whom he reads poetry. He tells her that it is on Sundays at 4pm and she says she's worried she might miss her regular tea and cake with the vicar and he looks surprised before winking again and warning her not to eat too much cake which is quite uncalled for really so Carol tells him that she'll have to eat ALL of the cake and drink ALL of the tea because the vicar has a gluten intolerance and a caffeine intolerance which is very unfortunate when people are always offering you tea and cake. Carol has no idea whether the vicar has a gluten and caffeine intolerance but she has seen her in the library before and she is a very pleasant but exhausted-looking Jamaican lady called Angela. Library Man looks concerned and asks her if she wants to take a book out and Carol is tempted to ask him for a first edition of *Don Quixote* however she does ask him for *The House at Pooh Corner* and *Lady Chatterley's Lover* and the Book of Mormon just to make his day more interesting. He fetches *The House at Pooh Corner* and offers to put the other two on order but Carol says no really it's alright don't bother they were only for the vicar and then she tells him she's joking because poor Angela clearly has enough to deal with already.

SUNDAY

Carol turns up at the local hipster coffee shop wearing her most artistic and complex outfit as she has assumed that she will be completely anonymous and therefore have the chance to reinvent herself as an intellectual of few words and many talents but three people are sitting at the table including her neighbour Johanna of many words and famous talents and all hope of reinvention is lost.

'Oh you don't need *us* you're fab *already* how *are* you have you found your *dream commission* yet Felix googled you again the other day and we can't *wait* to see what you're up to next freelancers are *so cool* not like *us* except lovely Gary here who couldn't be uncool if he tried *could* you Gary?'

Gary is a tall man folded up on a wooden stool like a cricket with indigestion. He has minuscule glasses and a black T-shirt that says 'Ask me about David Foster Wallace' so Carol does and instantly regrets it. The older woman with red hair and lots of tastefully placed tattoos of bees interrupts them and Carol would snog her with gratitude if it weren't for the orange lipstick. She is called Camille and Camille wants Carol to know that this isn't a writing group but rather a sanctuary for Carol's words.

Gary's offering for the word sanctuary this week is a response to *Infinite Jest* by David Foster Wallace and he reads his response delicately until everyone's ears are retracting into their skulls and their skulls into their necks.

Johanna has brought a selection of pastel life drawings and a poem about pastel life drawings. 'There's something so *liberating* about nakedness and the human *form* it's like a poem and I want to write like *that* not like *Infinite Jest* no offence Gary I cherish you as a *person* but there's just so much *negative energy* in the *phallocentric American canon*.' Camille squeezes phallocentric Gary's bony knee while looking like she vehemently agrees with Johanna. Johanna reads out her poem and it is quite interesting.

Camille has just written an episode of a TV soap and she dishes out the parts for everyone to read. Carol is surprised that Camille is writing TV scripts because she imagines her selling healing crystals at vintage fairs on rainy Saturdays.

MONDAY

Carol wakes up and falls asleep again and dreams that she is a naked mole rat and all of her veiny rolls of rat fat are spilling onto the hipster coffee shop table where Johanna is trying to spear them with a crayon.

She gets up properly at elevenish and feels depressed because the washing machine is broken. She puts on the least smelly bra and then takes it off again because she isn't going to bother going out today so she throws on her dressing gown instead and spends twenty minutes agitating the spots on her chin before finally sitting down at her computer which takes thirty-seven minutes to start up because it is so full of cookies and viruses like a snotty toddler.

Carol starts writing an article called HOW TO ACHIEVE YOUR GOALS (WITHOUT UTILISING YOUR TIME) and realises that despite always knowing exactly how long everything takes she rarely achieves any goals at all beyond making the newsreading public more depressed when they wake up in the morning. Carol remembers she is supposed to be showing Camille her authentic creative self.

Carol emails herself a draft of an email that she might send to some new editors then goes to the kitchen to boil the kettle. On her return she is pleased to discover that she has a new email in her inbox before she realises that it is of course from herself just a minute earlier so she goes back to the kitchen and discovers she has forgotten to switch the kettle on at the wall.

TUESDAY

Carol feels OK today. She has written almost a page and it has soaked up her sadness like a new sponge and now she is just a bland countertop in imitation marble. The page is about January which is the grimiest month. Carol imagines bringing it to the word sanctuary. 'It was supposed to be a vast humanist novel with unmistakable wit and insight but instead I am considering giving it to my counsellor on Wednesday so I don't have to talk.' Imaginary Johanna laughs a huge laugh while Imaginary Camille nods sadly and Imaginary Gary aka ImagiGary steels himself.

Carol looks out of the window at the drizzle which shouldn't be there because it's supposed to be snowing but then again it's better than August which is the month where half of the British population are just waiting for the leaves to die so they can put the central heating back on and the other half are delaying putting the central heating back on out of pride.

Carol's page says *the dull laundry month where I am such a miserable lead balloon that I can't be trusted to talk to people in case I make them droop or worse collapse inwards like miniature neutron stars in slow motion.*

Carol's page says *evenings are when nobody expects you to earn money or answer emails or dress yourself because they did that already in the morning or the afternoon when I was spending time with two-dimensional television people who tell you what they are thinking and don't expect you to say anything at all.*

Imaginary Camille's eyebrows are wilting and Imaginary Johanna is frustratingly sympathetic and ImagiGary is looking at her like he is pretending to be bored by everything she just said and also like he will rush home and furiously type up a CV and cover letter to give her next week. Dear Carol I am applying for the position of rescuer but only because you need me a lot. Yours charitably Gary.

WEDNESDAY

Carol realises that she is going to be late for her counselling appointment and texts an apology to Samir whose response is of course unreasonably nice. She wonders whether Samir talks to his plants when they are wilting or whether he just sits waiting sadly for them to open up.

THURSDAY

The Foreign Secretary is doing something terrible again and Carol considers becoming a politician so that she can tell him personally what she thinks of him and also so that she can become prime minister and make all of the cabinet ministers and enormously rich corporation owners and media barons pay tax and invest their money in environmental funds and donate their second and third and fourth homes to refugees and queue at the NHS dentist on a Wednesday with all the screaming children like everybody else. She remembers that she went to a private secondary school and that she hasn't been to the dentist in several years and feels guilty for the rest of the afternoon.

FRIDAY

Carol really must write something this week otherwise her personality will be eroded like a dandelion clock facing a light summer breeze and her brain will be clogged up by a gigantic wall of uncreativity and unthought so she tries to kick the wall over and type anything really anything at all but instead she gets trapped in a desperate cycle of checking each social media account in turn until there aren't any notifications anymore not even from bots or strangers. She goes to the supermarket without needing to buy anything and it is huge and fluorescent and desolate and Carol wants to cry but the wall of unimagination has filled up her tear ducts with brick dust and she is hard and compact and miserable and in completely the wrong place like a machine-washed tissue.

SATURDAY

Carol starts writing an article called HOW SUPERMARKETS MADE US HATE THE NATURAL WORLD and it is brilliant and she is very pleased with herself so she skips lunch to keep writing it until she is a hunched-over skeleton and the article is swimming in front of her at which point she eats some granola straight out of the packet and a hunk of cucumber that is lurking grimly in the fridge.

She spends the evening watching illegal clips of old comedy programmes on the internet with her boyfriend and he makes them an out-of-the-jar curry with cook-in-the-bag rice and tells her about his sore neck and his unpleasant boss and Carol tells him her boss is always unpleasant but actually she feels a little bit better about being self-employed and makes a mental note to buy her boyfriend a nice beany thing you can heat up in the microwave and put on your neck to relieve tension as long as you don't superheat it and make it explode and melt your skin irreparably.

SUNDAY

Carol takes *Atonement* to the word sanctuary because she has been meaning to read it and now she can at least start it by reading the first chapter aloud and hopefully it will be even more depressing than whatever Gary brings.

Gary has brought an essay about *Slaughterhouse-Five*.

Camille has brought a radio script and some oat and raisin biscuits.

Johanna has brought several erotic poems inspired by *Orlando* and Camille looks pleased. Camille suggests that Carol bring some of her own work next time.

Johanna invites herself round for tea and does all of the washing-up even yesterday's cereal bowls and the suspicious jam jars by the sink and she tells Carol about her new patio and her real estate colleagues and her candida infection until Carol's boyfriend comes home and then she tells Carol's boyfriend about her new patio and her real estate colleagues and Felix's coffee table made from repurposed motorbike parts. Carol asks whether the motorbike had a religious or a humanist funeral and Johanna laughs so much that Felix gets envious doing his gardening next door and knocks on the window and invites himself in for a few hours and tells Carol's boyfriend about their new patio and his real estate colleagues and his coffee table made from repurposed agnostic motorbike parts until Carol comes downstairs in her pyjamas to make a point.

MONDAY

Carol needs to take something to the writing group otherwise Camille will think she is just there for the biscuits. Perhaps she will write a terribly impressive but misunderstood work of speculative fiction which will predict the course of technology and politics for the next fifty years.

Ahead of Her Time Carol has a Pot Noodle for lunch and reads the contents page of *New Scientist* which includes cheerful article titles about cholesterol and addictive virtual reality and the International Space Station running out of funding and how people might survive a nuclear holocaust. Carol wonders whether people have sex in the ISS and whether you can get freeze-dried space lasagne.

TUESDAY

Carol picks up her toothbrush and realises that she has been using the same one for a very very long time so she goes to Superdrug and buys a blackhead-declogging-pore-minimising-super-cleansing-dermo-loving-micellar-technology charcoal face scrub and a toothbrush.

WEDNESDAY

The light outside is dirty grey and her feet are frozen and the nauseating energy from five packets of crisps and two large bars of chocolate and a Cup-a-Soup is causing her to claw at the walls. Her arms are made of glass and her torso of papier-mâché and her legs of dust and the tiniest draught will cause her to disintegrate all over the bed like a snakeskin. She stares at the patterns on the duvet cover until they are gigantic and then she gets up and washes her face and gets blackhead-declogging-pore-minimising-super-cleansing-dermo-loving-micellar-technology charcoal face scrub in her eye by accident which stings and stings and stings but at least she feels alive. She thinks about how ironic it is that when she is alone she spends half of her time wishing she were dead and half of her time terrified of anything that might possibly kill her including sepsis and chicken. She must be quite attached to living otherwise she wouldn't expend so much energy avoiding death.

THURSDAY

She is trying very very hard to find everything amusing and temporary and ephemeral but sometimes the nasty part of her brain wins and life piles a huge rhinoceros of pain on her shoulders.

FRIDAY

Really she just needs more money and exercise and sleep and a sense of purpose and to write a bestselling novel for which she will always be remembered and which will be so good that invading aliens will decide upon reading it not to blow up the Earth because humanity is worth something after all.

SATURDAY

The rain ran off the windscreen of the van. Squeak clunk squeak clunk the wipers fought in vain. Last week she had reported on a cheese festival and the week before it was a reptile beauty pageant. NEED A SUMMER BREAK? REVIEW OUR GROUNDBREAKING LITERAL-VIRTUAL FUNREALITY GAME. WE'RE COUNTING ON YOU.

Carol deletes a section that wouldn't go amiss in a futuristic telenovela then makes her way creakily to the fridge for a beer. Her hips shriek internally like unoiled robotic joints and she thinks about all of the books she wants to write instead of this one and how much she dislikes beer and how much she wants to go on holiday and then she notices that she has drunk the beer and has taken another one out of the fridge and she goes back to the laptop and starts typing.

Beer-Carol stops typing and puts a frozen pizza in the oven.

Beer-Carol is enjoying the nightmarish book although despite the satire and technobabble it will inevitably be consigned to the prehistorically-sexist-and-supposedly-non-existent-but-clearly-designated women's holiday section of most bookshops with a swirly font and a pretty pastel cover. She starts editing the next bit that she probably wrote yesterday but can't remember.

Clunk squeak clunk squeak. Literal-Virtual Reality. Maybe they'd put her in orbit and she'd fight off asteroids. Maybe they'd put her in the womb and she'd gestate for nine months. Maybe they'd put her in a top editorial job with a private jet. Maybe they'd put her in a damp bedsit with literal-virtual-actual cockroaches and pitiless bills. Jade got out of the van.

Carol smells burning pizza.

SUNDAY

'Really it's such a *gift* to see you stepping out of your cold journalistic *shell*' – Johanna is chewing a fountain pen unsuccessfully and her teeth are making little clicking sounds on the metal lid – 'but *what* exactly is the *overarching grand narrative* dear Carol? Are these people in Virtual-Actual-Hyper-Normal-Sexy-Fun Reality all trapped there as some kind of *scam*? Is Jade going to be *kidnapped* by the *government* for being a radical purveyor of *truth* and *insight*? Is this a book about *you*?'

Carol reads the next bit of *Funreality* and is just getting to the good bit when Gary turns up late and ruins the atmosphere completely. His T-shirt has a picture of a marijuana leaf and says 'There ain't no such thing as a free joint'. Johanna says that you don't have to be an anarchist to like marijuana and Gary informs Johanna that he isn't an anarchist but a traditional libertarian you know before the Americans ruined everything and Johanna laughs and says she's just teasing him because it's obvious that Gary doesn't own a large amount of property that he's anxious about being taxed on and then Camille interrupts politely and suggests that everyone share some insights on Carol's story and everyone does share insights until Carol is sure that she will never write anything ever again.

For example Camille reads the first page again for a very very long time and nods thoughtfully and says gently that a little more punctuation would not go amiss and Gary takes the page from Camille and reads it for a very short time and nods thoughtfully and Johanna takes the page from Gary without reading it and looks at Camille and nods thoughtfully and Carol takes the page from Johanna unthoughtfully while everybody is nodding and nodding and she agrees to add a few commas.

Gary's sacrifice to the sacred word altar is an unreasonably long stream-of-consciousness sentence about a squirrel he saw in the underpass.

Carol visualises an enormous fountain pen inking a full stop on Gary's forehead.

MONDAY

The house feels like a cage so Carol goes to the library to force herself to fill in job applications but the library is too big and cold and full of people who are rustling and coughing and fidgeting and muttering and slurping on their water bottles and looking at Carol over the tops of their computer monitors and Library Man comes over and nervously asks her about the writing group and whether she has lost *The House at Pooh Corner* or would like to renew it and did she get the emails and does she want to pay the fine although it's alright really because it's her first time and he can click the right buttons on the system and before answering Carol accidentally stares at him for so long that he looks like he might wee himself a little bit. Carol feels sorry for him and goes to the desk to pay her fine and renew *The House at Pooh Corner* and she tells him it is taking her a while to read on account of the syntax being very dense and the character development being very slow and Library Man laughs awkwardly and doesn't ask her about the writing group again.

TUESDAY

Carol's boyfriend is back from his work trip and she is relieved that she will now have some company while staring at the mildew on the ceiling and listening to the thuds and clatters from their nocturnal housemate who boils unrecognisable joints of meat at 4am in the kitchen with the windows closed. She last saw the housemate about six weeks ago and that was in the petrol station minimarket and they stared at each other like startled cats and made conversation about the rent and the weather and whose dirty pan had been on the windowsill since June and which neighbour might have stolen their recycling bin.

WEDNESDAY

At lunchtime Carol calls her brother for a whole hour which is probably his entire lunch break and he is so kind and serious and familiar that she cries.

THURSDAY

Carol is happy. She writes to twelve editors and applies to three recruitment agencies and seven full-time jobs and even the civil service and feels powerful and excited at the prospect of paying for all of counselling and council tax *and* a new coat. She will buy her boyfriend nice presents and shop in the premium aisle of the budget supermarket and visit her parents and take her friends out for coffee and pay off her credit card debt and get pet rabbits and donate to charity and go to the cinema and pay for online subscriptions without adverts and finally replace the broken bathroom mirror and splash out on a decent foundation that doesn't make her acne worse and she will feel magnificent or at least like other people do.

She gets up from the desk and goes to the kettle and watches it boil and pours it into a mug and realises she's forgotten the teabag but she adds a bit of cold water and starts drinking it anyway.

Carol checks her email and one of the editors has got back to her already and she sips the hot water and calls the doctor and starts her tax return and feels so normal that she doesn't recoil in shock when two more emails arrive.

FRIDAY
After waking at 4.48 and 6.55 and 7.00 and 7.05 and 7.10 and 7.15 and 7.45 Carol finally goes on a train to London and tries to ignore all of the chewing and typing and sprawling commuters who talk and talk into their empty phones as the signal dies.

*

The editor's office is very shiny and rather big. The editor is rather shiny and very small and called Bex and Bex asks Carol questions about herself and Carol doesn't say anything about the book or the mildew or the crippling self-doubt and tells Bex she likes going for walks and Bex says that Carol's journalistic experience sounds very interesting and will she be happy to wait a few days and Carol says that will be fine. Carol eats a chicken sandwich on the train and reads an article about the future of low-skilled manual labour in an automated world. Maybe she could write a book about a society in which everyone just eats and sleeps and watches TV and picks their noses and has sex because everything is run by machines and then she is very relieved when she remembers that is the premise of *Brave New World* so she doesn't need to write it and she can get on with journalism and with replacing the bathroom mirror.

In the evening she tells her boyfriend about London and the editor and he asks her why she is giving up on her book and she tells him she hasn't had any inspiration in weeks and weeks and she wants to go on minibreaks like everybody else and he cuddles her and says she's wasting her intellect and she tells him that if nobody clever goes into journalism then everybody will become stupider and stupider and then they order pizza and watch nine episodes of a comedy gameshow and feel strange.

SATURDAY

Carol feels almost like herself again although she doesn't quite know what that means but she is fairly certain that she hasn't been that self since December and nothing has felt right even her clothes and her voice and her bed and her favourite TV programmes. She is going to write challenging articles and thinkpieces and start to chip away at the crushing monolith of political injustice except that first she has to catch up on four episodes of the lesbian prison drama.

SUNDAY

Carol is just setting off for writing group when she remembers that she isn't going anymore now that she is once again an influential and motivated journalist. She calls her boyfriend who she suspects is buying her a birthday present in town and he answers the phone sounding very shifty so he is definitely doing that and she suggests coming to meet him in town just so he really panics and then she feels much happier about it being awful nasty disgusting weather outside.

At teatime there is a knock on the door. 'Is everything *alright* do you *need* anything really just *say* because we missed you today especially *Gary* and you know Camille brought camomile and cardamom cake for your *birthday* week at least I think that was why she did although she is cardamom intolerant and her apprentice keeps giving her *extraordinary* presents and how is your *book* coming along is it writer's block how *awful* you know you are wasted on the papers when they are just *deluding the masses* come on Carol please come next week please.'

MONDAY

A phone call early in the morning and Carol is miraculously awake enough to answer on speaker and shiny editor Bex is offering her a last-minute tight-turnaround 1000 words of accessible yet ruthless and concise yet detailed political analysis of what in Carol's opinion can be summarised as democracy being bad for democracy and All Hail the Foreign Secretary and

might even have the budget and space for a regular column

she looks at the bills on her bedside table and

won't get a better opportunity than this

she scrolls through another page of job adverts and sees a call-out for a virtual reality game reviewer and feels a little bit sick and

send a draft through tonight

Bex glitters impatiently through the phone and Carol looks at the ceiling and swallows and thinks – bitterly because of the bills and bitterly because of the mildew and bitterly because of that infuriatingly inescapable conscience of hers – if it's fiction you want Rebecca then there's a writing group at my local café so just turn up out-of-hours and wait for it to mysteriously appear

we're counting on you

and Carol hangs up.

Locale

Adam Trodd

We always just called it The Lane. It was a path between two
avenues in the same housing estate with cement bollards at either
end. Beer cans, carrier bags and other detritus gathered in its
corners and lay hugging the high garden walls at its edges. Animal
waste too was deposited there to petrify and crumble; nobody
ever cleaned in no-man's land. At night, older boys tattooed the
walls with slogans and images that meant something to them at
that time and marked them out as standard bearers for their tribe.

For us children, living on the avenues connected by The
Lane meant being combatants in a generational local war that
had been waged ever since the housing estate was constructed
in the mid-seventies. Roughly midway down its length, a small
buddleia bush, the roots of which had found meagre sustenance
in a crevasse between wall and path, became the most coveted
strategic position. Whoever reached and held the bush during
battle occupied The Lane thereafter and earned the right to
impose a tithe of passage on children from the other avenue,
who became second-class citizens under the new ruling power.
The tithe varied in accordance with the whim of the enforcer
and had been at various times: a Chinese burn, one strike of a

bamboo cane on the backs of bare legs, sought-after bubblegum transfers and at one point even a kiss, until the more gentlemanly among our number decreed that girls should be granted free passage unless it could be proven that they were spies.

Coming back to the old neighbourhood after so many years for the funeral of one our fiercest warriors felt like walking in slow motion through the terrain of someone else's past. His name was Fintan Egan, but we all called him General Black because of the dark hair that sloped in thick sheaves over his freckly brow. The priest used anodyne words such as 'untimely' and 'tragic'.

'C'mon, I'm gettin' out of here. It's fuckin' morbid,' Boucher said in the local after, placing his drained glass on the bar and tapping me on the elbow. Of us all, he was the only one who had stayed in the neighbourhood. He still lived two doors down from the Egans and they remained close.

'I'll get the lads,' I replied.

'Yeah,' he said, 'gather the troops.'

We stood in The Lane with our hands in the pockets of our suit trousers; five of us, minus our General. The buddleia bush was gone and the graffiti had not been cleaned off but painted over, and that layer of paint once more defiled by the insignia of new tribes with the same old things to say. Boucher took a permanent marker out of his pocket and wrote slowly, stopping between words to curse the uneven surface and to wipe his eyes on the sleeve of his ill-fitting jacket.

When he finished we stood back and read the epitaph.

> *Fintan Egan (aka General Black)*
> *1978-2015*
> *By his own hand*

Marble Mountain

William Prendiville

One day, towards evening, as the sun was declining over the distant hilltops, and dusk thickened the air like dust rising from the winding road, a figure appeared some way off, approaching the town slowly, steadily, until some minutes later we could make out that it was a man. At that time, we had been living in the town for about three years. My father was a doctor and we had moved there when I was at an age at which I remembered little before the town. We'd moved there because my father had found work there the year before, when he'd been having trouble with my mother and had left us for a year. But anyone could have told my parents that their marriage was disintegrating not because my father was unhappy where he was – not because he was dissatisfied with his current practice and needed a change so great that it had brought us from the cities in the east to this town in the middle of nowhere, on a large island off the coast, among mountains and fisheries, a lumber mill and a good Catholic school but little else, except for a ski-hill a half-hour drive away – but because my father and my mother were not suited to each other; and no amount of money, false promises or new starts could dissemble that fact. My father was popular with the town, my mother had the children, and for a few halcyon years, we were relatively content there. When my father and mother had started going out together again, often spending nights away at the closest city, towards the ski-hill, they hired a girl who lived down the street to babysit us. It was with her, on the dirt roads outside the town, by the river where she used to go motorbiking and where she would take us snowmobiling in the winter, that we saw the man approach.

Eden had been our babysitter for a couple of years; her sister had looked after us twice before giving the job to Eden, who was younger and more sure of herself. She was still then a tomboy, with straight dark hair cropped close to her head, bright splotches of freckles across her nose, and red energetic cheeks. The beauty that she would become when she'd grown, a stately if thickset figure with a daunting and imperious air, had not yet surfaced, and she was, as far as I knew then, solitary, someone who liked to spend time by herself but was affable and congenial with others at the same time, so that she was quite popular in our little town. People sometimes called her Eddy, though her mother, with evident disapproval of the diminutive, maintained 'Eden', shooting a glance from under her wrinkled brow whenever Eden's father used the name. He was apparently less perturbed than she by Eden's aversion to dresses, or her disinterest in the local high school dances, or even, I might say, in the pool hall, which I was forbidden to enter, where the big kids hung out, and which my friends and I, cycling there on our bikes, feigned to disdain, but to which we were all drawn by fearful curiosity for the raucous music and loud voices, or by the local dogcatcher's car parked behind it, the big dark car that would move slowly through town with one or two caught strays tied by a rope to its fender as it made its way to the small building behind the ice rink, from where we could hear the strays yelping and where, if they were not claimed after several days, with a momentary quiet settling over the place, they were exterminated.

The man we saw coming down the road, emerging from the shimmering heat the summer had suddenly brought after a bitter winter, was Craig Lawson; and on that fateful day, while Eden was squatted down to fix her bike, and my sister was crying beside her because she wanted to go home, I was the first to see him. Eden stood up after me, wiping the sweat from her brow with her freckled arm, her face, without her glasses, strangely naked to me, her eyes seeming somehow much smaller, like a bush had been parted and a startled animal revealed. She squinted, raising her hand against the sun to see who it was. Even my sister, who Eden was trying to placate, momentarily looked up to watch his slow approach. 'Shh, Cathy,' Eden said, bending down because Catherine had started crying again. 'We'll be home soon. Shh, we'll get you some monkey's blood when we get home, okay, Cathy? Shhh,' – monkey's blood being the name she'd given to soda water with cherry grenadine, which delighted us – and on hearing that, my sister nodded, sniffling, and quieted. Edith stood up again and Craig came at us unhurried, like he was fixed on his course, and we waited, watching him come slowly through the shimmering air and the bright sunlight and the dust lifting off the road against the pine trees; waiting for him in a silence pregnant with possibilities, until he seemed, through the wet and heavy air, to suddenly snap into view and, looking at us, eventually came to a stop, already smiling.

'Hi Eden,' he said, and his smile deepened.

He was several years older than Eden, and to us, a man. He had already graduated from high school, and Eden knew who he was because he had still been there when she had started going, although three years above her, and had dated Debra Tufts, who had been the prettiest girl in school and whose reputation, though she had long since left for the city and married, still lingered. He was someone, whether she admitted it to herself or not, who she had admired when she'd been younger still. She was startled now to hear her name come from him; and while she looked up at him as his smile focused on her in a way she'd never seen before, if she'd even seen him notice her at all, the tomboy that she'd been died away. It was as though she suddenly grew fully aware of herself, or aware of what she in body presented to the world, the world that had sprung up and was circumscribed in Craig's eyes, making her feel terribly bare. You could almost see it then. Her eyes were upturned, her face seemed to widen, as if something deep within her was rising and expanding in the gaze he fixed on her. She blinked twice, the smear of chain grease across her cheek shining in the sunlight, and she wiped the hair from her eyes with the back of her hand, surprised still at having heard her name, first, and her true name at that, with such startling familiarity, and then surprised at herself for not knowing whether to use his name, to show that she knew it, or just to say, as she did, timidly, 'Hi...'

The courting period didn't take very long, as reticent as Eden may have been in the beginning. She was still seventeen when they were officially recognised as a couple by the town, and the relationship lasted three years. She remained our babysitter, and was as dependable as she'd always been. She grew, if anything, more tender, more womanly, as if she'd suddenly grown up, and not wild and irresponsible as everyone feared she'd become in the incongruous company of Craig Lawson and in the passions of their relationship. She began staying out later with him; he would come down our street to pick her up in his car, with her mother frowning in disapprobation at the front window as she ran out to him, and her father lingering behind with worried care. But during that first year or so it was like she was glowing, like everything that had been latent in her, everything within her that had been trembling to bloom, finally flowered all at once, and her once boyish face – more marked now because she didn't wear her glasses anymore, except on the nights she stayed over at our place – seemed fuller and more tender and strangely appeased. She played less frequently now the maudlin love songs she used to choose from the stacks of my father's LPs after we'd gone to bed and which would reach us faintly from the living room, like something, some part of the adult world, that came out only after we were sent to sleep. On the nights my parents stayed in the city, when the roads were blocked with snow, Eden would let me stay up with her late at night because I insisted I was the oldest, and I would fall asleep beside her on the couch, looking out at the light from the streetlamps and the drifts of snow that would mount so high back then that there were some mornings when we, my family and I, couldn't get out and I would be sent by my father through the kitchen window to dig a space before the back door.

Whatever gossip there was, my father, as town doctor, often heard it: 'Tha' Lawson is up to no good with young Sprence, I tell ya,' he was told; and so he told my mother, and they spoke about it over dinner while my sister and I sat on either side of the table and listened in their growing silences to the clack of cutting on their plates. Craig Lawson's reputation about town was less than comforting. There were rumours about abusive scenes between him and his old girlfriend, and he hadn't had a steady job since graduating from high school, even though the truth was that there were few jobs to be had then and on the very day we'd met him, he'd been returning from the mill, where he'd gone to seek employment. And it was true that in the beginning of their relationship, my friends and I would sometimes see him emerging from the back door of the pool hall, passing around a smoke in the back lot, and him much older than the others. But he did eventually stop going there, and, besides, it would have been foolish to think that Eden had not heard or known enough about him beforehand. One evening, I surprised them on the couch together when I should have been asleep. They were sitting in the dark, with the light from a streetlamp through the front window lying across them like a faint gauze. Upon seeing me, Eden sprang up shocked and cried, 'Bobby! Go to bed! ... Craig,' she shouted, 'stop it!' – batting his hands from her, then taking me by my hand and leading me back to my room. 'I'm sorry, Bobby,' she said, but it didn't sound like she was really saying it to me, and Craig was never invited back into our house again. There were times during that first year when she appeared sad and fragile, and we'd suddenly hear the sad love songs coming down the hallway from the living room again, but whatever problems they may have had, they worked them out.

And how he'd changed! How Craig Lawson had changed! The long hair, which was in style at the time, had been cleaned and combed, and the small iron stud in his left ear, which the town eyed warily, was taken out and replaced by a more discreet crystal. There was an awkward and stiff politeness to him when he first met Eden's parents – there for Eden, conceding to Eden, when it was clear he would have preferred to be elsewhere – and a type of restrained disdain in his cordiality, with something that they, her parents, said afterwards was immature, even proprietary, in the way, when sitting on their couch, he had reached out and taken Eden's hand in his.

One Christmas Day, Craig was invited over to their house. It was never quite clear what his own family did, though his mother was dead and his father a drunk who lived past the tracks in the poor part of town, where we didn't go. My father and mother and sister and I had come over, having been invited, as we were every Christmas Day, by Mrs Sprence, and we'd dressed up for the occasion. The red plastic Christmas tree with tinsel boughs had been pulled out and set up again in the corner of the living room. The dining room table was laid out with pâtés and Christmas cake, which were there to assert her Scandinavian ancestry, one of the airs Mrs Sprence gave herself, in the same vein as the family photos neatly arranged on the tables, of husband and wife and the two daughters and then the family together, and the portraits that hung with a certain correctness upon the walls that lined the stairs, as if to say that *this* were the way the world should be, and that she, Mrs Sprence, dressed up now for Christmas, would accept no other. Eden's older sister was off at nursing school and had been unable to come. Mrs Sprence was sitting in her chair with her hands crossed on her lap. Mr Sprence was quietly drinking his rye. He looked too old to be the father of such young daughters:

his face was wizened, his hair dry, and his gaze, behind glasses, seemed always slightly distracted. When he spoke, his words were always ignored or treated impatiently by Mrs Sprence.

The snow had piled up outside and the sun was shining upon it. We found Craig in the kitchen, glowering. It was the first time he had been invited to the Sprences' for any formal occasion. He was uncomfortable being there and tried to hide it by being arrogant.

'Missus Sprence,' he proclaimed when he came back into the living room and sat on the couch, his leg cocked on his knee, 'you 'ave a pretty 'ouse.' He stretched his arm around Eden. 'An' a pretty daughter,' he said, laughing.

Mrs Sprence smiled thinly, nodding. 'Thank you, Craig.'

Everyone continued talking.

'Would you like another drink, Craig?' Mr Sprence eventually said.

''Ave you got a beer?' Craig asked, which made Mrs Sprence glance over from her conversation with my parents and frown at her husband.

'We have Golden and Labatts.'

'I'll 'ave a Golden!'

Mr Sprence rose from his chair and got it for him. Eden was visibly uncomfortable. Craig pulled her closer with his arm and pretended not to notice. 'Thank you very much, sir,' he said too politely when he got the beer, and snapped it loudly.

'Eden tells me you're working at the mill now...' Mrs Sprence said to him.

'That I am,' he said, flashing his eyes up at her as if seeking something more to what she said, then smiling. 'I begun there four months ago.'

Christmas carols were playing over the speaker. Mrs Sprence smiled thinly. He seemed to remember himself then, putting his hand on Eden's knee as a sort of apology, and leaned forward to take one of the home-made shortbread cookies on the table. 'These are good cookies,' he told Mrs Sprence.

'I'm glad you like them,' she said, heavy with irony.

'I do,' Craig replied, pretending not to have noticed, then added with the same irony, 'I think my pa used to buy the same ones,' leaning over to take another.

*

Eden was undoubtedly in love with him, for he had been up to that point – and could later be said to have been throughout her whole life – her first and only real boyfriend. And, despite the surliness that sometimes came over him, from that prickly and false pride he carried with him like some tin trophy – as we had seen that Christmas, after which my mother had glanced up at my father on the way back home from the Sprences' and my father had said sternly, 'Not now,' which I saw as meaning he didn't want to discuss it in front of the children – it should be said that Craig Lawson, even on that very Christmas Day when he put his arm around Eden and pulled her to him as some deliberate affront to her mother, was, for a time at least, smitten with her, too. The whole town used to speak about them: about how Eden was just a pup and that Lawson was too old for her, how they would see his car (perhaps the one thing he loved more than Eden) waiting by the high school for her to get out, him sitting with his elbow cocked in the window and the music loud till the bell rang when, from some odd sense of decorum, he would turn it down, his face angry-looking or strangely impassive, looking at no-one, until Eden would emerge and get in his car and he would lean over and kiss her. *That no-good lout*, people would say, *just like his father, no wonder his mother died young as she did, God rest her soul, having to deal with the likes of the two of them her whole life, crushed between them, as if God had sent them to squeeze and crush every drop of sin from her, and she suffered it in her quiet and stolid way, she did, till the day – she wasn't yet fifty then, was she? – she gave up the ghost, and flew straight up to heaven, God rest her soul, and left the old man with the bottle (not that he, the husband, noticed she'd gone anyways) and the young one wild and free and doing whatever he wanted in this world, as if there weren't any consequences to pay for your actions!* They, Craig and Eden, would often be seen together walking down the main street of town, his arm draped about her shoulder, his head held high as a cock's, his chest puffed out as if he were breasting the air, but all with something too self-conscious about it, even as he was talking with her, as if with one ear he was half-listening to whatever Eden was saying and with the other he was constantly on his guard, ready to take offence.

The summer of her graduation, Eden and Craig moved in together. It came as a shock to everyone, including my parents, though the town had grown used to seeing them together. By then, my parents had come to see Eden as more of a family friend than a babysitter. Her relationship with Craig had caused a definite rift between her mother and her, and it was said that the two didn't really talk anymore, with Eden keeping to her bedroom in the basement, while her mother and father's room was on the second floor, and that the only time they gathered together again as a family was when the older daughter Anne came home on vacation from college.

Eden announced the news of her move one day as she was sitting at the kitchen table drinking tea with my mother. My father was there, considering her sternly, as if she were almost, but not quite, part of the family. She had let her hair grow long and called my mother now by her first name, as though it were adult talking to adult, woman to woman. She was eighteen then and her body had not yet taken on the amplitude it would when she was older. Her long brown hair was pulled back in a ponytail. Her face was freckled from the sun and flushed with excitement. Her eyes twinkled as she talked about the coming move. She sat at the table with her sleeves rolled up and a necklace hanging from the unbuttoned top of her blouse, brimming with suppressed excitement but attempting to look older than she was by trying to contain her enthusiasm, although her eyes, and her smile, like a rising sun, and the nervous tapping of her finger on her teacup, betrayed her.

'This is a very big responsibility, Eden,' my father said. 'You can't move in with someone and move out as you please.'

'I know.'

'Have you thought about the commitment you're making?'

'We're only going to try,' Eden said. She never called my father by any name, though she looked at him now with that smile that had something in it of respectful distance. 'He was going to get a house for himself anyway,' she explained, turning her attention to my mother and smiling more broadly again.

'I think it's a great idea, Eden,' my mother said, reaching out and putting her hand over Eden's and shaking it. She was also smiling, wistful. 'You can only try.'

There had already been a few scenes between Craig and Eden, so there was cause for concern. Their fights grew to be infamous, although, surprisingly, she always won. If she wept alone in her room, no one saw it. We only saw her face sad and pale and withdrawn, with something vulnerable and childlike about it at first, when the troubles had just started, as if she could not understand, not the details, but, essentially, why they were fighting. And these fights and the temporary departures of Craig from her life were further confirmed, although she said nothing about them, by sightings of him at the pool hall again, glowering, or getting raucously drunk with his friends; once, on such a night out, he hit a friend who had ventured to make some lewd remark about Eden, and after one punch held his friend up with one arm and with the other fist still cocked told him, 'Don't you fucking mention her again!' The town grew to know they were fighting when he was sighted about town alone for two or three days, passing out drunk on friends' couches, and a light was left on in the kitchen of the single-storey house they'd moved into, just on our side of the tracks, where Eden waited sadly until eventually and inevitably he stumbled home and told her, 'I loves you, Eddy,' and she took him back again. They had few fights in public, though everyone always knew when things were going badly, before he began openly seeing other women. Once, towards the end, when things were very bad, her father, who she worked for at the cinema he owned, tried to talk to her about it.

'Eden...' he began.

'It's too late now,' she said sharply, cutting him off for the first time in her life.

But all this came later, long after she sat at our kitchen table, with my mother's hand on hers, shaking it with congratulations. My sister and I were told to go out and play while my father lectured Eden about something we were not meant to hear and which embarrassed her, because when she came out again towards the front lawn where my sister and I were playing, she was flushed. She stopped and squatted down and played with us for a while, then she patted our heads and we watched her walk off down the road, under a low June sky.

*

It was as though, after that, everything changed for her so quickly and dramatically that it must have become, deep within her, intolerable: and then at one point it all stopped again, for good. I remember when she was older and divorced, with two children of her own who lived with her ex-husband, a thin older man who had once been her teacher, on the other side of town, her body fuller and used now, but like something she sat in without being conscious of it, without it belonging to her, in the way we sit in a chair. Beauty still clung to the fleshiness of her face, like the rays of some dying or hidden light, and whenever we came to visit – for we had left the town a long time before – she would greet us and sit back down again in her chair by the window, in the house where she lived alone, with fierce and lonely solitude.

She and Craig moved into their house that summer when she was eighteen, and they lasted longer than people expected.

Eden seemed for a while to have calmed Craig down and Craig seemed to have fully brought that beauty in Eden to the surface. There were some nights that showed what was to come. Craig, making good money, would drink, often going straight from the mill, his hair stiff, the day's heat still lingering on his burned neck, the wood dust clinging to his used tartan shirts as he stood at the bar drinking with the older men from the mill, his face taking on a slightly amazed look, his eyes growing merry at first, then seeming like they were going to jump out of his sockets with a kind of intolerable enthusiasm. 'Hey Jason, get Eddy a drink, will ya?!' he would shout whenever Eden showed up, laughing at his own jokes, putting his arm around her, until the moment, if she couldn't convince him to leave beforehand, his head would begin to nod, his enthusiasm would abruptly dim, and she would end up carrying him back home. Her mother now refused to have anything to do with her. After about a year's absence, she came and started babysitting us again. There was a strange look of diffidence in my mother's eyes when she first arrived, and she spoke to Eden with a sort of straitened familiarity.

'Hello, Eden,' she said, when Eden appeared at our back door again for the first time. 'Everything's as it's always been,' – looking like she wanted to say more but couldn't. 'We'll be home by eleven.'

'If there's any problem, Eden, call us,' my father said peremptorily, appearing in the doorway of the living room before my mother followed him out again. Eden, as though suddenly exhausted, picked up my sister, put her on her lap and looked ahead, distractedly.

The winter that came that year was fierce. It howled in early and dumped so much snow upon our little town that there were days when everything was shut down. Everyone said they hadn't seen snow like that for years. It brought with it an early ski season, and on the days when the schools were closed, we were packed into my father's jeep and drove our way to the local ski-hill. That's what people called it, a 'ski-hill', but it was more a mountain than anything else, with trails splintering over its surface, set back from the road beyond the foothills of endless pines. We spent every weekend there, skiing during the day and sitting in the cheap lodges in the evening waiting for my father at the bar, sometimes having to wait so long that it was decided in the end that we would bring Eden with us, too. And even then we sat, with Eden looking after us, and my mother now free to join my father, listening to the voices and music coming from the other room, like a whole other world that we could hear but not enter, and so tired by the end that I could hardly remember my mother waking us up and putting us in the jeep, and my father driving us back along the highway, and Eden quiet in the back seat beside us while my parents exchanged words in the front – 'Look, Marie,' my father saying, 'I'm fine!', 'You shouldn't drink so much,' 'If you want to drive, you can drive,' 'I'm only thinking of the children,' – until we arrived back home again. Just how much was happening in Eden's life then was hidden from us behind the cheerfulness she put on when she played with my sister and me, and the silence she maintained when she was around my parents. But one night I overheard a conversation between my parents in the kitchen that shed some light on the troubles we could only guess at.

'He's not to be trusted,' I heard my father saying. 'I've heard things from patients, Marie. He's about town with some other woman, some tramp he's found...'

'It's not her fault,' my mother interrupted.

'I don't want her around the children anymore,' my father said.

'She—' but my mother turned then and saw me in the doorway, shot a look at my father, and I was sent back to my room, where my sister was still sleeping.

One day in February, we all packed into my father's jeep. There was a bright blue sky and a light breeze was wheeling snow from the high banks along our driveway. We had been woken early and given breakfast. My father sat in the front seat beside my mother, with my sister and I in the back, and we drove down the street to pick up Eden at her parents' house, where she had recently returned to live. She was sitting in the front window, a dark, immobile figure behind the clouds moving across the windowpane. She came out as soon as we arrived, looking like she hadn't slept, trying to smile. My mother tried to be cheerful when she opened the back door of the jeep, but it felt like a cold silence entered the jeep with her. My mother and father exchanged glances, and we drove down our road in the early morning quiet with the bright clouds passing above us and the banks of snow towering beside us and the road still empty.

'Ready for another day of skiing?' my father said.

'It looks good today,' Eden said.

'Eden, dear,' my mother said, turning around, 'if... if you're tired, you don't have to... it's not necessary for you to...' then looked back at my father, as if seeking what to say.

'I'm okay,' Eden said.

'It won't be a long day,' my mother promised.

The story, as we heard it later, was that after several well-publicised fights, followed by increasingly tenuous reconciliations, during which time the small house she lived in with Craig by the tracks remained eerily silent as though to reproach all the town gossip, Eden had finally left Craig. She had moved back into her room in the basement of her parents' house after he had begun impudently parading around town with another woman, or, more specifically, after she, the other woman, many years older than Eden, had one day crossed Eden's path in the main street of town and smiled at her, then chortled as Eden passed. Craig made the woman suffer for it afterwards when Eden had finally left him; he threw a drink at her in the local bar when she came in weeping, begging, 'Why, why are you mad at me, baby, why?'

The whole town was talking about the incidents, though no one said anything to Eden, and about how, it was said, Eden's mother had taken her back in without a word, neither of reproach nor sympathy, and how the bed in her old basement room was made up again stiff and cold, as if it had stayed that way from the moment she'd left to the moment she returned. Craig had tried to approach her many times after that, but she wouldn't talk to him. When she had stopped working at her father's cinema, where he used to try to see her, we would see his car driving up and down our street, but he never dared show up at her house. Until the day he did, and her mother answered the door while Eden was still in the basement, and Craig demanded to talk to Eden, and her mother just stood in the doorway – a tall, thin, cold woman who never seemed to age – and told him, without once bending her impassive gaze to his wild, shamed, impotent fury, or even pretending that Eden wasn't there – told him simply and coldly, before closing the door so that its unhurried click was like a certain, last reproof, 'Don't ever come back here again.' Then she, the mother, went back downstairs and pretended she didn't know Eden had sat listening; only looked at Eden and walked back upstairs again, with Eden looking up after her and not saying anything either. Craig began going around town shouting, who was she to take his girl from him, did she think them better then him?, and continued to drive up and down the street, as though just to let them know he was still there. One evening he even stopped outside our house so that we could see his car in the dark from our front window, but he never came in, as though he were not sure if Eden was there or not (which she was), or if my parents were there or not. It was around that time that I had overheard my parents' conversation in the kitchen.

We arrived at the ski-hill while it was still early. Eden had not said much for most of the ride up. She had sat, depressed, in the back seat and eventually my father put on the radio to cover the silence. But when we got to the ski-hill, the mood changed somewhat. The sun was shining bright upon the hill, and we could see from where we were parked people covering it like ants, and my sister seemed to have suddenly grown so full of energy that it was all we could do to keep her still and put on her snow pants and boots and skis. We all skied together, until my father left us to ski the Black Diamond slopes up at the top. It was the type of day when the sun seems to be pushing its way back up some long tunnel, scattering the winter winds before it. The snow reeled up blue and crimson against the blue sky, the sun was warm, the air invigorating, and even Eden, despite herself, seemed to be slowly cheering up. We had had lunch and were at the bottom of one of the lower slopes when my mother, pointing to me, said, 'Why don't you take Bobby off skiing on the bigger slopes for a while, Eden?' and put her arm around my sister: 'I'll look after her.'

We went off to the chairlift, and as we stood in line, Eden was smiling. 'You can handle it,' she said to me, never really treating me like a child. And we skied then and enjoyed it, going up and down the mountain, with the slopes so packed it was like the whole town was there. We did a few more runs and were standing in line when I saw Eden's face drop and I turned and saw, though he hadn't seen us yet, Craig Lawson standing further up with his girlfriend – the same woman who had laughed at Eden, the same one he had thrown a beer at in the bar – towards where the chairlifts arrived with a rusty clank and pulled people back up the mountain again. I don't know what he was doing there; it was just a coincidence. He didn't look like a skier. He wore jeans crusted with snow, and no hat. His matted brown hair was slicked under his goggle strap, and he wore the same bulky red lumber jacket he wore around town. He stood looking up the mountain, lifting his face to the sun and turning every now and then to answer his girlfriend in a cursory manner, before they both pushed onto the landing and turned to meet the chair coming towards them. They didn't see us, but when we arrived up top, they were still there, apparently arguing because the woman was too frightened to turn right, onto the more difficult slope Craig wanted to go down. We had no choice but to ski past them, and when we did – when Craig looked up, no longer listening to his girlfriend, and saw it was Eden – it was like we were pulling a look from his face of dawning recognition and incredulity. I could feel his gaze following us like a cord tied to my back, and I knew, without Eden having to tell me, not to look back.

We skied quickly down the slope, but when we arrived at the bottom and were standing in line again, we saw him, midway up, flying down the mountain as best he could without falling. Behind him, his girlfriend, in her pink ski-suit, was looping from side to side, so that he had to stop every once in a while and wait impatiently while she tried to keep up. He arrived at the bottom, with his girlfriend just behind him, looking for us frantically. When he saw us, it was like his eyes were clamps, and he began, without a moment's thought, trying to clamber through the other people waiting in line. 'Craig! Craig!' his girlfriend was calling, confused, scurrying after him; and when they had both got to as far as they could come, standing now almost right behind us, she stopped as though she'd been struck, and seemed to physically retire behind Craig, hurt, and glaring hatefully, not at Craig, but at Eden. Eden was staring straight ahead. 'Eddy...' Craig said, breathing hard, then 'Eddy!' – raising his voice when still she wouldn't turn around. The lift came, Craig was held back, and we were joined by two people from the adjacent line. But we heard Craig arguing with the controller, and we heard his girlfriend, complaining, in a hurt and weak voice, struggling to assert some authority, 'Craig, can't you just for—' 'Will you just fuck off!' we heard him yell, then he turned back and watched us swing off the ground, his eyes dark and angry.

Eden turned to me on the chairlift and I could tell by her face that she was trying not to act shaken. 'Don't worry, Bobby,' she said, 'there's nothing to be scared of.' She tried to smile, to reassure me, but her smile was like something abstracted from her face, hanging weakly in the air between us, and her eyes looked like they were trying to cling to something in the wind. We broke off the main slope, down trails that ran through the trees, to a lift that was less busy, about halfway down, and took that back up again; and the whole time it felt like we were racing against the shadows of the clouds running across the mountain face, racing against or away from something, with Eden leading us across the mountain through higher slopes, where the air was thinner and colder and where even in the sunlight the snow blew in our faces like sand, making our way back towards the other side, until we ran into Craig again, and this time he was alone, standing by the bottom of the lift, peering up the slope before he saw us, too. Eden's body seemed to contract when she saw him. It was too late to go anywhere else. She tried to ski past him to the lift but there was a clumsy clattering of skis, and Craig, with a naked urgency on his face, stopped her. 'Eddy,' he said immediately, 'she never meant nothing to me. Eddy... Eden...' Eden, glancing back at me, tried to push past, and when he reached out and took her arm, everything that had been welling up inside her, that had been churning there in her silence on the lifts and slopes trembled on the point of breaking, and she tore her arm from him. 'Leave me alone, Craig!' she snapped. 'Come on, Bobby,' she said gently, and just as gently pushed me ahead of her. We were on one of the trails higher up on the mountain then, where the lift was for two people only. Craig got on the one behind us and began calling out after Eden, without caring about the people turning around before us or the people below stopping on the moguls and looking up. Eden wouldn't turn around.

What happened then was that, abruptly quiet, and with his sudden silence filling up with determination, he followed Eden down the slope. There were large moguls everywhere, and she broke away from me, and I saw the two of them bouncing through the sunlight and snow and the other skiers. Craig almost lost control several times, but with a will that seemed to envelop him, like some outside force that brought his reeling arms and splayed body back in again, he kept after her; and Eden almost fell a few times too, because the moguls were so high. Eden veered off towards the right side of the slope, where the snow was packed heavier after a day's skiing and which fell steeply into a dark valley of trees. Craig was yelling after her again. Eden looked frightened, and when she glanced across as he managed to speed up beside her, it looked like she was going to weep. The two swept further right. Eden yelled something at him that I couldn't hear, but Craig continued to follow after her, scarcely aware of the people before him. He was yelling something at her again, with the back of his head turned to me, when I saw Eden glance ahead at something and turn to him with her eyes frantic and her mouth opening like she was going to say something but then suddenly – and it was a split second – everything seemed suspended, soundless, in the expression that came over her face and drained it mute, like a wind being sucked back up into the sky, leaving everything abruptly still, with Craig alone continuing to move, like some figure across a momentarily frozen background, and with the tree shooting up before him like something implacable, irrevocable, rising through the snow and hissing air to meet him. I don't think he even saw it. I think he was still yelling something to her, though the words were unheard, and the thud that came then was quick, solid and dull, as though the tree had been hit with the blunt end of an axe, with a small, slight cracking, like the snap of a branch. Eden shot out onto the slope and stopped and looked back, then looked at me, pale and trembling, her eyes wide and beseeching, standing just below where the body lay motionless among the moguls and sunlight, her face looking like something that had been ripped apart, as if her desperate speed had torn it asunder to reveal the face of some frightened child, of incredulous, impotent and injusticed innocence, before her body crumpled and she too fell, light and soundless, into the snow.

*

In the house where Eden grew old, and where we used to visit her, she would meet us with a determined cheerfulness that did not seem to diminish with the years or after her divorce. She was the only reason we ever came back. The mill had long since closed down, and Eden had spent a while working as a nurse in another city before eventually returning. She had remained close to my mother, and my sister had come and stayed with her once after we'd left, as had I. She stayed there until she died, not yet fifty, and alone, of cancer. I only heard about it when it was too late, because as we had grown older, we had lost touch. No one had ever mentioned Craig on our visits, and most everyone left in town had probably forgotten him. But I remember how sometimes, if we stayed there long enough, Eden used to sit in that front room among the pictures of her children and her vases of dried flowers – that room that was like a room no one ever really lived in, that was just there for guests – looking out the window through the sheer curtains she never pulled back, like she was waiting for someone or was watching someone go. She never married again or dated. Her children have grown up and have children of their own. I came back for the funeral and met them. Her house had been cleared and everything packed up, and among her things they had found a creased picture of her when she was sixteen, with a man that no one recognised beside her. Her son came up to me and showed it to me and asked me if I knew who it was. I looked at it for a moment and looked at him, he who hadn't really known his mother, and folded it again and gave it back. 'Oh,' I said, telling him at least most of the truth, or as much as I was willing to tell: 'It's just someone she used to know.'

Atoms

E J Saleby

She ran her tongue over his teeth in a final taste that ended him. When he was gone after her promises, she showered in the scaled cubicle, her skin puckering in the mist and toes gripping the tiles. There was mould in the corners, black spores gathering, and she held her breath. She dried herself on his towel and its embrace reminded her of her father. His toothbrush was too large and the other one was not hers so she used her finger, squeaking in her mouth like a cloth on a mirror. Minty and soaped, she was clean on the surface at least.

In the bedroom she found her underwear and dressed for the night before as though remembering an accident. Sunlight caught the dust in the air that was floating galaxies of dead skin. Particles of him and her. They were covered in each other. She sat on the bed where they had been. It was alive with creatures that she could not see. She knew they were there. Tiny horned microbes, many-limbed and bustling amidst the sweat and semen. She rubbed her bare arm, smooth from the wax. The tiny hairs on her landscape would sprout up soon. She would turn to liquid one day, she thought. She pictured herself decaying into his parquet, black goo and putrescence on the varnish, a feast for the beasts.

The air was heavy with his absence. She went to the windows that were too large to understand and peered behind the blinds. Daytime roared with a searing light and the raging of the city below. She turned her back on it. He had left his watch in his hurry, curled and stopped on the wooden floor by his bed. She picked it up, slipped it over her fragile wrist. She wound it, noting her chipped thumbnail and her swollen knuckle, the erosion of colour on the tip contrasting with the growing purple. The watch slipped nearly to her elbow. She did not fit but the cogs ticked against themselves and the universe spun again. She held the face to her ear and was thrilled by the regularity. There it was. The attempt to make sense of it all.

Her high shoes were in the hallway, pressed together where he had tidied them. The front door was closed and she skated over in her tights, fixing the deadbolt and security chain once more. His mobile rang quietly and she recognised it on the side table by the dangerous lilies. Her vest top was smeared still in their pollen where she'd brushed against them before when she was listing and the corridor was at an angle. Her fault. Such strength in their colour. He had helped her take it off.

She lifted the phone, swiped her finger over the screen and he was back.

'Hello?' he said.

'Hi.'

'Rachel?'

'Hi.'

She listened to the university behind him. The quiet echoes of pages and thinking.

'It's me. Why do you have my phone?'

'You left it here.'

'Where are you?'

'In the flat.'

'What?'

'In the flat.'

'You can't...' he began to say, but she did not let him finish. There was so little power left to her but she held some now in her finger. She swiped him away and leant in to smell the lilies, their scent tunnelling up her nostrils. The amber pollen clustered with intent and she stared at it for some time. She was a bee flitting from one flower to another. She was not ready to leave yet. She could sense him in his panic, his mind unused to the muffling of fear.

In the kitchen there was coffee and some fruit. The beans were ground into powder in the bag, crushed and buried and broken. She made herself a cup that was too hot for a long time. She sat with her feet on the table and watched the steam rising in front of her toes. His watch ticked gently, too high on her wrist. It would stop again soon. He might come back, of course, but she doubted it. He had a lecture now, another this afternoon, and then the meeting he had bored her about for so long last night that she had kissed him anyway. It had worked, her tongue in his mouth. It had been years, he said.

He was probably terrified she would turn up there now. It was her lecture too, she thought. It didn't matter. Quantum physics, string theory, the multiple layers that proved it was all nothing, all at the same time, everywhere. She was there right now, in another universe. Screaming at him in laddered tights across the lecture hall, her dozing peers turning and staring. Mad Rachel. Running down the wide steps to where he stood as if paused in time. Sobbing in her seat high up at the back, her knees tight against the chair in front, her coat next to her, retching so loudly he had to stop mid-sentence, the PowerPoint frozen on a star or a telescope or a theory only they could understand. Or arriving, making notes and leaving without acknowledgement, not a word, not a gesture. She was here now. It was all happening. Right now. Right then. All the time. She needn't do anything.

Rachel sipped her coffee, its bitter molecules sharp on her throat. The heat released the coffee particulates into the water. No wonder it was so strong. She decided to explore his flat while she was disturbing his lecture and making notes quietly at the back and not here.

Down the corridor in her tights, the coffee stained in spotted tracks behind her. She knew his bed and his imprint and the smell of his wife on the pillow. She wanted to sense him again, the esteemed and learned man. His study was off to the right and surprisingly small, an afterthought of the builders, perhaps a miscalculation in the drawings. A large old desk with green leather embossed on the surface. She fingered the seams as though tracing a boundary. She lifted the paperweight, an enclosed nebula. University of San Francisco, Faculty of Physics, Conference 2002, she read beneath. He was her age then – nearly, anyway. Perhaps they would meet.

She sat in his important chair and placed her hands where his were so often, her naked arms in the leather dip of his elbows. They were touching again, she thought, and sipped his coffee. 10.12, the watch told her. Their lecture had started. She wondered if he knew she was sitting there now, in the university amphitheatre, his words rising to the tip-tip-tap of the laptops above him. What were the students really looking at, he had asked her last night with the sheets on the floor. She'd liked his insecurity then. Naked together, she held the power. Like now, she thought.

When the phone began ringing it had a different tone and she was surprised and momentarily baffled. A landline, she realised, and smiled to herself. Of course he would have one. They all did, his generation. She left the study and hunted its call, enjoying herself. She hoped it would be one of those phones with numbers embedded in a plastic circle. She could be Audrey Hepburn in a hotel in Rome. Where was the lobby? She tracked it to the table with the lily and his mobile, an insistent lump of plastic tethered to the wall beneath. She picked it up, its looping coils like a helix. It could be anyone. There were so many of us.

'Hello?'

Rachel said nothing.

'Hello? Richard? Is that you?'

Rachel listened to her breath in the receiver. It journeyed from her mouth and through the wires and back into her ear but travelled so far to do so. She sounded underwater.

'Richard? Are you ok? Richard? Say something, darling!'

The woman's voice had the early shrillness of age, soft tones worn down like eroded joints. Rachel breathed out again, a sigh like the end.

'Who is this. Who is this?'

'Nothing,' said Rachel. 'This is nothing.'

She held the receiver in front of her and looked at it. The woman's voice emerged flattened and shrinking as she returned it crying to its cradle. Silence again at this altitude. She wondered what she looked like, this woman whose place she had shared.

She could search her out, rummage through the drawers and the bathroom cabinet. She could try on her skirts and stand behind her suits at the bedroom mirror where he had watched himself in the morning glow. He had been so proud.

There was no need, she decided. They knew each other enough already. She had tasted her in him.

Her shoes were still there, arranged neatly together under the lilies by Richard when he was still in control. She tucked her toes into her heels. He was regretting it all, she was sure. It did not matter. None of it did. It had barely happened.

His mobile rang once more, displaying the university number. Richard again. She walked to the front door on her toes, her footsteps punctuating the floorboards. She slid off the security chain and wrenched the deadbolt aside. It gave with a gasp that reminded her of the lab. Of him.

He was still ringing. The landline started up too, and for a second or perhaps much more or less they were in unison, calling for her in waves of sound that refracted and reflected but that she ignored.

They were only atoms. Him and her and her as well. All of them. Buzzing particles of energy, vibrating against each other for a time, again and again and even after they were dead. Whatever that meant.

She slipped out of the flat, between the spaces they had left open for her. His watch slipped down to her wrist as she closed the door behind her. It was still ticking, but that did not matter.

The Rabbit

Suzanne Ghadimi

'Please,' I said in desperation as I looked across the open bonnet of my car. It was 2.30am and we were in the garage. It was December and it was cold in Aberdeenshire. Colder than usual.

'I just want to...'

'You have to stop!' I begged.

'...fix it,' he said.

He was leaning over the car engine, holding a torch in one hand and a small spanner in the other.

Ten minutes ago, I'd woken up alone. I had searched the house looking for him, then searched it again calling his name. It didn't occur to me that he might be outside, because it was the middle of the fucking night and where would he go? I screamed his name and began to cry, then noticed his slippers by the front door. If his slippers were by the door, then he must be outside somewhere. At 2.30am on a Friday morning. This Friday morning.

I was out of the door in a moment and set off the bright motion sensor security light the same instant I stepped on a sharp pebble. I hadn't stopped to put on my shoes. I was hopping around on one foot in my pyjamas, half-blinded, when I stopped crying and started to get angry. I noticed the garage door was up and a light was on. I limped into the garage and saw him.

'Forget about everything else, I'm going to kill you myself,' I shouted at my husband, filling all the corners of the garage with my voice. I started to cry again.

It was over two weeks ago that he had received the letter giving the time and date of his appointment with a consultant urologist. I knew that it was not going to be good news. Prompt appointments from the NHS are never good news.

The waiting room was lovely and full of worried-looking people. Couples, mostly; middle aged or older. Just like us. The walls were painted a quiet blue and the chairs were comfortable. Inspired by the unimaginative and unthreatening John Lewis design.

We sat holding hands tightly until we were called.

We sat with his consultant, in another thoughtfully stark room, as she explained the diagnosis and listed the treatment options. Then she said everything again. There were a few diagrams, a few statistics, and pamphlets. Lots of pamphlets. She asked us to let her know by the coming Friday what treatment we had decided on.

'Arrangements need to be made,' she said.

We then sat with a nurse who offered the really nice kind of biscuits that people will often save for Christmas or very special days. My husband ate seven and would have had more, but that was all the biscuits she had put on the cheerful paper plate.

'Do you have any questions? About what the consultant told you?' she asked, and my husband said 'No,' no – he couldn't think of anything. He was holding the small collection of pamphlets in one hand and a biscuit in the other.

'You're probably in information overload,' the nurse said. 'It's a wee bit to take in.'

We were given phone numbers, an email address, and a few approved websites to look at if we wanted. She also talked about the treatment choices. I stopped listening at some point and thought about the beautiful biscuits and about everyone in that lovely room still waiting for their names to be called. I hoped there would be enough biscuits for everyone.

'Well, that's you then,' the nurse said as we thanked her. 'Nae bother,' she said, cheerfully leading us to the lift.

A week before he received the letter, my desktop Mac had made an odd noise and frozen. It was nine years old and I had never backed it up. Never. But before I confessed this to my husband, I was able to start it in safe mode and copy my recent and important files. I sat and stared at the familiar machine and began to feel a choking panic rise in my throat. What would I do without my computer? This computer. This computer my then live-in partner and my now husband had bought me when his old laptop I'd been using had died. He bought me a brand-new Mac and it was beautiful, strange and so wonderful. I loved that computer and now it was about to die and I didn't know if I could cope with that. He came into the office where I was silently crying. He asked what had happened and I told him and then he hugged me. He found it sweetly amusing that I was so attached to an old computer.

We came home from the appointment with the pamphlets. He went straight into the office without taking his shoes or coat off. He stood looking at my old Mac that was clinging to life in safe mode.

'Right,' he said. 'I think I'll give it a go.'

He sat on the floor of the second bedroom with his laptop balanced precariously on an old chair. He had watched countless YouTube videos already. My old Mac computer was on the floor beside him where he had dragged it. He dismantled it. Carefully, he laid the parts out all around him on the floor and labelled each and every one. He was meticulous.

I wasn't expecting this to be the first thing he'd do when we came home from the hospital. He just sat on the floor watching video after video as people on the internet took apart, fixed, and then reassembled old Mac desktop computers.

I was sitting staring at the very small screen of the laptop I was now using, wishing it was last week and that it could always be last week and that the appointment had never happened, when he wandered into the office. He seemed quite happy.

'I think it's the graphics card that's gone. I ordered a new one from eBay, it'll be here in a day or two,' he told me, then asked, 'What's for dinner?' I told him he could have whatever he wanted, that I'd make him anything.

We were putting the dishes in the dishwasher afterwards when he noticed the grouting along some of the tiles and kitchen counters. It had cracked and, in some places, come completely away. He ran a finger along an edge. 'I can fix this,' he said, and went off in search of sealant.

He said later he would run to B&Q first thing in the morning for sealant as his had mysteriously disappeared, and then he would fix that shelf.

'What shelf?' I asked.

'The broken one in the cupboard,' he answered.

'The one that's been broken for three years?' I said.

I was standing looking out of the kitchen window at the back garden when he came home. It was grey and cold. He had the tube of the stuff he went for, but he also had a tin of paint and an assortment of brushes, which he left in the hallway. 'I thought I'd touch up the skirtings while I'm at it,' he said. I made him some coffee and had another cup myself.

'Bugger,' I heard him say a while later.

I helped him drag the now entirely useless and even more broken shelf into the garage. It wasn't easy getting around all the mess that had been in the cupboard, on that shelf that was now cluttering the hallway. He stood scratching his chin, looking around the garage, then asked if I wanted to go back with him to B&Q to look at new shelves. I said no curtly and went in to make some more coffee. He could pick out a new bloody shelving unit on his own. I tripped over the tin of paint as I walked down the hall and swore loudly in the almost empty house.

He had been gone for a bit when I went into the office to look at the news on my laptop, with my fifth cup of coffee in hand. I saw the small pile of pamphlets by the printer. The top one said 'Treatment Choices: What is Cryotherapy?' and I knew the one underneath said 'Know Your Prostate', both written in an unthreatening and empathetic font. I called his mobile as I stood looking at the pamphlets and asked him to stop on his way home and pick up some cream; I told him I had run out. I listened to his comforting voice as he happily said he would.

I poured out the half-full container of cream that was in the fridge after I hung up. I stood looking out of the kitchen window into our large back garden and noticed the rabbit. He sat in the sallow winter grass looking towards the house, as he had for a while now. He had suddenly appeared one day.

I wondered what he saw, what he thought of – if indeed rabbits had thoughts. I wondered why I thought of the rabbit as 'him'. I found an odd comfort in having a rabbit in our garden watching over us, if he was watching over us. *What if he wasn't watching over us?* I suddenly thought. I called my husband back and asked him to also get some biscuits – the really, really nice ones.

'A package came for you while you were out,' I said when he came home. He looked about excitedly and I handed it to him. I didn't ask about the shelves.

After dinner, he escaped back into the spare bedroom to work away. He attached and reattached bits and cables inside the complicated computer; he fitted the new graphics card. It was a warren of pins, circuits, and metal. Even one small thing missing and it wouldn't work or even turn on. 'Such a complicated and delicate machine,' he whispered as I stood watching him from the door.

Later, I sat on the floor with him, holding the torch for better light as he tried again and again to put things back together. Until now it had not worked, but a moment later the start-up sound boomed into the tensely quiet space. I felt a wave of relief as the screen began to glow and the image of an apple appeared. He laughed with joy at finally getting everything right.

My computer worked. It begged for my password. I watched as my home screen appeared and felt oddly safe. This was normal and comforting. This was what I had so hoped for.

'Right, what's next?' he said as he looked about the room.

'What do you mean?' I asked him, but I knew. I looked at him and wanted to hold both his hands tightly in mine, those hands that he could not let sit still.

He was in his pyjamas.

It was still 2.30am and I was still crying. My car was still between us and I was equal parts angry and frightened.

'Just stop,' I said. 'Please.'

His face was taut and tired and so very beautiful.

'I can't,' he said. 'I need to fix this.'

I walked towards him and stood on something else sharp. I was spinning again, hopping with even less grace and swearing astonishingly at my lovely, thrawn, and exhausted husband. He watched in stunned silence. I regained my balance and stomped towards him, trying to grab the spanner out of his hand, but he held tight to that cold and soulless piece of metal. After a brief and surprisingly fierce struggle, it spun from our hands, arched in the air and landed in the darkness just beyond the garage, close to the garden path. I sat down on the freezing cold and dirty garage floor. My husband sat down beside me. We looked at each other.

'Please...' I said.

'I can't...' he said.

A sudden and unexpected movement caught our attention and we looked over to where the small spanner had fallen.

The Rabbit

The rabbit sat looking at us.

My husband looked at me. 'Isn't that the...'

'...from the back garden?' I said.

He was so perfectly still.

Then he turned and hopped back along the darkened path towards the back garden.

'Surgery,' my husband said. 'I've decided on the surgery.' I leaned over and rested my head on his shoulder.

'We're going to be OK,' I said, looking out of the garage, noticing it had begun to gently snow.

Cold Turkey

Niki Baker

The snow reflects moon-silver, softening the Norfolk landscape, and the wind carries scraps of carols on its wings. Tom shakes himself to clear snowflakes from his snood, his wattle flapping. Tom's a bigger turkey than me. He teases me about my 'superstitious nonsense', but I have this nagging feeling. Two children walked past yesterday and one said, 'Nearly Christmas.' Whatever that means.

I sidle over to the hole in the fence, squeeze through and plop into the field, where the world is big and the white is deep. Giddy with excitement, I set off in big fluttery leaps.

After a while, snow is c-c-caked on my f-f-feathers and my legs are t-t-tired...

I wake up inside a metal box, where it's *really* warm. I hear footsteps. One side of the box disappears and is replaced by a woman's face. She looks me in the eye and then makes a horrid shrieking noise. I rush out and she suddenly lies down on the floor.

Outside, it feels colder than ever. The woman's voice is shouting things like, '...told me it was dead...' and '...going vegetarian...'

I find a cosy corner in the barn and wait for my feathers to grow back.

Touching the Sun

Clare Reddaway

The pebbles hurt the soles of her feet. She doesn't care. Hurting is good. Pain is what she deserves. She steps into the water. The sea is deceptive. The shallow, nibbling waves with their light froth of white are not the warm waters of the Aegean. They freeze her ankles, her shins. She shuffles forward and flinches as another patch of skin is iced. She can see a steep drop into deep water, only a few feet away now. If she steps off the sea cliff she will be submerged. She teeters, scared of submersion, scared of the shock of the water, scared to make the decision – then she plunges head first into a breaking wave. The shock makes her sob. She forces herself to open her eyes. The water is murky, churning with sand. The shafts of sunlight turn her skin corpse-white. Twisting, she breaks the surface and swims jerkily, powering the blood around her body, craving warmth, survival. It is long, stretched-out seconds before her body adapts. Until, with a deep breath, she relaxes. Her strokes slow and smooth. She starts to swim out, away from the beach, towards the horizon. The water comforts her, holds her, supports her. It feels warm, buoyant, womblike. Is this what it would be like, she wonders, if she dared? Agony. But a short agony. Followed by this, which is a form of bliss.

She flips onto her back and floats. The sun is hot on her face. It is hotter than is normal for Dorset, hotter than it should be. She closes her eyes and instead of black sees red with yellow lines and shapes that ooze and float. She opens her eyes and makes herself stare straight at the fierce white disc in the sky. Perhaps the sun will blind her. If she puts her thumb in front of her eyes she can blot it out. Make it disappear. She heard on the radio on the way to the beach that they have sent up a probe. They want to touch the sun. It will land on the surface. It won't melt like the wings of Icarus and plunge to its destruction. They won't allow it to do that. They are too clever. Too clever to be burnt.

She knows the heat of the sun. She felt it the first time she brushed past him. His skin touched her skin and the heat shot through her body as though she had plunged head first into a wave of fire.

She shivers. It is August, but the water is too cold for stillness. She turns over and starts to swim. Her arms cut through the water and her legs kick evenly, she turns her head every third stroke to take a deep breath, she can feel the pull of the water as she drives through it, she points her toes, reaches her arms, cups her hands, she is efficient, she is a fish, a seal, a shark. She is at one with the water. It is thick, salty, heavy. Like the liquor you cook fish in. Like the taste of a man. Like his skin, like his mouth, like her mouth, after. She licks her lips. They are as salt as water.

Her limbs are stretched and warm. She pauses, bobs, sleek as an otter. She is a long way out. She looks back to the beach. Her husband is crouching down beside Sarah. Their heads – one blonde, one brown – are the same height, though Sarah is only three. They are both staring at the barbecue. They look solemn and purposeful. Perhaps they are cooking the sausages.

She sees Sarah reach out her hand. She wonders if Sarah will burn herself. She wonders if her husband has noticed. She waits for the stab of anxiety. It doesn't come.

She looks around. The cliffs are burnt honey in the late afternoon sun. They curve round the beach like cupped hands. Beyond the cliffs, around the point, is the harbour of a small seaside town. It has fish and chip stalls around the dock and a winding cobbled street of colourful painted houses that climbs a hill to a small ruined castle. She knows this because she has been there many times. She knows that beyond the town, further along the coast, the cliffs become higher, more sheer. They cut straight into the sea without the gentleness of the pebbly sand where she has been sitting all afternoon. She has seen the waves crash against these cliffs, battering them even on the calmest of days. She has been told that this is because of the winds and the currents. She doesn't know anything about wind and currents. But she does know that paths wind up from the rocks at the base of these cliffs. They are old paths, hard to find, secret and forbidden and perilous, doubly difficult with bare feet. But they are there.

She is a strong swimmer. For weeks, she has been watching the progress of the man who is swimming around the edge of the country, and she has wondered. She has seen him swim beyond beaches, alongside cliffs rising out of the waves, she has seen him being swept along by the currents and she has thought: maybe she could do the same. She swivels and starts to swim towards the headland. Towards the secret forbidden paths.

She must conserve her energy. She must alternate her strokes to stop herself from developing cramp. She sweeps her arms out into a circle and her legs, froglike, follow. She thinks of her life, of the safety, of the certainty. She thinks of her husband. He is tentative and gentle and kind. She thinks of the man whose skin is as hot as the sun and she thinks of how he will throw back his great head and laugh that booming laugh and sweep her into his arms when she comes to him wet as a mermaid from the sea. Naked and free and with nothing. She thinks of how she will leave wet footprints on his floor and cover his bed with salt and bring him no possessions or trappings or expectations and he won't care. She is swimming to him. Her stroke grows jagged with excitement.

She is like the probe journeying through space to the sun. It has so far to go. It will penetrate the sun's atmosphere in a quest to explore the solar storms that rip the surface with flares and bursts of fire. How much more thrilling than the fog and drizzle that blankets her life now, full of placid certainties and humdrum grey. She wants to fill her life with firestorms.

A wave hits her face and fills her mouth with water. She flounders, but rights herself. She is gaining on the headland, but not quickly, not given how hard and how long she has been swimming. The currents must be against her, the tide must be turning. She glances back at the beach. She sees her husband. He is standing now. He is staring out to sea, out at her. He sees her look back at him. He lifts his hand. He waves. Sarah is in his arms. She has buried her head in his shoulder. He is comforting her. He is comforting their child.

She stops.

Sarah is crying. This time anxiety strikes. The steel thread lassoes her and reels her in. She turns. She must get back. Her limbs are heavy and tired. Her strokes are still efficient, but slower. Each pull is hard, every reach cracks her muscles. She is chilled now. Her skin is puckered and tight; she is shivering.

The sun has lost its heat. It is no longer searing white. It is deepening to a homely orange as it dips down towards the horizon, it is benevolent, safe, invoking autumn leaves, clementines, pumpkins. Why did she go so far? What was she doing? Now she is swimming with the current. She is carried towards the shore. She is within reach, she is by the sea shelf. But the undertow tugs her back out, she feels his fingers on her legs, stroking, intimate. She has made her choice. With the last of her strength she struggles over the shelf and into the shallows. The waves whisper on her skin as they let her go.

In the past, her husband would call her Venus when he saw her rise from the waves. He would run to her and wrap her in a thick towel and hug her close and kiss her wet head. Today he does not even smile. Her legs are shaking and she is all goose pimples and bleached skin. Her teeth are clattering as he throws her a towel.

'You were gone a long time,' he says. 'I wondered if you were coming back.'

She smiles a warm and forgiving smile. She strokes her tummy, where a new life is forming.

'I have something to tell you,' she says.

She meets his eyes.

They are as cold and dark and infinite as space.

'Is it mine?' he asks.

Misper

Katherine Pringle

Strong boots stomp the tarmac and stop right next to Geoff and me. Wet leather and sheep muck leap up my nose. There's a strange hand in my fur, big-fingered. I lick the palm – urgh, tastes of engine oil. And the voice that belongs to the hand shouts over the beast in the sky:

'That missing girl... I saw her. About ten this morning. Trudging along the path between the end of my field and Carn Wood. Real slow, staring down at her feet. Looked just like that photo in your hand. What's her name, Erin? Aye, she had that long red hair. Just fourteen? Same age as my own daughter. I thought to myself, now that one should be in school. But no bag. Nothing with her. Really looked like she was going nowhere.'

Geoff talks fast into his radio. The wood skulks up on the dark hill, branches shaking. Come on then, they say, come in and see what we're hiding. Dare you.

But Geoff turns and strides, straight through the gate to the long house. And I'm right on his scuffed black heels.

The door flies open while the bell is still ringing. Her breath is loud and fast, like she's running. There's a silver *Mum* on the top of each slipper. Unravelling.

Mum doesn't want me in there.

'Stay,' says Geoff. I lie down at the foot of the stairs, for him. 'Good boy.'

They tuck their voices behind the kitchen door. Hers is high and watery as she says:

'A sighting? Oh, thank God. She's OK, OK. Might walk through that door any second.'

Geoff's words are calm. Hers heave and rock:

'Carn Wood? God no... No, not that place... Where Alice... Yes, you know, her sister... Erin thinks she remembers, but she was too young, so young. We should have moved away, but I couldn't, I couldn't... Oh, but what am I thinking, she won't have gone near the wood – she's forbidden, she knows that.'

Geoff talks quietly. Then she says:

'No, she doesn't tell me what happens at school. I never know what's in her head. Last week she kept singing some song... I heard it through her door. Over and over, like she couldn't let it go... had to get it right. Then this weekend, just silence.'

I get up off the mat and have a good sniff at a sleeve slumped on the bottom stair. Right cuff limp and chewed. Smells of bottled flowers, dried ink, bus fumes, ripped-up leaves. All mixed up. And something else – I stick my nose in the air. Flakes of a girl. Left behind. Whispering:

I couldn't do it. Stand on that stage and sing. They were all laughing, I could hear them. Laughing at me. I had to run.

A chair drags behind the closed door. Slippers pace the floor tiles, round and round. Mum says:

'Look at that sky... I need to bring the washing in but I can't stand that awful helicopter drone. It'll be dark soon. How will she cope out there without me? She's just a child.

Surely she'll be home soon... You'll be home soon, won't you, my darling? You'll be home if you can.'

Those flakes zing up my nose: soft like dust, spiked with life.

I cried on the bus home. They all saw. Alice wouldn't have mucked it all up like that. I'm nothing. Nothing. I'll never be the star.

Mum's voice twists into knots:

'I should have seen it... Her hair wasn't washed this morning, her shirt was crumpled. She pulled away from me when I tried to hug her, didn't look back. I shouldn't have let her go, should've gone after her when I found her cardigan. She doesn't like the cold... Oh God, she's out there alone. She's got nothing with her. Nothing. I can't stand it, I can't breathe...'

Silence in the kitchen. The sky howls.

Geoff opens the door, lifts my lead. 'Let's go, Scout, my boy.'

But not yet. He has to get on that radio of his again.

It's dark by the time we're good to go.

Geoff's wearing his earth-caked wellies; the beast is quiet. I know what that means. It's our search now. At last.

Deep into the striped gloom. Needled branches prickling the clouds. Shifting air, stuffed full of pinecones and ferns.

His deep, calm voice says: 'Control, Control. 1642 commencing search of Carn Wood. Over.'

My lead comes off – that's better. Shake my head free.

He fastens the bells and lights round my neck. 'Ready to play, Scout?'

Am I ever?

'Good boy. Go find. Go find.'

He sends me up towards the ridge. Nose-first into the wind.

Light-pawed. Ferns skim my fur. Ah, stretch the legs, lick the night. Here I come, ready or not.

Geoff paces our spine, steady and straight. That's Geoff. But I'm off. Away and back, away and back. Always back. And he's watching me with his torch, like I'm the boss here.

Yup, just doing my thing. My collar shines red. Bells jangle on my neck – the song of this night game. Chase the wind, feel it build as I run. It knows I'm trying to make friends with it. But it's playing hard to get. You'll never catch me, it cries. You'll never grab the things I hold.

Well, that stirs me right up. Just you watch, I shout. I'm on your tail. What tricks have you spun? I don't know where you've hidden that prize yet, could be anywhere. But if it's here, I'll find it.

Keep going, keep going. Running the hill. Rough tough ground, the ferns won't let up.

Back to his heels. Nope, I tell him, nothing there, trust me. He knows I know. Look over here? I'm on it, don't you worry. And I'm off again.

That wind's weaving through the ferns, leaping up the tall trunks, sailing into the sky. Leading me on a wild dance.

A fizz tweaks my nostrils and wheels me round, sharp. Hello? My tail springs up like a flag. Hang on. Nose in the air – sniff, sniff, sniffing. Tickles a bit. Can't quite get it… almost, almost. Got it.

It's her, the cardigan. A billion pieces of her drift here. Crying:

The world's going on without me, I can't feel it. But I won't leave a gap. I'm too small and hidden.

Nonsense, I shout. I'm breathing you in right now. I call back to Geoff: We're close.

I'm alone. I'm cold. The trees are swaying and whispering: You're missing, you've always been missing.

You're not alone. I'm in here too, giving that wind a run for its money. I'm on your trail.

I used to look at this wood from my window and wonder if Alice was still in here. Today it was so quiet and dark, I didn't want to stand on the edge anymore. A little voice said: It's better in here. But I don't know these long shadows and I can't see the way out. I'm lost, just a ghost like Alice. But no one will find me. I don't shine as bright as her.

The wood is full of you. I'm going to find you, pull you out. Then I'll do the winner's dance.

Go, go, go! I smash into the night. Off the path now, far from the torchlight. Ferns fly in my face as I bound up to the ridge. I'm boiling; I stick my tongue out to cool off. Where are you, where are you?

Someone is coming. Closer and closer. She's with me now. But I don't want to be like her anymore. I don't want to be a ghost. Go away, go away. She's behind me, I can't see her. But I know she's there. Stroking my hair, and saying in a little voice: There now, my sister, there now.

The wind shrieks, She's mine! And snatches her off. I stop. My nose feels dry. I don't know which way to go. It's all muddled up.

The torch is small behind me. Watching. He still thinks I'm leading this game.

No chance. Been chasing the tail end of something. Old scent, must be. Lofted up and stashed at the top of this ridge. Stuck between the fern fronds, tangled into the branches. She was here once, but she's been blowing about this place for way too long.

Told you, spits the wind. Told you I'd win. I'm the boss here. I've been up to this all day. Spinning and brewing. You'll never find her, she's gone.

Geoff strides up to me, panting. 'What've you found, Scout? Good boy, show me.'

Nothing, I say. Nothing. I hang my head. I hate this stillness. I need the bells in my ears again.

The wind cackles. Geoff scratches the fur between my ears as he pours water into my bowl.

'It's not over, Scout, my boy,' he says. 'We'll find her.'

He digs a plastic bottle from inside his search jacket, twists it open. Ah, good plan, Geoff, spot on. I slug my water.

He holds the bottle at arm's length, squeezes it three times. White powder comes puffing out and hangs in the torchlight like a ghost on camera. Till the wind charges through it, stretches it thin, snuffs it out.

'Aha,' says Geoff, shining his torch on the map.

Yup, I saw it too. The path of the wind. We caught its sneaky dance. It's blowing in behind us.

Geoff looks back down the hill. 'What've we missed, Scout?'

He switches on his phone map and we stare at zigzag red lines.

'Let's see, good ground coverage here. But there's a gap right there.' He points at a hole in the red mesh, and a thin blue line. The river.

I growl. Couldn't hear it. It's been drowned out by the pesky wind.

I stand tall on the ridge and shout up to the flailing trees: The boss, you say? I'm the hero. I'll win this game. You'll see.

And I'm off, bells ringing. Fast down the slope, right up the nose of the wind. Down, deep down where water drags over sharp stones.

The river's sunk low. Tree roots poke out from the bank like bones. Cold air, dead still. She must be here. Must be.

I track the limping flow. Nose to the clouds. Ready to catch, ripe to be caught. My tail quivers. What's that? A spark. And another one. A swarm. Hot like fireflies. That's her. She's snagged me again, she's reeling me in.

Bright scent, pooled over the water. Getting brighter. I can taste it, could almost lick it up like a treat. Nearly... nearly... nearly there.

Bingo.

I leap the last bit, arch-backed, over and over. Take that, demon wind. I'm lit with the winner's fire.

White face, closed eyes. Red hair tugged by the water – looks like rusty seaweed. I want to paw it out, but this game's not over till the torchlight shines on her.

I race up the bank to the far-off beam. I run to Geoff, push my front paws on his chest. She's over there, I yell. He leans over me, mouth smiling in a line, but his eyes aren't. They're searching the dark ahead. 'Good boy. Show me.'

Back the way I came. He's right behind me. I find her again for him. Here she is. Cardigan scent, mixed with soil and sweat.

I nudge her hand with my nose. Gently does it. Cold skin. She's not moving. I try again. And again.

There's torchlight on my face.

A deep voice says, 'Control, control. 1642. Misper found...'

A siren screams. For me?

Mum leans low, stroking my hair and staring like she can't take her eyes off me. She's saying, 'Oh my Angel, my Angel.' Her cheeks are dripping wet. Her arms are around me. Just me.

The black-and-white dog is dancing with a rainbow ball. Bells ringing and ringing. He found me, even in the dark.

It was easy, I say. You were shining.

The Search for Atlantis

Max Dunbar

13.9

It was always the spring or the autumn when the signal came – something to do with the lengthening of days or nights, and the drawing in and tightening of air that came with the change of seasons. Dr Winterburn wondered if everybody felt this dreamy restlessness at such times, or was it just him? There was a tightness of definition to the dimensions of A&E reception as well, as he walked through it, doing his purposeful doctor's walk and noticing things he perhaps wouldn't have otherwise: the aggressive smell of cleaning products, the shit and blood and puke hosed down from the walls, a troupe of teenage girls squeezed onto two plastic chairs, all showing the inflammations of pellagra on their faces and hands, one of them doing something Jimmy Winterburn hadn't seen since his own school days – playing with a paper fortune. Bite. Lift. Count.

He reached the main doors and walked out into the cool middle evening, never to return. The breaks, sprains, breakdowns, overdoses, sunstrokes in his waiting room would all have to wait a little longer; they would have to call Ms

Burnell in for consultant cover, or even Mr Rowbotham, heaven save us and preserve us. Too bad.

When people asked why he had become a doctor, Jimmy would tell them that he wanted to do something useful with his life – and, if he was tired or not thinking straight, he would add: this time.

Now he was the top A&E consultant in the Nottinghamshire area, with a permanent post in a major teaching hospital, a happy marriage, three amazing children, a house he owned free and clear, far from the increasing disorder and unsafeness of the city.

And it didn't mean a thing to him, any of it.

He walked until he reached the Trent Bridge. The A60 was closed, perhaps a new curfew, maybe because of the latest spontaneous demonstration – Jimmy Winterburn worked too hard to keep up with the news. Barriers had been flung up, too, as an anti-suicide device. This was no problem. Jimmy climbed the plastic walls with ease and levered himself onto the bridge parapet. He barely broke a sweat. His body was forty-seven, and he'd looked after it well.

Jimmy strolled along the bridge road, enjoying the night air, still noticing everything – a black zeppelin in the distance, the charred pillbox of the tollhouse, something black and crumpled near the sports end, perhaps the remnants of a small fire. He thought he heard music and that made him think of Louise Atherley, all those years ago... how on earth had he forgotten her?

Light caught his eye and there it was, a floating symbol in pink blocks and lines, like something from a 1990s video game... or an image you'd see if you closed your eyes too fast on a summer's day.

He had to take a running jump to clear the bridge.

Bite, lift, count, Jimmy thought, hurtling over the river.

The pink covered everything.

Lines and bars disappeared and Dr James A. Winterburn, tall, handsome and distinguished, went with them.

Count.

Lift.

Bite—

1.1

Someone asked if he was okay and he heard his voice say something back; it had felt like a stumble, a headrush, and Mads said *whoa, Scarborough warning!* Someone else – it sounded like Rahman, Rahman was his name – grabbed onto him and said *Jimmy, it's only eight o'clock for fucksake!*

But Jimmy was fine. He recognised now this other bridge, the motorway bridge that led to the high green space between LS6 and the city centre. He reassured his friends – god, how *young* everybody looked! – and said: 'Rahman, there's no way I would make the schoolboy error of getting hammered before the party! That's more characteristic of an inept student type like yourself!'

'Bloody *stew*-dents!' Mads cried.

They were laughing now as they reached the grass, for students was exactly what they were, and freshers at that, living in a shared terraced house in the Hyde Park area of Leeds, and it was almost the end of that first year, and the Drydock had thrown itself open for the summer party and was shining like a happy lighthouse over the freeway, and now he could see clusters of other young folks, sitting and lying and laughing and dancing, and Mads was twirling her glowstick, the one she always kept with her just because it annoyed him and he'd said it was too Crasher '95, and catching him looking, she said now: 'If you're not careful Jimmy, I'll start blowing my whistle.'

The medical-scientific knowledge he'd gained on the last go round – all those man-hours, textbooks, shadowing, lectures and exams – was still there, but it was fading slowly, like the images on an old TV when you pull the base. And the memories of that life were being crowded out by sensation, by the energy and euphoria of this younger body. He was nineteen and fit and free in this year of '99, and if he cared to buy a thing, he could.

Jimmy's mission that night was something he never talked about, not even to Rahman or to Mads. His friends stopped to greet Flavia Johnson's crew, and in their handslaps and exchanges of hugs and in-jokes and plans (something about a month away in a cottage somewhere) Jimmy slipped into the Drydock's lower bar – and there she was, the girl who looked like Laura Prepon, dancing to Reef's 'Place Your Hands', standing out from the shuffle and press of bodies, making even that stupid song look good. He ordered a beer from the old man behind the bar (a fellow of around sixty summers with cropped grey hair and a Roman nose who caught his eye and nodded in familiarity, though Jimmy didn't think they'd met) and tried to work out how he would speak to her. That was the problem: he had the young man's shyness again.

Someone clapped him on the arm. Monkey Harris was a guy who looked like a student but wasn't. He was a guy who hung around the student and club scene. Monkey Harris said: 'Jimmy! How's your bones?'

And then, in what he perhaps imagined to be a discreet whisper, Monkey Harris asked if he wanted some drugs.

8.5

It seemed like a good idea at the time, and who knew, maybe the coke would give him the courage and articulacy to approach the girl who looked like Laura Prepon and win her over. In fact, once you got past the general dodginess of Monkey Harris, his product was pretty damn fine. Jimmy got completely aced on it, wandered around the grassland, bludgeoned the night with long, intense soliloquies. He didn't see the girl who looked like Laura Prepon again that night, but Jimmy didn't care. There was time. He was young again.

That summer Monkey Harris got him a job in a nightclub down by the docks – the place was called Club Eternal, although Monkey Harris, who'd read a little Nietzsche when he actually was a student, called it the Eternal Return Etcetera. Jimmy had an aptitude for bar work and enjoyed the scene; it was only much later that he realised the club was run not by the named licensee but by the tough, taciturn fellow who ran the door and who also happened to be the Leeds face of a major drug distribution operation.

By this point Jimmy had a fairly major coke problem, and had been 'asked to leave' the Hyde Park terrace after he kept bringing back bar staff and bouncers and other interesting characters at five in the morning. Around '01 he realised the girl who looked like Laura Prepon was slipping from his grasp, because he was well into the sleepless hardcore elements of the student drug scene, from which most undergraduates kept a sensible distance.

By the time of his graduation, Jimmy was working the club pretty much full time. He had an apartment on Clarence Dock and a marble coffee table and a punk session girlfriend who was just as strung out as he was. As well as slinging drinks, he had secondary income from other jobs, such as collecting money from pubs, clubs and dealers, and certain one-off missions – perhaps the scariest being to drive from Leeds to White City at midnight with a kilo of heroin in a hidden well under the boot of his car.

The Eternal Return closed down in 2005, after a member of the United Service Crew was shot in the eye during an argument on the dancefloor in the middle of a Roni Size set. By then he had plenty of work, and the reputation that came with it. He was pulled over for minor motoring offences, searched in the street, at one point even arrested for jaywalking the Headrow. *Just so's we have your prints on file,* the arresting officer laughed. *You never know, Jim, they might come in handy!*

As it happened, Jimmy's print records were indeed used as evidence at the Crown Court, where he was put on trial for shooting Roger 'Bendy' Wharton in 2012. Jimmy couldn't at all see what the fuss was about, because Roger 'Bendy' Wharton had, according to Jimmy's intel, been arrested for importing herbal dope and subsequently done a deal with the CPS, which could have led to life sentences for most of Jimmy's firm, as well as the seizure of homes, cars, the new place in Provence and god knows what else. Besides, he presumed that Roger 'Bendy' Wharton had millions of realities to be alive in, and it wouldn't kill Roger 'Bendy' Wharton to get murdered in just one.

Not that Jimmy said this in court. He entered a guilty plea, hoping to be out of the joint inside a decade – 'Ride it, mush,' as a criminal acquaintance of his always said, 'they can lock the locks but they can't stop the clocks.'

But as the years went by, and his tariff came and went, and the parole knockback came time and again, he realised that he had pissed too many people off, that the authorities were going to make an example of him. He got older and felt his field of reference narrowing, his memories emptying. One day on the library computer he happened across a news story – *Experimental novelist Louise Atherley, 45, takes Booker Prize* – and it took him a beat to recognise the name, and the face. Months went by when nothing mattered to him except prison politics and his little routines.

By the early 2020s he had a PlayStation, and played it through the long lockdown hours. At night, he dreamed of the video games he'd played as a child, Super Mario and Zelda and the New Zealand Story, where you could die but there was always an extra life, always a reset option and another chance.

He had served twenty-two years when the signal finally came. It had just turned April, and they were bussed out to pick strawberries on this farming complex near Middlesbrough, something to do with labour shortages (Jimmy knew all about this, he read the newspapers religiously every morning). He had been picking for almost five hours, his fingers were cramping and fruit juice was trickling and hardening inside his shirt, it was approaching the top of noon, and he glanced up and saw it – the shining pink symbol, hovering over a row of oblivious sweating men in plastic gloves and prison tracksuits.

The guard saw him run but never had a chance of catching him: Jimmy worked out whenever he could, and even in his fifties he could still move at a seamless, covering speed. Jimmy Winterburn raced through the field, trampling stalks and grass, shoulderbarged another prison officer who had been looking in entirely the wrong direction – and then *leapt*, and the guard chasing him saw Jimmy merge into a flash of pink light.

Then the light was gone, and it had taken Winterburn, J., HH12W26272, with it.

1.1

'Went crazy, wouldn't leave her alone,' Flavia Johnson was saying when they reached her little gang, 'lost his job, had a place in Kirkstall, watching that show over and over again,' and he was tempted to go into the Drydock, he could hear the Reef song playing and knew that the girl who looked like Laura Prepon might be dancing to it, and it was so good to have this energy again after decades of prison time... but Jimmy knew what he was doing. *Let her come to you.*

They sat there on the grass with Flavia Johnson and her academic society crew, passing a bottle of wine from hand to hand, and Jimmy propped his back on his palms and took his time to enjoy the dry grass, the stars overhead, the noise of traffic and music and dialogue. He zoned out, and a little later felt somebody knock into him. 'Whoa!' Rahman shouted. 'Scarborough warning!'

He looked up, expecting to see Monkey Harris, but it was her – the girl who looked like Laura Prepon, the girl he'd glimpsed on the concourse and in the Social but never actually spoken to. 'Apologies, man, Jesus,' she said, and her accent wasn't American but the posh, throaty drawl of southern girls. 'It's hotboxed in there, I'm sweating like a *bitch*.'

'You are a disgusting old baggage, Louise Atherley,' said Flavia.

'God, I *know*. Pass me the Lambrini.'

'You better not act like this in the cottage,' Mads warned.

Jimmy could have sat outside there all night, chatting about books and the scene and the state of the world. He clicked with Louise Atherley, clicked almost audibly with her, and when Mads tried to set up a game of spin the bottle with her damn glowstick, Jimmy demurred, not wanting to show the craving for intimacy on his face. But Louise Atherley said, 'Goddamnit, don't be such a *gentleman*,' and she pinned him down and gave him a long, messy snog.

They spun the bottle for another couple of go-rounds, then started dancing (Reef had given way to a Manics retrospective), and as happens in the press and depth of the night, Jimmy lost track of her, and didn't see her again all summer – he wasn't close enough to Flavia and her group, who belonged to the high-end academic strata of the scene. When college opened again he went to every scheduled class, and also joined numerous literary and philosophy societies on a networking mission. Housemates and tutors alike were amazed by the new, sober and motivated Jimmy Winterburn.

He caught up with her finally outside a lecture theatre. A plastic sign outside gave the lecture title: 'The Map and the Territory: Deconstructing the *Choose Your Own Adventure* series'. Louise Atherley recognised him, remembered his name, he could see it in her eyes. She didn't remember spinning the bottle, but she was happy to go for a drink with him and to chat about her summer – they had gone to Flavia Johnson's cottage in the Ribblesdale, and there she'd had an intense romance with a Rhodes scholar from Long Island who Louise just called 'the Prep'. The Prep, it seemed, wore V-neck sweaters, had his hair cut at a specialist London stylist and treated his women poorly. Louise seemed glad to be shot of him.

That second year they got into a routine: drinks on the terrace bar and in the Arts Café, spoken word readings and galleries and arthouse movies. Jimmy didn't press his suit, beyond the random brushing of fingers and arms. There was an obvious chemistry and warmth between them, but Louise had a focus that didn't accommodate romance. For her dissertation she was writing a long, complex social novel based on ideas she'd had during the *Choose Your Own Adventure* lecture.

'The concept would be like the original Montgomery-Packard series,' Louise said, over dinner in the Japanese bar opposite the Drydock. 'You get to a decision point in the story and choose from two or more options. But instead of space adventures or finding Atlantis, the story is going to be about real life – going to work, falling in love, the adventures and tragedies of the everyday. I mapped it out.' Their plates rested on an enormous A3 cartograph of the book – a mad array of coloured lines.

'Have you read Christopher Hitchens?' Jimmy asked, remembering now that Hitchens wouldn't publish this line for another ten years. 'He says the real tragedy of life is that we have many more desires than opportunities. We only get to go round once. I used to love those gamebooks too, and that's why they were so popular – it's like video games, it's a world where you can always go back, always reset yourself and take another path.'

Louise nodded. A strand of her black hair had got caught in her Laura Prepon-style glasses, and she took them off to deal with it. 'But it's not at all ideal, because books and video games are finite. *Journey Under the Sea* has forty-two endings, *Grand Theft Auto* has hundreds of secret missions, but at some point you're going to reach every ending, complete every mission, and look under every rock. In real life, though, it seems like there's endless possibility. This book will probably kill me to write.'

'Because it'd be like a complete representation of life's possibilities. Loops and switchbacks and dead ends. Hey. There is an ending in one of the *Choose Your Own Adventure* books that's impossible to reach.'

Louise had unhooked her hair strand. 'Really?'

'Yep. The book is *Inside UFO 54-40*. There's a two page spread of the city of Ultima. It's like paradise. But you can't actually get there if you follow the rules.'

'So how d'you get to Ultima?'

Jimmy smiled, and took her hand. 'You have to cheat.'

That was the first night they slept together.

3.8

Jimmy hit the first place that didn't have shutters slung down and a plague mark painted on the door. The bar was packed, because it had solid walls and steel bars over the windows. The old man behind the counter said: 'Back again?'

'Again? I've never been here before.'

'Doesn't matter.' But the old man was someone Jimmy almost recognised... the same long nose, cropped silver hair, skin like light on old wood. 'Take your order?'

'Give me a normal coffee. Can you do that?'

The old man nodded and turned to the coffee machine. Over the steam and clatter he said: 'Crazy out there.'

'Tell me about it,' Jimmy said. He had the Westminster beat for a liberal daily, and he had been covering the bailout debate. It had ended abruptly when angry men overwhelmed the security guards, burst into the chamber and started shooting. A detachment of armed police arrived in seconds, started shooting back, and Jimmy had made a discreet escape through the Strangers' Bar.

The old man served his coffee. 'I'm just glad I got my generator round back. Enough for two, maybe three more days. After that, god knows. Maybe they'll have got the power back on, and maybe not.'

'It's fucking crazy. I'm just glad my wife's out of town.'

'Want a game?'

'How d'you mean?'

'I keep board games. For, you know, hipsters and whatnot.' Indeed, among the businessmen and public sector workers crowding out this place there were some playing Scrabble or Connect 4. The old man took a game from a stack behind the bar and handed it to Jimmy – The Game of Life. 'I think you may enjoy that one.'

Jimmy perched on a table next to a woman sobbing into her cashmere wrap. He remembered playing The Game of Life when he was a kid. He even remembered the advert that had promoted it.

Louise called on his mobile. 'Where the fuck are you, Jimmy?'

'I'm in Shoreditch and I'm alive,' Jimmy said. 'Where are *you*, more to the point?'

'Don't worry about me, babe. I'm at the cottage – Flavia's here,' and he heard Flavia shout hello in the background. 'And the Prep.'

'The Prep?' That was a name Jimmy hadn't heard for a while. Hadn't the Prep gone survivalist crazy and moved to the Hebden boondocks?

'Yeah, he's back now. He says everything that's happened, the banking crash and all, it's because society's got too *mechanistic* and *chemically orientated,* that we need to *get back to the land*. He says he predicted the whole thing. He runs a craft shop now. But fuck his shit. How are you?'

'Don't worry about me. The power's still on at our place.'

'You have to leave the city, Jimmy.'

'There's no way – they've closed two of the gates, the others have been taken by the Levantists. You stay up there as long as you want. I'll ride this out.'

'As soon as, Jimmy. I'll be back as soon as. I love you.'

But Louise did not come back for a long time. Jimmy stayed on in the city, thinking: *we spent so long trying to get into London, trying to establish a life here, and now the cashpoints don't even work*. But those had been good years: the wedding in Soho House, the nights out in Hoxton and Shoreditch, the evenings of comedown sex and TV boxsets, the long, friendly, muddled lunches with friends and colleagues, Jimmy establishing himself as a serious journalist while Louise completed her postgrad work and held parties and salons and, whenever she could, worked on her novel – the *Choose Your Own Adventure* book, well over a thousand pages long, the map bustling with lines and loops and switchbacks, a novel she worked on well into the night.

The next time he caught up with Louise, in fact, was in 2017, at her book launch. By then things had settled down, and it felt churlish to complain about the suspension of

Parliament and other bourgeois things, because at least the power was back on and the streets were not actually on fire. The launch was at the old Groucho Club building, now turned into a Community Meeting Point. Jimmy gatecrashed out of curiosity. He had thought that Louise Atherley's complex postmodern novel would have been too controversial to publish in this day and age, and indeed it was. Instead Louise was promoting a memoir called *Wickering: How I Survived Apocalypse on the Ribble Valley.*

Another surprise was that Louise was introduced by the Prep, who hailed her book as 'an indictment of the materialist and neoliberal regime that led to the financial crash of 2008, and an exemplar of socially responsible communitarian literature that will be studied and enjoyed for generations to come.'

Louise read from the memoir. There were long passages about making things out of wicker, and long passages about walking on the hills, interspersed with brief references to the credit crash and the riots. Jimmy listened as best he could and drank shots of whisky from a flask – discreetly, though, as alcohol had been formally banned in 2013 and everyone else was drinking from the juice bar. After Louise had finished her reading, she and the Prep did a short demonstration on how to make things from wicker.

Jimmy had to wait for the Q and A to pass before he could catch Louise face to face. 'This is a surprise, and a departure – what happened to your social novel?'

'Well, in the Ribble for so long, I had time to think,' Louise told him. 'About the novel, about our marriage – I mean, I'm so sorry I haven't been in touch, and so glad to see that you're safe. It wasn't easy up there for a while – we had to hunt *sheep* by torchlight, and cook meat over open fire. Tucker – the Prep – he taught me a lot. He made me realise that I was torturing myself with this project and it would never end. He helped me burn it, Jimmy.'

'You *burned* your novel?' Jimmy's voice rose; several heads turned. 'But it was awesome! You used to read passages of it to me, and there was that one time, when you were crying and saying you'd never finish the book, and I held you in my arms and said—'

Louise's expression sharpened. She pulled Jimmy down a corridor and out of a fire exit. 'Listen to me. Things have changed. We, we had a good run, and I loved you, but you're very much the sex and drugs and rock and roll part of my life – and like I say, things have changed.' A man from a Community Patrol glanced at them, and Louise lowered her voice. 'You know mine isn't the only book that's been burned in the last few years. This will be a good future, for many people, but if you don't fit, bad things can happen. Tucker's an important man – he's going to get the Community Development ministerial post. And being with him has made me realise that the summer of '99, the one I spent with him, it made a greater impression on me than I knew at the time, and I have a future with him, even,' – she held up a hand to forestall any objections – 'even if I don't agree with everything he thinks or does, he listens to me and I can change things.' She hugged him. 'Goodbye, Jimmy. Be safe.'

The next time the reset option came around, he was eighty years old and living in an exile commune in Finland.

1.1

'Scarborough warning,' Rahman yelled at him, but he wasn't going to stumble, he knew exactly what he was doing now, the point was to get to Flavia and seduce her and make damn sure he was invited to the Ribble Valley cottage this time round, maybe kill the Prep, or at least turn the Prep around, be a change agent and shape whatever was going to happen in this world. But there were so many moving parts, he needed a beer to think it over, and so he strode into the lower bar of the Drydock where the Manics were playing 'Revol' and the girl who looked like Laura Prepon was dancing above and apart from the standard student one-two shuffle – Jimmy marvelled again at the fluidity and grace of her movements. The 'Revol' song ended and another one came on, a sample of dialogue from an interview with the writer Hubert Selby Jr.

The old man served him his drink, and said: 'You're back again?'

'I don't believe we've met,' Jimmy said, but could he be sure? That was the problem with these constant iterations – you kept thinking you saw people you knew, and when you did know people, you kept confusing the different versions of them. You thought: *is this the one where I spend five years hiking around Latin America, or do I wake up tomorrow in bed with the Amazon dominatrix?*

'Oh yeah, we've met many times.' The old man wiped stray ale from the cover of his book – a collection of short stories by Ray Bradbury. 'You keep coming here and coming here and thinking this time everything's going to be perfect. You never accept that life's never going to be a succession of flawless, momentous moments. The princess is always in another castle. You can be happy and fulfilled all your life but at the same time there will be moments of boredom, torpor, anxiety, and at the end of it, you die.'

'I can't help but think you're being a bit negative,' said Jimmy.

Monkey Harris appeared at the bar. 'I got the perfect cure for that, Jimmy. How's your bones?'

'And you can bugger off too,' Jimmy told him.

The old man said: 'Can I ask you something? How do you know this is even real? How do you know you ain't hallucinating, locked up somewhere, or dying – or living in Kirkstall, taking too many antipsychotics, drinking yourself to pieces, watching *Orange Is the New Black* over and over again, developing an obsession with the actor who plays Alex Vause, and then with a woman you once glimpsed who looks vaguely like her? I mean, why *this* girl? You could have married Mads, she was the first person you slept with, she fell in love with you—'

'That could be,' Jimmy said. 'Or it could be that *everyone* has this ability, this reset option. I don't want to miss out on anything. I'm so afraid, and I don't want to miss a thing.'

'I've given you this little speech before,' said the old man. 'And you didn't goddamn listen the first time around.'

'Maybe. But when I hear the music, I'm gonna dance.'

He finished his beer and loped onto the dancefloor. When Louise Atherley saw him, her eyes lit up for a moment; she gave him a smile of amused tolerance, or diversion – and took his hand.

17.9

They were in Missouri this time, under siege at the university. There were rumours that the National Guard was coming, but their students were with them, there were amusing placards stacked like plastic chairs and lists of their demands pinned to the wall, and they had never felt so alive. He poured a glass of wine and walked onto the balcony, where a counter-demonstration was protesting in their favour.

'Hey, Slipping Jimmy! Wine me, baby,' said Louise, from inside – she often called him Slipping Jimmy, after the *Better Call Saul* character. He poured her some of the Chablis, but she was looking at her tablet. There was a fire on it. Louise glanced at him. 'Fuck me,' she said. 'North Korea. There goes the eastern seaboard.'

The Cloud Loom

Jasmin Kirkbride

The rain begins with that soft, familiar sigh of release. No
pitter-patter – not from this altitude – but a sense of falling with
no confirmation of receipt. One long, diminishing descent.

His heart sinks and he rolls over, hiding his face in the pillow
for just five more seconds, trying to blot out the inevitable.
The mean, repeating rainfall days stretch out behind and into
an imagined beyond, dreaded only because a cave of memory
decades long tells him it never used to be this way.

He sits up to confirm by sight what his marrow knows
already, watches rivulets of condensation slide down the
panes, interrupted by leadwork and caught motes of dust. He
scoops one under the pad of his finger. Stops it in its tracks.
The light flickers and the mist falters beyond his silent room.
Yes, raining, and where the drops fall, the world below will be
washed away.

'Sudhev.' His voice is hoarse with just-waking as he calls
his assistant. 'We must check the mills.'

In the next room, the soft rustles of a man dressing. The
same outfit as he – the so-called King – wears: fast-drying silk
overalls with oiled canvas trousers and a fur-lined sealskin

coat atop, cotton socks with leather soles, and wellingtons lined outside with waterproof feathering. All so worn and weathered they are as a second skin.

Sudhev sticks his head around the door, already wearing his vapour mask with the undefined brow and the smoked-glass eyepieces, a tight bind ending in a filtering snout. In this light, with the curtains half-drawn, the mask makes him look more creature than man; and perhaps, from a human view, they are. 'Ready when you are, Sire.'

The King nods, picking up his own mask and stroking the heavy golden star pinned between its brows. The only indication that he bears the ultimate weight of the mills. When the others cannot weave, the buck must always stop with him. 'Very well. Let us see what is to be seen.'

The mask sits heavy on his face today, almost unneeded, the mist outside is so light. Centuries ago, when the King was newly raised, a man could drown within minutes of stepping into the clouds, but now... He gazes up at the bland, white face of the sun beyond the lowing fog. Now *this*.

Sudhev still treads with the timid steps of an apprentice. He remembers being human too closely, while the King barely remembers at all. He has been up here so long he enjoys the vertigo-giddiness of fifteen thousand leagues beneath his feet – is comforted by it, even.

The mills have slowed by the time they pass the turbines. The feed of mist dwindles and the wheels churn one long, lazy thunk after another as they droop into slumber. None of the productive clatter the King was hoping for.

Inside the mill-house, he examines the loom, catches the fresh threads as they emerge from the spinners. Clear spiderwebs, white under his dark skin. Too thin for weaving, this can never be the stuff real dreams are made of. He has been waiting for this day for decades – has felt the stories thinning year on year as the rain cycle accelerated and the mills were starved of vapour. There is no time anymore for the clouds to seep and stew, for them to collect the billion fleeting thoughts from the Earth's floor below. Where once dreams flourished in a person's mind, now only a barren silence remains, fertilised by the skinny anxiety of some forgotten but crucial act. The King was taught to weave with fat, ethereal yarn, oozing raindrops like tears of ambition. No more tears, no more hope, no more tales. Just the falling, purging rain.

Outside, the precipitous sigh increases. A grave roll of thunder turns beneath the mill-house.

'Do you think the sun will come out again today, Lord?' Sudhev's voice is tight: he knows not the looms of old, but he can sense the wrongness in his training. That bitter ichor of a lost but unknown thing at work in him as well; he who has yet to learn to see beyond the dream and into its weaving.

The King ponders, only for a moment. He feels the shift in the light on the back of his neck. Plucks the thread beneath his fingers. It snaps, falling in a wet, spattered line across the floorboards. Yes, the sun will come out again today.

His brow darkens. 'What does it matter? It is their own fault if they do not dream tonight. They turned the mists into water. They washed themselves away. Besides,' – and here he exhales sadly – 'what point is there in making stories when there are so few left who wish to dream?'

AUTHOR BIOGRAPHIES

NIAL GIACOMELLI currently lives in Hampshire, England with his wife and two young children, and spends his days writing radar software to track the position of commercial aircraft. Fairlight Books published his debut work of fiction, *The Therapist*, in 2019.

ABI HYNES is a drama and fiction writer. Her short stories have been widely published in print and online, including by Litro, Interzone, Splice and Neon Magazine, and she was shortlisted for the Bath Flash Fiction's 'Novella-in-flash' Award in 2017. Her plays have been performed in venues across the UK. She graduated from Channel 4's 4Screenwriting Course in 2018 and she is currently working on TV and audio dramas.

SARAH DALE has recently completed an MA in creative writing at Birkbeck University, London, gaining a distinction. She runs her own practice as an occupational psychologist, and lives and works in Nottingham. She is currently working on a series of short stories. @creatingfocus

MARGARET CROMPTON began exploring poetry, short fiction and drama, after fifty years in social work (practitioner, lecturer, editor, writer). Several of her poems and stories are published both online and in print, and some poems are set to music. Her plays are performed by Script in Hand and published online by Smith Scripts. Present challenges are novellas and children's fiction.

SOPHIE VAN LLEWYN was born in Romania, but now lives in Germany. Her debut *Bottled Goods* was longlisted for the Women's Prize for Fiction in 2019. sophievanllewyn.com | @sophie_van_l

LEE WRIGHT was born in Warwickshire and is a widely published author of short stories, poetry and non-fiction articles. He holds a master's degree in Creative Writing from the University of Leicester and began studying for a PhD in Creative Writing in 2020. He is currently writing his debut novel.

MAGGIE LING was an illustrator and cartoonist before swapping dip pen for iMac. Many of her stories have been placed in international competitions, including a shortlisting for the Bridport Prize, published in *Unthology 1*, *Unthology 5* (Unthank Books), the Asham Award-winning *Something Was There* (Virago) and in her debut collection *Appetites: stories of love, sex and death* (Troubador).

JUDITH WILSON is a London-based writer and journalist. She graduated with Distinction from the MA Creative Writing at Royal Holloway, University of London, in 2019, and won 1st Prize for the London Short Story Prize 2019. She is writing her first novel, set in London in the 1860s. www.judithwilsonwrites.com

SAM REESE is an award-winning writer, researcher and teacher Hailing from Aotearoa. Currently a lecturer in creative writing at York St John University, he is the author of the short story collection *Come the Tide*, and non-fiction works on jazz, literature and loneliness, and the American short story.

YVONNE DYKES is the seventh child of nine children and her family is a rich source of inspiration in her work. She is a Londoner, born and bred and proud of her Irish heritage. She attends City Lit, where she is working on her new manuscript under the guidance of author Jonathan Barnes. Her novel, *Brondesbury,* was self-published in 2016.

OMAR SABBAGH is a widely published poet, writer and critic. He has taught literature, creative writing and philosophy at the American University of Beirut (AUB) and at the American University in Dubai (AUD), where he is currently associate professor of English. His novella, *Minutes from the Miracle City,* was published by Fairlight Books in 2019.

DAVID LEWIS is a reader for Electric Literature. His writing has appeared in *Talking Points Memo, J'aime mon quartier, je ramasse, Chelsea Station, The Fish Anthology, Liars' League London, Willesden Herald: New Short Stories 9, Kaaterskill Basin Literary Journal* and *The Weird Fiction Review.*

CHLOË ASHBY is a freelance writer and editor. She has written about art and culture for the *TLS, Guardian, FT Life & Arts, frieze* and many others. She's working on an art survey with White Lion Publishing, which will come out in March 2021. Her debut novel, *Wet Paint*, will be published by Trapeze in spring 2022.

HANNAH STEVENS is a freelance writer of fiction and non-fiction with a PhD in creative writing. Her work has been widely anthologised and featured in many literary journals. Currently Hannah co-directs Wind&Bones a company exploring the crossing-places of creativity, writing and social justice.

ANNA APPLEBY was born in Newcastle upon Tyne in 1993 and tragically lost her Geordie accent in a collision with the South. She floated around looking for a voice but eventually gave up and wrote things down instead. Most of the time she can be found in Manchester, composing music and eating crisps.

ADAM TRODD'S writing has appeared in publications such as *Banshee*, *Ellipsis* and *The National Flash Fiction Day Anthology*. He has been shortlisted for the Cúirt Prize and the Bath Flash Fiction Award. He has won both the Benedict Kiely Short Story Competition and the Book of Kells Creative Writing Competition.

WILLIAM PRENDIVILLE was born in Cork, Ireland, grew up in Canada and now lives in Paris, France, where he works as a journalist. He is the author of *Atlantic Winds* and *Love Is Nothing But The Fruit Of A Long Moment*.

E J SALEBY lives near the coast, and can usually be found on the laptop, at the piano or outdoors. He studied Literature at university and has been writing ever since. He has worked in too many jobs and enjoyed most of them. He is currently working on his debut novel. @ejsaleby

SUZANNE GHADIMI is a Canadian-Scottish writer and artist currently living in Aberdeenshire. She graduated with a BFA in Studio from Emily Carr University in 1999 and completed her MLitt in Creative Writing from Aberdeen University in 2018. Her first short story *Pixies* was shortlisted for the Aesthetica Fiction Prize in 2018.

NIKI BAKER has earned recognition for her travel writing, poetry, lyrics, flash fiction and short stories. An active seeker of wild places, she has escaped to rural France with her soulmate, who is also a writer. Niki's first full-length novel will be published in 2020. @NRBakerWriter

CLARE REDDAWAY'S stories have been widely published, have won and been shortlisted in many national competitions, and are frequently broadcast on BBC Radio Bristol. She reads her stories at events throughout the south-west, and runs a regular live lit night in Bath called Story Fridays. Find out more at www.clarereddaway.co.uk.

KATHERINE PRINGLE has worked in publishing for many years as a book designer, but writing is her first love. She tries to grab as much writing time as she can alongside looking after her two young daughters. Katherine seeks to create a strong sense of place in her stories, often inspired by her homeland of Ireland. She was the winner of the Fabula Short Story Contest in 2016, and is currently writing her debut novel.

MAX DUNBAR lives in West Yorkshire. He blogs at maxdunbar. wordpress.com/ and tweets @MaxDunbar1.

JASMIN KIRKBRIDE is a writer and editor. She is currently undertaking a PhD in Creative and Critical Writing at UEA, exploring climate change in science fiction and hope in ecocritical dystopias. Her fiction has appeared in magazines including *Fictive Dream*, *Ash Tales*, *Haverthorn* and on the cover of *Open Pen*, and has been shortlisted for awards including the 2019 EVENT Magazine Speculative Fiction Contest. www.jasminkirkbride.com.

FAIRLIGHT BOOKS

JAC SHREEVES-LEE

Broadwater

*'This Farm, these people, these blocks, these roads
are my home.'*

Welcome to Broadwater Farm, one of the most well-known
housing estates in Britain. A place where post-war dreams of
concrete utopia ended in riots, violence and sub-standard housing.

In this collection, Tottenham-born Jac Shreeves-Lee gives voice
to the people of Broadwater Farm. With evocative language
and raw storytelling, she compassionately portrays their shared
sense of community. A community with a rich cultural heritage,
comprising over forty nationalities, generations old.

*'The truth and humour in this intensely fine and
lyrical short story collection shines a light that is
ultimately uplifting.'*
—Martina Evans, Poet and novelist

'A voyage both unforgettable and searing.'
—Onjali Q. Raúf, activist and author of
The Boy at the Back of the Class